MW01241580

SOMETIMES A
SOLDIER COMES
HOME

A NOVEL

JESSICA CIOSEK

GenZ
The Future of Publishing

Supervising Editor: Emily Oliver, Stephanie Marrie
Associate Editors: Destinee Thom, Allison Macdonald

Cover Designer: L. Austen Johnson, www.allaboutbookcovers.com

ISBN 978-1-952919-51-0 (paperback)
ISBN 978-1-952919-52-7 (ebook)

GenZPublishing.org
Aberdeen, NJ

DEDICATION

For Bob who has always believed
For Ava and Quincy who willingly shared me
And for my grandparents:
Eleanor, Roger and Burrell (Hank)
without whom I and this story would not be.

"You gain strength, courage and confidence by every experience in which you really stop to look fear in the face. You are able to say to yourself, 'I have lived through this horror. I can take the next thing that comes along.' You must do the thing you think you cannot do."

—Eleanor Roosevelt

PROLOGUE

Roger heard only the bullet. It whirred and buzzed like a mosquito on a humid August night. He cocked his head and the bullet pierced the thin, vulnerable flesh on the underside of his chin. Had he not reached forward, the bullet would have struck him square in the forehead. It was meant for him; not in a malicious way or from the deliberate human intent that had already claimed so many millions of lives in this war, but rather in a divine, preordained way. His number was up. He was not meant to return from the war. He was not meant for anything more, not meant to be a father to his three small children, not meant to grow old with his beloved wife. The simple truth of the matter was that his life would end as a Private First Class in the US Infantry assigned to guard duty in Wetzlar, Germany while awaiting transport back to the United States in the aftermath of the Second Great War of the world.

In the final moments between bullet puncture and the furious bleeding out of his life, Roger conjured Eleanor. He found her at the sink in their tidy, bright kitchen. He could see her as if he were there with her, by her side one last time.

Small-framed and delicate, she was wearing a yellow housedress, her fine dark hair pulled away from her face, though a few stubborn little wisps curled at her temples. Yellow looked beautiful on her. It pulled the glints of gold from her dark hair and added light to her deep blue eyes. She looked weary but content, tending to the needs of their small family on yet another ordinary afternoon.

"I'm sorry, El," he said.

She looked up, seeming to hear his words. Her face twisted in confusion.

"I love you."

Her eyes went round with fright. She tipped her head, as if waiting for something more. And there was so much more he needed to say, but his visit ended as quickly as it had begun, and he was left only to hope that today had been an easy day for her—that the children had all been in terrific moods, playing in the yard and going down easy for naps. And that she had been able to find a little respite for herself while the children slumbered. That was his final wish for her: a pleasant, ordinary, forgettable sort of day, because soon enough, August 20, 1945 would become forever a dark day on her calendar, and he was so very sorry for that.

PART ONE

~~CHAPTER 1~~

ELEANOR

I f I'd known, I wouldn't have let him go. I thought about it some in the days that followed, how we should have run off, taken our little ones and set up life in the deep woods until the whole thing was over. Might not have been the right thing to do, but if I'd known, I would have done it anyway. I swear I would have. But it was wartime and any soldier's wife knows—when they call him, he goes. And so we agreed, Roger and me, to be brave. We convinced our young selves, with kisses and hugs and no small amount of tears, that if we played by the rules, things would work out. Whether they did or they didn't is a matter of perspective. One thing I do know for sure now is that you never, ever truly forget what you lost, no matter how life carries on.

I fixed him breakfast the morning he left—two eggs over easy. They weren't on the ration list, but they weren't so easy to come by, either. I fried them up in a dollop of bacon grease. Cooking grease was to be turned in for the war effort. I knew that, but

I had squirreled away a little jar in the back of my icebox anyway. *Just in case,* I'd told myself. And sending my man off to war was the biggest "just in case" my simple life had ever known.

It was August when they required him. The day had hardly begun, and already I could feel the promise of heat and humidity in the air. My tidy yellow kitchen shone bright with the morning sun. I felt a thin trail of sweat trickle down my back. But I stood over the stove anyway, watching those egg whites change from clear to pearly. This was one morning I intended to make sure every little thing came out just right. I flipped each egg gently, one at a time, and struggled to push away the terrifying thought that this might be the very last meal I'd ever cook for my husband.

"Smells like old times," said Roger, coming up behind me. I jumped a little, startled by his sudden appearance.

"It's the closest I could get to real bacon right now."

"We take what we can get, darlin'," he said, slipping an arm around my waist. I flipped the burner off and slid the eggs onto the waiting plate. Turning away from the dish, I put my full attention on him. He was dressed in his navy blue church suit with the thin maroon tie I'd given him last Christmas.

"Well, don't you look spiffy," I said, rubbing his lapel. Thin yet muscular, Roger towered over me.

"Gotta look good for my lady," he teased, his pale blue eyes looking down playfully into mine. Roger was the kind of man a woman felt safe wrapped up against, so I tucked myself up tightly into him.

He pulled me close. The musk of his Aqua Velva aftershave sent a thrill to my middle. I reached up for a kiss. His lips met mine and we kissed hard and deep. It was the sort of kiss you might save for late in the evening, but we couldn't afford to miss any chances.

A bright "Hi, Mommy" interrupted us. We turned, and there, in the kitchen archway, stood our little girl, Carol. Dressed in her summer nightie, the pink glow of sleep was still warming her cheeks.

"Morning, sweetie," I said.

"Morning, sunshine," Roger said. He let loose of me and swept Carol into his arms, carrying her to the table. At three years old, she was the apple of her daddy's eye and he hers. I went back to the stove, oleo-ed a piece of toast, and poured a cup of hot chicory coffee. Real butter and regular coffee were long since on the ration list. It was a warm meal with compromise for the war, but I served it with every bit of the love I had for my soldier. For Carol, I plopped a scoop of oatmeal into a small bowl and tucked a square of toast beside it.

"Breakfast is served," I declared, faking good cheer. I sat down in my usual seat. The thought of food wasn't agreeing too much with me, so I sipped at my coffee and listened to Roger and Carol prattle on.

"Eat up, sweet pea," he said to her. "We gotta stay strong for the fight." Roger flexed his arm and growled playfully. Carol took a dutiful mouthful and did the same, trying to growl through her oatmeal. Roger had been doing that with the children since the day his draft notice arrived. At first, it had felt like good fun, but that morning the truth was more real than I ever wanted it to be. I blinked back tears and looked off out the kitchen window, as if whatever was out there could somehow offer me a way out of the inevitable.

Then a yelp came from upstairs and brought me back to the morning. "Barry boy's awake," I announced and popped out of my chair.

"Sounds like it," said Roger, straining a smile at me. We both knew what we were trying not to think about.

I climbed the stairs to gather our second-born. Just a year and a half old, Barry was a darling little cherub with bright blue eyes and curls just like his father. He stood at the rail of his crib, sleepy-eyed but ready for the day. I freshened him up and carried him downstairs on my hip.

"It'll be okay," I whispered, pressing a kiss to his forehead. He leaned into my shoulder. This little boy hadn't the least idea what it meant that his father was going off to the fight, but it soothed us both anyway.

"There's our Butch," Roger said as we came into the kitchen. He swung Barry into a hug and buckled him into his highchair. I fixed another bowl of oatmeal. And there we were, a family of four around the breakfast table, just like any other morning. The sun shone across the table as happy as you please, but all I felt was the ache of a coming good-bye. I scooped a spoonful of oatmeal for Barry and fed him with the care of one trying to prolong a moment forever.

Roger stabbed a crust of toast with his fork, swabbed up the last of his egg yolk, pushed it into his mouth.

"That was just the sort of breakfast I need to get me off on the right foot," he said contentedly, laying his fork and knife along the edge of his plate. The flat of the knife caught the sun's beam and shot a sunspot across to the far wall. It caught Roger's eye. "Well, look at that, would ya?" he said. "Mr. Sun has come out to play." He picked his knife up and maneuvered the sunspot along the wall, singing *You Are My Sunshine* as the light danced up and down, all around the kitchen. The children followed the spot, mouths wide with wonder. Roger warbled the final word then dropped the knife. The sunspot disappeared.

"All gone," Roger whispered and held up his empty hands.

"All gone," Carol echoed. Barry twisted himself around in his highchair, hunting for the spot. Roger grinned and flipped the fork back into the beam.

"See there," he explained, "the light bounces off the fork, then shines on the wall."

Roger showed them his trick over and over, on and off, on and off. It was an ordinary moment of a father playing with his children, but at the time all I could think about was my tender, loving Roger going off to a war with guns and knives, bombs, grenades, and enemies. It didn't suit him, didn't suit him at all. At his core, Roger was a carefree soul quick with a joke or a laugh, full of love and good cheer. He wasn't a fighter. I swallowed hard and checked the clock.

"I'd best go and get myself together," I said.

"Okay, I'll keep an eye on these rascals." Roger winked, but sadness tinged the bright blue of his eyes. For weeks, a heaviness had hung about him. He never said it, as men won't, but leaving us was breaking his heart. I kissed him and scooted from the room before my tears spilled over.

I took each stair slowly, placing my feet heavily on the thin stair runner and trying to convince myself that he was only going off to training—he might never see the fight. Or maybe he'd come down with some curable illness that would put him out of the fight. Or maybe, or maybe, or maybe. Oh, I would have given anything to keep him home. But it was 1944, and war had been dogging the world for some time. Posters hung in every store window—advertisements for bravery: "Uncle Sam Wants You", "Grow Your Garden for Victory", "We Can Do It". Bulletins and updates interrupted the radio shows regularly. The music hours were a mix of heartbreaking goodbye songs and dance numbers too happy by half. And, every day at noon, radio star Kate Smith would call on God over the airwaves to bless us all. Ration books, scrap metal drives, war bonds and blackouts. It was a way of life none of us wanted, but we did what was expected and prayed every night for it to end.

In fairness, Roger and I had been lucky. The Army's policy was to call the family men last, which was why Roger hadn't been drafted until now. In the meanwhile, he'd been going right along to do his part for the war effort. Flint had been a factory town since back before the Great Depression, and now all those factories were working overtime. The AC Delco plant had been retooled to put out machine guns for our boys, and Roger was one of the foremen who oversaw that work, day in and day out—nights and weekends, too.

Now, his draft number had come up and it was his responsibility to go. I wasn't arguing with it, this wasn't a time for arguing, but I was as frightened as any war wife would be. Not that there was anything much to do with my fear, what with the whole world wrapped up in it as well. Even the ladies' magazines, so bossy and sure of what a woman ought to do most of the time, could only say: "Wear a cheerful smile for your man." Some bit of advice that was, but I wore it anyway, as best I could.

At the top of the stairs, I listened for a minute to Roger playing with the children. I would miss the low hum of his voice in the house, the comfort it gave me to hear him first thing in the morning or at the end of a day. A voice is something that fades in a person's memory, without anything to replay it. That was something I remembered about Daddy; when he left there wasn't any more thunder—happy or mad—in our house.

"I will hear Roger again," I softly promised myself, but I wasn't sure I could believe it.

I got myself fixed up for the trip to the train station with some mascara and a dash of pink lipstick. I was just buttoning up my yellow dress, Roger's favorite, when I heard Mother pull the side door open.

"Okay, I'm here!" she hollered, letting the screen door slam. She had agreed to watch the children while we went off to the train station.

"Morning, Mother," I said, hurrying down the stairs to meet her. She stopped just inside the side door and fussed around in her lump of a handbag. Short and round like a cartoon hedgehog in a child's picture book, Mother was wearing the slate blue dress she favored and had her hair fashioned into her usual gray-brown cap.

"Need some help?" I asked. She didn't bother looking up.

"I'll be along," she replied, waving me off.

"All right, then." I went into the kitchen.

"Mother's here," I said, winking at Roger.

"Yes," agreed Roger with a smirk. "She surely is."

It was mostly my family we had near us in those days. Roger's folks still lived up north, on the farm in Kalkaska, Michigan. Roger and I had moved down to Flint just before the war. There were good factory jobs to be had, and Roger and I were anxious to try city life for a while. So, we packed up and made our way down. In time, most of my family moved down, too. Roger's sister followed later, but his folks stayed put. We drove up to see them a couple times a year, or they'd visit us. But with gasoline and rubber on the ration list since the beginning of things, Ma and Pa Mitchell hadn't been able to see Roger off. Instead, they'd spoken with him by telephone for a good while last night, said their good-byes, and wished him a safe return. It wasn't the best way to send a son off to war, but there wasn't any other way.

Mother plodded into the kitchen. She dropped her handbag onto the chair.

"Morning, Mother," Roger said.

She looked him up and down and nodded ever just so slightly. "Morning."

In her hand she held a small box tied up with a pale blue ribbon. "Brought some cookies for the children," she said. "Mrs. Gaines had them left over from a war bonds party." Mother worked as a housekeeper for Mrs. Gaines and regularly brought her leftovers and cast-offs to share with us.

"Isn't that nice?" I remarked.

"Cookies?" said Roger, smiling. "Who said the children could have cookies?"

"Daaaddy...." Carol pleaded. Roger laughed and swung her up onto his lap. He was prolonging the morning as best he could, and I didn't blame him a bit. Barry squealed, so I wiped his face and gently plopped him on his father's lap. Roger wrapped the two of them into a hug, nuzzling and kissing them. Sadness pressed itself against the back of my throat, but I swallowed hard, and decided to enjoy these last few minutes, if nothing else. They laughed and fooled around until Roger glanced at the wall clock.

"Well," he said, catching his breath, "it's about that time."

"I imagine so," I said, trying for a brightness I couldn't begin to feel. The children seemed to sense the change in the air; Carol's eyes turned watchful. I lifted Barry from Roger's knee. As he stood, he picked up Carol. I'd seen Roger pick our daughter up effortlessly a thousand times, but this time she looked almost heavy in his arms. I couldn't imagine how heavily it weighed on him to leave our small family.

"Daddy loves you, little mop top," he said, kissing her cheek and setting her on the floor.

He turned to our son. "Daddy loves you, too, big boy," he said, running a hand along Barry's cheek. "You be brave." He kissed his forehead.

Mother took hold of Roger's arm. "You keep your head low, now," she said firmly, looking him in the eye.

Roger's face tightened under her gaze. "I'll do that."

Mother gave his arm a squeeze. She wasn't the sort for sentimentality; her responsibilities lay heavy on her and seldom lightened. So, it surprised me when she took a moment to encourage Roger.

"All right, then," she said. I passed Barry to Mother. She rested him on her hip without a word. The room took on a heavy air.

My voice broke the tension. "They've had breakfast. Leave the dishes in the sink for me."

"Don't you worry about us," Mother assured.

I turned towards the children. "Be good for Grandma, now."

Roger pressed last kisses to each of their foreheads, then gathered his bag and took my hand. We hurried out the side door.

Out on the driveway, Roger pulled me close into him. "And here I thought your mother hated me," he said.

"Me too." We busted into giggles, laughing like our old selves, like teenagers, like young lovers with no dark horizons. I slipped my arm through his, pulled in tight. We could be carefree for a just little while longer.

He opened the car door for me, and I slid across the vinyl front seat of our Buick to sit alongside him, thigh against thigh despite the heat. He draped his arm over my shoulder. We hadn't ridden like that since before Carol was born, but I intended to savor the presence of him until I couldn't anymore.

"The car's all tuned up," he said, backing out onto the street. "You ought to drive it once a week to keep it running nice. The tires are in fine shape, so you don't have to worry about that."

"Okay," I said.

"And rubbish night is Thursdays, but the tin collector comes on Friday."

"I know all about that, honey," I said.

He looked over at me, a half-smile on his lips. "I suppose you do," he said, and squeezed my shoulder.

"It'll be fine." I patted his hand. "Don't you worry about us."

"I will worry."

"Not any more than I'll worry about you." I kissed his cheek, resting my head on his shoulder. We drove along, the thrum of the car the only sound between us.

As a girl, I hadn't thought too much about finding love. I hadn't expected love was thinking too much about finding me. Then I met Roger, and love wasn't hardly enough to describe how I felt. There was a part of me that didn't believe it could last. I suppose I was expecting he might vanish someday like my own daddy had. But he didn't. We'd married and made a life together. Nearly five years as husband

and wife, and still it felt like magic. I'd look over in the dark of night, or the gray of an early dawn, and there he'd be, my very own love of a lifetime. Every morning, every evening, a plain gift he was to me.

I studied him, too, until I knew him better than I knew myself—the gentle slant of his forehead, the smooth curve of his chin, the peppery follicles of his clean-shaven cheek. I knew him the way any woman comes to know the man she loves—from hours wrapped up next to him, dancing, whispering, kissing, making love. I was so lucky, more lucky than I ever deserved to be. I couldn't believe I had to let him go.

"And the garden," he said. "It's all weeded and those tomatoes are starting to ripen, so you ought to get out there every day if you can. Should be good eating real soon."

"Jean and I talked about canning some for when you get home."

"Now that sounds like one of many things to look forward to."

We laughed, but we both knew all this common talk was just a cover for our unspeakable fear. It trembled just below the surface, black and thick, weighing every conversation, every glance, every touch with a grim uncertainty. At the traffic light, Roger stopped the car. We kissed, long and slow. I put my thoughts only to the tender sensation of his mouth against mine, and not one thing more.

Too soon, we were at the train station. Roger pulled the car in easy and parked it in the second row.

"Don't want you to have to walk to Timbuktu to find it." He handed me the keys. They dropped like lead into my hand.

We climbed the stairs to the train, sweaty palm against sweaty palm in the summer heat. But we held tight; not willing to let go until we had to. On the platform, people stood in clusters of twos and threes. Stoic fathers stood with their hands shoved deep in their pockets; worried mothers fussed and plucked at their fresh-faced sons. Quiet couples like Roger and me stood in pairs, leaning into each other, whispering and nodding, passing secrets of love and promise until the bitter end. We found a spot among them. Like a bored old bull, the train hunkered not 30 feet from us, spitting and steaming, waiting to take our men away. We ignored it as best we could. Roger wrapped me in his arms.

"You're beautiful, El," he whispered tenderly against my ear. "I love you. I'll always love you."

"I love you, Roger. Every day for the rest of my life." I dabbed at the tears gathering in the corner of my eyes. Roger handed me his handkerchief, his own eyes red and worried. There was nothing left to say. I pressed my head against his chest and listened to his heartbeat, drank in the musky scent of him. The train whistle blew. I jumped.

"Oh no," I whispered. My heart pounded. My hands shook. Roger pulled me close. "All aboard!" the conductor hollered. Around us, the quiet murmuring became a chorus of good-byes and

— 15 —

shuffling footsteps. We kissed again, greedy and grasping this time. It was a kiss full of everything the two of us had, all our heres and nows, all our hellos and goodbyes, all our promises and dreams. It was a kiss full of a lifetime, for a lifetime.

"Don't go," I whispered, and I meant it, I did, until I saw Roger's face. He looked at me with such a mix of hesitation and fear that I would have pulled those words right back out of the air if I could have.

"I wouldn't, El," he said, his mouth curved in a frown. "If I didn't have to."

"I know, honey. I'm sorry. I love you."

He smiled as best he could, kissed me ever so gently, and stepped out of my arms. Holding my hands to his chest, he looked into my eyes.

The conductor cried, louder now, "All aboard!"

"I'll be back," he whispered. "I *will* come back," he repeated, a firm determination in his voice. And I believed him—heart and soul, I believed him. We kissed one more time, and he let go. I never will forget the feeling of his warm fingers letting loose of mine, slipping out of my grasp. As he made his way toward the train, every ounce of me wanted to grab him back, to run up and take hold of his elbow and drag him as far away from the train, the station, the stupid war as I could.

Gathered in bunches now, the men funneled slowly onto the train. We wives, girlfriends, mothers, and fathers hung back. It was the hardest thing to say goodbye to the men not knowing when we might see them next. But it was a time of duty. We all knew it, the men most of all.

"Come back, Roger! Come back to me!" I hollered, my hands cupped around my mouth.

He turned, there among the thick of them all, and our eyes met. "I'll be back, Eleanor," he answered. "I promise I'll come back." And I heard him even though he didn't yell. Around all the noise, above all the commotion of people moving here and there, and the fuming, impatient train, I heard him. He sealed his parting promise by blowing me a kiss. My heart lifted. He would come back, he would. Men came back all the time.

I kept my sights on Roger's curly head amongst the crowd for as long as I could. I stood on my tiptoes, inched forward, and stretched to keep ahold of him with my eyes. It wasn't long before the train was full and the platform empty of our brave men.

The whistle blew three loud blasts. The wheels began their steady roll. I scanned the windows for him. I dashed toward the train, pushing past the small crowd, praying for just one last glimpse. Then, there he was—his bright blue eyes, that curly hair. He waved, blowing eager kisses my way. I waved, blowing kisses back.

"I love you, Roger!"

I ran along the platform until it ended. There at the very edge, I looked on as the train chugged away, feeling as if it were pulling my heart along with it. Slowly but surely, it picked up steam, traveling faster and farther, getting smaller and smaller, caring not one bit that it was taking my love away. I squinted, keeping my focus on the red caboose.

The track curved and the train disappeared, a wisp from its steam trail the only evidence it had ever been. I watched the vapor curl into the thick blue sky until there was nothing more to see.

When I turned to leave, I found a few other people lingering on the platform, mostly women, their eyes shot through with red from crying, the tips of their powdered noses pink and rubbed raw. Though in that moment we were dallying there together, each and every one of us was utterly alone. I caught another woman's eye. She could just barely fake a smile before turning away. My eyes followed her as she ran off, her shoulders shaking under the weight of deep sobs. That was all it took for me to break. I dropped onto a small bench and the tears came like rain, guttural cries gushing from my throat. And I let them. I'd been holding it all in so long, so hard, for Roger, for the children. Now I could cry, really cry. So I did.

After a while, an older woman sat down on the bench next to me. She didn't say anything, just sat. Dressed smartly in a trim summer suit, her hair a smooth dark blonde curled into an updo, she had a calm air about her. It made me feel a little foolish carrying on like I was. I dabbed at my eyes with one of Roger's hankies and took a deep breath.

"You're stronger than you know," she said, turning to look directly at me. Her eyes were warm but serious. I shook my head, bit my lips, not yet trusting myself to speak.

"You are," she pressed, nodding once. "We like to think our men are the strong ones, and we let them think that. But men are the brave ones. They step in to fix problems. That takes courage. Women hold a place for them to come back to. And holding that place with all the worry, all the heartache, all the belief—that takes strength. Men are brave, but women are strong."

I let her words hang there in the thick morning. The last thing I felt at that moment was strong. Any strength I could've had had been drained from my very depths when Roger boarded that train. In fact, the only thing holding me up right then was the wooden bench and my own sense of good manners.

"I just put my third son on that train," the woman went on. "My third son of the four I have. He's only eighteen. Already, his oldest brother's been lost. The middle one's in the thick of it somewhere. And now the next one's been called. My very heart is broken. Shattered into three pieces." She paused. A tiny band of perspiration glistened at her hairline. "But I carry on," she said, dabbing at her brow with a handkerchief. "I've got another boy and a girl at home, so I carry on. That's the strength of women—we keep going. They go to the fight and we stay here and keep things going. We do it because we have to, but mostly, we do it for them. It's as simple as that."

"Hmm," was all I could think to say.

"You have children?" she asked, blinking at me like an old owl.

"Two—a girl and a boy."

"That's reason enough, then," she said. "They'll be needing their mother now more than ever."

"Yes," I replied, not requiring a reminder that my little ones had only one of us now. She stood, stepped in front of me, bent to meet my gaze. Her perfume wrapped itself around me like a flowery embrace.

"Even tears don't take the strong away," she said, patting my hand. Then she walked off, a firm step to her stride, shoulders held just so, returning to her life without her three boys.

I'd never put much thought into whether I was or wasn't strong. But as her flowery scent faded in the morning heat, I figured there was a lot I was going to learn about myself in the days ahead, whether I wanted to or not. I walked alone down the platform steps, my sandals crunching too loudly across the gravel parking lot. In my head, the woman's words played again and again. "Stronger than you know, stronger than you know." *We'll see*, I thought. *We'll see.*

CHAPTER 2

ROGER

Roger pulled out of Eleanor's comfortable arms with all the reluctance a man has ever felt. *This is courage*, he told himself. *This is bravery—stepping away from all you love and into the world's greatest unknown.* It was expected of a man in times of trouble, so he took a deep breath and fell in line with the others. Thick shoulder to thick shoulder, the earthy heat of the other men enveloped him, carrying him along. He steadied his knees, planted his foot hard on the steel train step, and pushed himself up into the muddled, hot car.

"One last look," he whispered, and pressed through the crowd to get to the window. He scanned the platform full of waving arms and worried faces until he spotted Eleanor, her yellow dress like a beacon in the crowd, her familiar beauty a comfort as his whole world shifted around him. Her eyes swept the train's windows; she was searching for him, too. He slid the window down.

"Eleanor! Eleanor!" Roger's voice called over the din of other farewells. She found him. He blew a kiss. She blew several more back at him. The train whistled, jerking into motion.

"Come back!" Eleanor called. "Come back to me!"

"I will!" he answered, the word "will" sinking under the dense air like the thin promise it was. "I will come back!" he cried, emphasizing the word "back" with a barking grit. He *would* come back to her.

The train began its slow roll down the track. Roger clutched the window's open edge, feeling as if the very thread of his heart was unraveling. With each passing second, it became more and more clear that he was leaving his love, his children, his whole life behind. He threw a final kiss to her and kept his eyes on that yellow dress until it was only a speck. The train picked up speed and curved away along the track. She was gone.

He flopped onto the worn Naugahyde of the train seat. The wheels churned a steady rhythm like a drumbeat of departure. Wind whipped through the car, clearing the tension of good-byes still lingering in the air.

Around him, the other men laughed and joshed, introducing themselves to one another. Roger couldn't muster the wit nor the ease to join the fray. Instead, he turned toward the window. The way he saw it, a family man was damned if he did and damned if he didn't in this cotton-pickin' war. Either a man stayed behind and saw to providing and protecting the home front, or he went on over with the other men and did his duty, leaving the wife and children to their own best devices. Neither decision seemed even halfway right for a worthwhile husband and father. There was a threat, to be sure, and a real man ought to confront it. Courage, bravery, and standing up to fight were the duties of a good man. But so, too, was seeing to the safety and security of his home in times of trouble. Torn between his duty to the country and his responsibility to his family, Roger had chosen not to enlist. Instead, he had waited to be called. The War Department would find him when they needed him, he reasoned, and they surely had.

In the meantime, he had planted a garden in the corner of his backyard—a "Victory Garden," they called it. It was meant to keep the family fed so farm food could go to the soldiers. He took his turn every other week on the neighborhood civilian watch and worked extra hours down at the AC plant. He collected tin and carpooled to the factory. He did his part. When the War Department finally called for him, there wasn't anything more to discuss except how to best keep Eleanor and the children safe while he was away.

They had worked it over time and again, he and Eleanor. She wanted to stay in the house with the children until he returned. With her mother and sisters nearby, she argued, she'd have plenty of help. "It's change enough with you going away," she'd reasoned. He would have preferred she and the children went up north, tucked in safe with his folks on the farm, far away from Flint and its factories that could become targets if the enemy came near again.

She couldn't imagine it, living with his parents without him. "I love your mother, Rog, but it would just be strange for all of us."

Roger had initially agreed with his wife, but as the day of his departure drew nearer, trepidation set in. He'd brought it up again on his last night.

"How about this," he suggested in the bathroom before bed. "If things go on too long, you'll go up to the farm?"

"I thought we settled all that," she countered, meeting his eyes in the mirror. She rinsed her toothbrush, he wet his.

"We did, but there's no telling how this is all gonna go," he said, his words muffled by his toothbrush. "I might be gone for a good while."

"Maybe not," she said reflexively. It had become a habit for her to remind them both of the slim chance that he'd never have to see action, that the war might end before he shipped overseas. She said it every time. To Roger, it was foolishness—he'd been called, and he would go—but he let her say it. These last days with the woman he loved would not be spent in petty confrontation; he knew he would regret that more than anything. He twisted the faucet off. She handed him the towel.

"*El*," he pleaded as he dabbed at his chin.

"Okay, yes, if it goes on too long," she acquiesced.

"Promise?"

"Promise," she agreed. "I won't stay here if I can't manage."

"But you won't go to the farm, will you?" Roger threw the towel over the rod.

"Probably not." She smirked. He pulled her into a hug, held her tight, soothed by the familiar curve of her body against his. Eleanor was a delicate thing, her skin soft and nearly alabaster, a girl in need of protection or at least great care. The thought of having to be away from her for days, weeks, even months on end was impossible to consider.

"Always a mind of your own," he said, kissing her temple.

"That's why you married me," she replied. "Or so you claim."

"Among other things." He kissed her hard on the mouth, then led her to bed.

As they had every night since his draft notice arrived, the two of them made slow, tender love. It was an unspoken ritual they'd fallen into, a kind of reassurance they took in one another. Without speaking, they explored each other in ways they might otherwise have been afraid to, careful and patient, gentle and thoughtful. It might be hours before they slept. Neither hurried, neither spoke, sharing only the moans and sighs of pleasure and connection.

Much later, Eleanor rolled over and lay across his bare chest. He kissed her hair, curling his arm protectively around her.

"It'll work out, Rog," she said. "It will."

"Mmmm," he softly hummed in hopeful agreement. She drifted off.

The warm curve of Eleanor soothed his soul, but his mind wouldn't rest. His thoughts raced, confused, searching. Around him echoed what seemed a never-ending battle cry of masculinity, a certain honor in the sacrifice of war. He mimicked it, like good men do, but he couldn't lay any true claim to it for himself. He did not want to go, did not want to leave his family, did not want to fight. And so he wondered, what was it that drove men's souls in times like these? Where did true courage come from? There were battles that had to be fought, battles that were necessary and right, and men had to go and fight them. Of course he knew this; he was neither naive nor simple. What he could not get a hold of was how each man came to have the courage to do what had to be done, how each man found it within himself to fight.

The truth was, Roger often felt as if he were playing at the game of being a grown-up, and this was just one more version of pretend, the sort of pretend he had played with his sister, Bea, when he was a little boy.

"You be the daddy," she'd say, plopping Pa's church hat on his head and pushing his feet into the old man's dress shoes. He'd drag the shoes around on his too-small feet, deepen his voice, and tell stories about going into town "to see to some business." Now, the church hat was his own and the shoes fit snug on his own size elevens, but Roger had yet to feel like he was the sort of man his father was: a man of honor and purpose, a man who knew what needed to be done and did it without comment or complaint.

Like a dutiful son, Roger had tried to emulate the old man; he had married a good woman, found work of the sort that could support a healthy family, did what was expected, what was asked of him. Still, there was a nagging feeling that he had no right to be as fortunate as he was. Despite being a child of the Great Depression, the good life had come easier than expected. Having such advantage made him question his right to it, as if the struggle ought to be greater for a man to be so lucky. As if life and love had to be earned before they could be fully enjoyed. And so, the war. Was this the price required of him? Pay it and he could feel worthy of his good life? If he were lucky. If he survived.

Roger fixed his eyes on the landscape, hardly taking notice of the patchwork of passing houses. Eventually, the homes thinned, giving way to open fields and farmland. Roger watched it fly by, lush and green. Soon enough, their bounty would be harvested. The fields would turn brown, fade, rot, and be buried by an unforgiving plow. The cycle of planting, tending, growing, and harvesting would begin again come spring. *We live, we give, we age, we die. But do we live again?* He fixed his eyes intently on the fields, comforted by nature's promise of renewal.

CHAPTER 3

ELEANOR

A pinching headache settled in behind my eyes as I turned the car up our block. There the house stood, same as always, our darling white three-bedroom tidy with its green shutters and screened-in porch. We'd bought it only a year before. Our very own house. I pulled into the driveway and looked for some difference in the place now that Roger was gone. Would the house come to feel his absence? Would the paint dull, the shutters droop? So far, they looked the same as they did every other day of the year, homey and sturdy. I wondered how long I might expect that to last.

I pulled the car into the driveway, carefully snugging it up to the back wall of the garage before shutting it off. An uncomfortable stillness laced with the heavy odor of oil wrapped itself around me. I paused and looked around. The garage belonged to Roger and his things, mostly. His workbench stood along the passenger's side wall. Above it, every tool he owned hung neatly on a tack board. Next to that was a metal cabinet with drawers holding every nut or bolt a person might need, carefully organized by size. Below the workbench were bins filled with ropes, rags, and scraps of wood. Like with like, all of it in easy reach. It was a simple system devised by Roger. I had always appreciated the tidiness of Roger's things, but now it felt like a hug he'd left behind for me. It brought me comfort to believe that he'd intentionally left his things all in place and easy to find just in case I might need something while he was away.

I clacked across the driveway in my sandals and pulled the side door open.

"Yoo-hoo, it's Mommy," I called, expecting to hear little feet come running.

Instead, I heard Mother. "Now, you sit right here. We've only got just a few pages left to finish," she barked. Next I heard, *"And who will help me grind the wheat?"* The voice she used was squawky and a little grumpy. *Sounds like Mother,* I thought, though I was sure she was trying to sound like a little red hen. I smiled to myself.

"Not I, said the duck," she quacked.

"Not I, said the dog." This voice was like a whiny old man. I came around the corner into the living room.

"Mama!" Barry cried, but neither he nor Carol dared move. The two of them were tucked on either side of Mother, and she had her hand rested firmly on Barry's leg. I suppose she figured that if she was taking the time to read, they were darn well going to listen. I put a finger to my lips.

"Not I, said the cat." Her cat voice was a high-pitched meow. I sat down next to them on the

sofa, pulled Barry onto my lap, gave Carol a little rub on the back. Mother had always been a tough taskmaster. I tried to be gentler with my children.

"Then I'll do it myself, the little red hen said." On Mother went with the story until the Little Red Hen told off all the other lazy animals and ate the bread herself.

"Well, that is a lesson, isn't it?" she said, closing the book. "Everyone needs to chip in and help when there's work to be done, right?"

Carol nodded. "That's right, Grandma." Barry didn't say anything; he just leaned into me. I kissed his head, taking in his toasty little-boy smell.

"I'll put the book away, Grandma," said Carol.

"Good girl." Mother fixed her eyes on me, searching my face for any evidence that I'd been spilling tears over Roger's leaving. I knew she was ready with a scolding if she spotted it. I held my breath, hoping I'd wiped away the evidence.

Mother Hazel Osborn had no patience for self-pity. She had her reasons, not the least being that her own husband, my daddy—and the only man she ever loved—had up and left one day midway through the Great Depression and never returned. She never talked about it, but it grew in her a hardness.

The fifth of her nine children, I was ten when he left. Hard in his own way, Daddy didn't talk too much, but he could be fun. I remember him twirling my sisters and me around the front room on a Saturday night, laughing and carrying on. He'd eventually get Mother to dance with him, too. They must have been happy when they started out. In those early days, there was an ease that would come over her face when she'd catch sight of him walking up the block.

"Here comes your daddy," she'd call, her voice softening from the edge it carried through the day. I do know Daddy was the only one who ever could make Mother really laugh in that "let loose" way a person needs every now and again.

But those days were when I was young. By the end, I don't think I saw a kind word between them, let alone a smile. Whatever Mother and Daddy had when they started out got lost under the weight of no work, no money, and a bundle of kids to feed. By the end, they argued more than anything. Lots of hollering and slamming doors, and Daddy sipping out of his tin flask like it was some kind of medicine. Then he was gone. He went out to find work one morning and never came home.

I remember the worry that troubled Mother's face that evening. There had been stories of men leaving their families in those hard days of the Depression. The belief was that they'd gone off to find work and that when they did, they'd be back with pockets full of money and life would be good again. But Mother didn't harbor any hope of that. The day after he left, she took what clothing he'd left behind and put it in the drawers of my older brothers. She tossed his collection of pipes into the fire. If we ever asked after him, all she'd say was "Daddy's gone," and turn away.

His disappearing left Mother with nine children to feed, clothe, and raise on her own. She had to become the man and the woman of the house, mother and father to all of us. She did the best she could; I surely couldn't fault her there. At first, she took in washing. Then she cleaned houses. It wasn't easy and times were hard, but not once in all those years did I ever see my mother cry. There wasn't any room in that house for tears.

There was one night I remember in particular. All of us were sitting around the dining room table. We'd had the little bit of dinner she could afford for all of us, some biscuits and lard, I think. My younger brother, Jack, five years old, sat across the table from me, his white t-shirt dirty from a hard day's play.

"Mama?" he said, his dusty face pitiful under that blond brush-cut. "My belly is hurting. Couldn't I please have a bit more to eat?" Now, Jack wasn't one for good manners, so for him to say "please" meant he really was after whatever he was asking for.

I remember Mother hung her head for a moment and the room went quiet. Then, she pushed herself up spine straight in her chair. "We've all had our share of what we've got for now, Jack. And those tears aren't going to help," she said. "Tears are nothing but a waste of the little bit of strength you've got left to go on. But you have a cry if you need to. And I'll bet you all the bread in the bakery that once those tears are cried out, you'll open your puffy eyes up to find yourself in the same place you started, only with a raw nose to show for all your blubbering." She looked around the table, meeting all of our eyes each in turn. Then she pushed her chair back, carried her empty plate to the sink, and walked out. Mother was hard, but I still believe it broke her heart to have to tell her own hungry child he couldn't have any more to eat. But, from that day on, she reminded us regularly that tears didn't solve a thing.

"Tears never put food on the table," she'd say at the first sign of a quivering lip. "Tears never mended a threadbare sock." And that, to her credit, was how she had raised nine children on her own.

"Raised them right," as she liked to say (which was debatable when it came to my older sister, Helen, but I never argued).

So, I sent a hard smile back at her searching stare that morning.

"He's off, then?" she asked, standing to leave.

"Yes, he's off," I answered. Barry slid down from my lap. "Little bit of a crowd at the station."

"Hmm." Mother smoothed her dress and headed toward the door. "I think Barry may have the sniffles."

"Is that right? I'll have to keep an eye." I slipped off my sandals. "Thank you for the sitting."

"All right, then," she said without looking back. "See you Sunday for dinner. Goodbye, children." As she lifted her hand to smooth her hair, I remembered the woman at the train station, *"Stronger than you know,"* and I understood the truth of her words. Mother was a strong woman to have done for the bunch of us like she did for all those years. But those days had made her bitter, too. Even now, when her hardships were mostly behind her, she rarely smiled. As I watched her go, I wondered what a different kind of strong might look like.

Carol slipped her hand into mine. "Mama?"

"Tell Grandma bye-bye now," I said, giving her hand a little squeeze.

"Bye, Grandma," she called. The door slammed and the house fell quiet.

"Mama?" Carol asked, nearly whispering. "Can we have a cookie now?"

"No cookies with Grandma?"

Carol dipped her chin. "No."

"Well, let's go get us a couple." I picked her up and in we went to the kitchen.

"Barry, cookies!" Carol called. He toddled in. We untied Mrs. Gaines' fancy grosgrain ribbon and sat around the table eating gingersnaps, orange drops, and soft molasses curls (no chocolate, that was on the ration list) until the whole box was empty. And as I sat side-by-side with my two little ones, munching cookies to salve our sad good-byes, it occurred to me, like it hadn't until Roger boarded that train, that the responsibility for our life was mine to shoulder now. Roger was serving the world. I had to do my duty here at home. Caught up in my fears, I had only thought about missing him. But, alone with the children for who knew how long, it felt like I had a purpose, too, like I had a reason to find my strength. I wasn't sure how, but I did feel like his leaving had tasked me with figuring it out.

CHAPTER 4

ROGER

The train picked up speed, traveling through farmland and forest with the kind of determination that assured a man he had no choice but to be carried along. Inside the car it was loud and close, the steady rhythm of the train's wheels lulling the men into a weighted silence.

After a while, the kid seated next to Roger thrust a meaty hand his way. "Kelly," he said, loud enough to be heard over the train's churning. "Kevin Kelly, PFC."

Roger took the young man's solid hand in his own. "Roger Mitchell," he replied, turning gratefully away from the window and his thoughts.

"Draftee?" Kelly, a red-haired boy, thick and freckled, asked, his eyes darting a quick inspection.

"I am," Roger answered. The other men seemed to sit up, perk their ears at the kid's barking, confident voice.

"Family man?" Kelly continued his interrogation.

"A wife and two children," responded Roger. "My little girl is three, and my boy's a year and a half."

"Young ones."

"Very young to be doing without their Daddy," said Roger solemnly.

Kelly eyed him. "It's got to be done," he said firmly.

"Sure looks that way." Roger shrugged.

"Better world when it's over. I believe that." At this, several of the other men adjusted in their seats and craned their necks to get a look at this kid, wondering, as Roger was, at the stuff this brash soldier was made of.

"You've been over, then?" Roger asked.

"I have," Kelly answered, betraying nothing. "Where's your basic?"

"Arkansas, they tell us."

"That's about right, isn't it?" Kelly laughed. "They tell ya a lot of things in the Army."

"You're on leave?"

"They brought me home for a spell. But I'm going back," he said, nodding as if convincing himself.

"That right?" Roger wasn't sure what it meant to be "brought home." As far as he knew, once you were over there, you were over there.

"Did my basic at Camp Grant," Kelly continued. "Me and my kid brother went over together."

"He going back, too, then?"

"My brother? Nah." Kelly looked down at his knees, his assertive front faltering. A silence fell between them. Roger waited. The other men waited, too, all of them anxious for some glimpse into the true story of war. Eventually, the kid lifted his head, his face pink, his eyes sad but hard. "Colin's never coming home. It was D-Day. It happened that we landed together. I made it up the hill. Colin left it all on the beach."

"Oh, that's terrible," Roger said. "I'm sorry for your loss."

Kelly pulled a long breath and reclined in his seat. "Not as sorry as those Krauts are gonna be when they see me coming back for 'em."

"They say it was hell that day," Roger said.

"Oh, man, was it," Kelly replied. His voice went flat, quiet. "Hell and then some." He looked past Roger, settling his gaze somewhere outside the train window. "When the fighting was over, some of us went back down the hill. Casualties and wounded everywhere you could see. I ran around looking for Colin, yelling his name, hoping I'd hear him yell mine." Kelly paused, looked at Roger, his eyes filled with a kind of unending disbelief. "And there he was." Kelly's voice thickened. "Splayed out like he was faking it, arms flung wide, legs spread, looked like he was trying to make a snow angel there in the sand. My kid brother. His eyes still open, his mouth pulled wide like when we were kids and we'd scream 'Geronimo!' before we jumped off the garage roof. Only now Colin had a red hole ripped through his middle." Kelly rubbed roughly at the pale stubble on his chin. "I'll never forget it. I carried my own brother to the edge of that beach." His voice cracked. "Loaded him onto the transport and watched him taken away."

"Helluva thing," Roger murmured. The man seated in front of him shook his head and made a quick sign of the cross. The train's wheels beat a rhythm like an honor guard for the kid's young brother.

"They called me home after that, on account of my being the only son left," Kelly explained. "I have three sisters, but Colin was the baby. My mother's favorite. She's never gonna get over it." He pushed himself up in the seat, bravado threading his voice. "So, the way I figure it, I might as well go back over there and take a few more of those Jerrys out while I can. For my mother and for Colin." He gave Roger a sharp nod and became a soldier again. The only reminder of his pain was the hand he swiped at a wrinkle in the knee of his uniform. He rubbed hard at that knee. Roger couldn't think of a thing to say that didn't sound either foolish or stupid.

"Glad it was me folded his arms across his chest, closed his eyes," said Kelly after a while.

"I s'pose that is some small comfort," replied Roger.

Kelly nodded. "But nobody should have to look at their kid brother with a hole clear through his heart."

"No, that surely isn't right."

"Not much right about war." Kelly spoke like a man much older than his years. "Of that you can be damned sure." He leaned his head back against the seat. "But you'll find that out soon enough. I'll be getting some shut-eye now. You might think about doing the same. Sleep's one of many things that gets awful hard to come by over there."

"All right, then," Roger said, but he knew his thoughts wouldn't let him sleep for some hours to come.

The kid leaned his head against the rest, closed his eyes, then popped them open again. "You're doing the right thing," he said, "for those little ones you got. You'll see when you get there. It's gonna take the lot of us to settle this thing, but we'll be glad we did when it's over." The kid crossed his arms over his chest and closed his eyes again. Roger stared out the window at the empty country roads, feeling hollow but more determined than he had when he started.

CHAPTER 5

ELEANOR

Around five o'clock or so, my sister, Jean, rolled up in her big red Cadillac. I was at the sink, peeling carrots for dinner, when she pulled in. Roger and I got a kick out of her in that car. A tiny blonde gal, she had to sit on a pillow to see over the steering wheel, but she didn't care. She loved her Caddy, and it suited her. Small though she was, Jean was a pistol, always dressed to the nines, her bleached hair pulled into a tight chignon.

Carol clapped her hands when Jean walked in, squealing, "Yay! Auntie Jean!" Barry jumped up and down.

"Hey, look at this gang of misfits." Jean pulled both children into a squeeze. "Now I know how your daddy feels coming home from the factory every night," Jean said. She looked over the children's heads at me.

"How'd it go this morning?" She raised her eyebrows.

"Fine, fine. They still made him go."

Jean laughed. "Damned Army. Were there others going?"

"Some. A crowd, but not like in the early days when Earl and them went."

"Maybe that means the thing is gonna end soon."

"I can only hope."

"Brought you something," she said, letting go of the children and reaching into her purse. "It's a blue star flag for the window." She held it up. "So people know your man is gone."

"I know what it is," I said, taking it from her. The fabric was a thin nylon, red with a white rectangle in the center and a blue star in the middle of that. Through the top ran a wooden dowel strung with a yellow cord. I held it up. "My own blue star flag," I said softly, thickness gathering in my throat. "I always wondered how a family got ahold of one of these."

"They have them down at the plant. We keep a box in the office," Jean said.

It was nicely made, the blue star centered just right and the red border bright and chipper against the white. I'd have liked to tell them to keep their old flag and send Roger back home, but the children had their eyes on me.

So instead I said, "Why not?" with a shrug.

"Why not," Carol echoed, with her own little shrug to match mine. I hung the flag from the window latch over the sink.

"Maybe I'll put it in one of the front windows after a while."

"Put it where you like," Jean said. "I just thought you ought to have one like everybody else."

"Thanks, hon," I said, and returned to peeling the carrots. "But enough about that. You know Mother came to sit this morning."

"Can't believe it," Jean said, helping herself to a carrot stick.

"Well, you won't believe this, either. As we're about to leave, she grabs ahold of Roger's arm and says, 'Keep your head down over there.'"

Jean's face stretched into wide surprise. "*What? Our mother?* I don't believe she did anything but give him a kick in the pants." She snapped the carrot between her teeth.

"We couldn't believe it, either."

"Well, I'll be danged, Mother has a soft spot."

"At least when someone's going off to war." I said it. I laughed. Jean laughed, too, but something twisted up a little inside me, dark and jangly. Jean sensed it.

"Well, don't you worry," she said, quickly. "She'll have no use for him when he gets home again. You can count on that."

"I'm sure she won't." I took a bite of carrot just to give that worry in my gut something to gnaw on. The children were milling around our legs like kittens.

"I'll get dinner going, if you'll keep these two happy," I said. "That's what Roger would do."

"I'll do just that, my dear wife," she joked, pulling Barry onto her hip. "We'll make the best of it. Maybe even have some laughs while we're at it."

"You always do make me laugh, Jeannie girl."

Jean gave me a reassuring smile. "Oh, almost forgot, I brought a melon. Left it in the car. C'mon, kids, let's go get us a watermelon." They traipsed out the door, Jean leading the way in her work skirt and heels. I went back to the carrots, a smile on my lips but an ache in my heart. Jean was good fun and my favorite sister, but there was something missing, and there would be until Roger was back here in his own house, with his own family, where he belonged.

CHAPTER 6

ROGER

Roger had seen a newly dead man once in his life. Of course, he'd been to funerals here and there, old men and women cleaned up and tucked neatly into a casket. But one time, when he was a boy of twelve, he bore witness to the end of a man's life. It was the hired man who worked the Weaver farm. Ol' Henry they called him, an odd man who had seemed ancient to Roger at the time. He was quiet, tired-looking, leathered by the sun, and seeming always to have a certain weight on his shoulders. People claimed he drank and lived in an old lean-to out in the woods along the river. Roger never believed it. The man's clothes were too clean, too neat for living in the woods. Roger believed Ol' Henry had someone somewhere who looked after him, worried about him. Someone other than just the Weaver family caring that he showed up to work their old mule.

It was the mule, Daisy, who handed Henry his final hat in this earthly world. One summer afternoon, hot as blazes, everyone sluggish and short-tempered, Roger had been lazing around the Weaver farm with Billy Weaver, a boy he'd known most of his life. Looking for some way to ignore the heat, they'd wandered out to the field, kicking dirt and talking about heading for the stream out beyond the tree stand.

About halfway there, they'd come upon Ol' Henry at the edge of the bean field. Henry was fussing at the plow side of Daisy's harness, untangling the straps or something, Roger couldn't quite make out what. Whatever it was, it had Henry standing squarely behind Daisy's right hind leg. Now, one might suppose an old farm hand would know better than to stand behind a mule's rear legs, but what a person knows and what a person does is often at odds when they've been doing it for a very long time. Ol' Henry had been tending to Daisy for nearly ten years by then.

As Roger watched Ol' Henry work, a summer-sized bee managed to land squarely on Daisy's right haunch. Ol' Henry seemed none too bothered by the bug. He got the leather strap fixed in place and started flipping it to make sure it was moving right. Well, that lash smacked the bee square out of the air just as it was rising off Daisy's backside. The bee fell back onto Daisy's haunch and, angry as a buzzard, stuck its stinger as deep into her thick hide as it could manage. Daisy snorted in protest, then kicked out. Her kick landed squarely in the center of Ol' Henry's chest and knocked him clean off his feet. Roger remembered the old man calling out a startled

"Oh!", his face in full surprise. He dropped solidly on his seat, the heat-dried dirt puffing up in dim clouds around him. A toothy smile crept across his face. He looked on the verge of a hearty chuckle, as if laughing at himself for such a foolish mistake. Then his eyes fell shut. He collapsed straight back onto the parched soil and lay still as a stone.

Roger and Billy ran over. Billy bent and tugged at the old man's shirt.

"Hey, Hey, Henry, wake up, old man." Henry did not move.

Billy straightened. The boys looked at one another.

"Think we should throw some water on him?" Roger asked.

"I think he's dead," Billy whispered.

"Dead?" Roger echoed faintly, not because he didn't hear Billy, but because it seemed impossible that a man could be alive one second and gone the next, right there in the bright, sunny, ordinary farm field.

They stood there transfixed, two boys in the pressing heat, staring down at Ol' Henry. The man looked perfect in death, his eyes closed, the lines on his face eased into calm, looking as though he'd fallen peacefully asleep at the edge of the field. Roger could still recall the unexpected quiet of sudden death. Daisy snorted and fussed to fill the silence. Her jerking movements made it seem as though she was trying to look over her shoulder. The boys both took a step away from the old mule.

Billy ran and found his father. Roger stayed with Ol' Henry. Afraid to touch him, Roger kept his eyes trained on the man, searching, hoping for some sign of life, a twitch, a gasp, the quiver of an eye. It never came. Then, Billy's father and mother came running, Billy leading the way. Billy's father shooed the two boys away. They shuffled off reluctantly, turning back for another glimpse here and there, saying nothing. From an oak in the field's tree stand, Roger and Billy watched in silence as Henry was carried to the house on the back of Daisy, the very beast who'd dealt him his mortal blow.

It did happen that Ol' Henry wasn't as old as his name would indicate—forty-two, said his lady friend, Darlene. And it did turn out that Ol' Henry had a woman who took care of him, washed his clothes, and fed him a warm dinner in a tiny rented room behind the courthouse. She and Henry had in common a fondness for the drink, according to the church ladies. Still, Darlene managed to put together a quiet farewell for the man and see that he got a proper burial. Then she left town, they said. Roger never knew if that was true, but he did expect he'd see a good many more dead men before he was back home again, and it was likely they'd all leave someone behind.

CHAPTER 7

ELEANOR

I t was strange to tuck into bed without Roger, stranger still to wake up without him. There was a quiet in the bed where sweet nothings used to be, only my toothbrush leaned in the bathroom cup, only my nightgown hung on the bathroom hook. His half-full Aqua Velva bottle still stood on the top shelf of the medicine cabinet. All of it felt like a reminder of what love couldn't overcome.

Downstairs, in our tiny breakfast nook, his chair sat open and waiting, warm coffee on the stove but no one to kiss with that brown breath. Not a lunch to pack or factory duds to wash. The end of the day turned long and dull with no hope of Roger rolling in from work, a little sweaty and smelling of the gritty factory.

When he was home, he'd fill the place up with his laughter, his kidding around. Just his being in the room made our little house seem right. Without him, there was a spot left wanting. Men take up space in the world, the way they carry themselves, big and wide, voices rich and deep, musky odors coming off of them when they swoop you into a hug. Remove them and a hole opens up, a gap where that man ought to be. At least, that's the way it was for me.

Still, I got breakfast around, same as always. The children fussed and dawdled, same as always. The room was a little emptier, but the routine stayed the same. Oatmeal for breakfast and little-kid chatter.

"More sugar, please," said Carol.

"Okay, a little more, sweetie," I said. "But we're rationing." I watched the fine white grains spill over her lump of oats and thought about how we used to spoon sugar over our oats without a care.

"We're gonna have to be very good while Daddy's away," I said, trying to bolster myself as much as anybody. "We have to eat all our breakfast and take our naps. And we must write letters to Daddy every day."

"Daddy wants a cat picture," Carol chimed in.

"That's a nice idea." I fed Barry a bite of oatmeal. "Maybe we can make it for him after breakfast." I'd written my first letter to Roger just last night. Nothing special, just a run through of our day after he boarded the train, and a long bit about how much I already missed him, how I wasn't sure I cared to go on without him. I knew what he'd say reading that: "You have the children to keep you going while I'm away." He'd said it a hundred times if he said it once, reminding me I wasn't alone. He was right, but the love you have for your children is a different kind than the love you share with your sweetheart.

☆   ☆   ☆

On Sunday, we traipsed over to Mother's for dinner. Just the previous Sunday, we'd made this walk as a family, with Carol perched high atop Roger's shoulders and Barry boy on my hip. Now, I had Carol by the hand, Barry on my hip, and we were making slow, steady progress, just the three of us. The afternoon was as hot as could be and I was feeling every degree of it, my feet straining against the straps of my sandals and a curl of sweat damping my hairline. When Mother's quaint little cracker box of a house finally came into view, I was ready to drop. I had an idea I might fall into Mother's favorite oversized calico-covered chair and never get up again.

I pulled the back door open and gave a tired, "Hello." The children toddled in ahead of me.

"In the kitchen," my sister, Helen, called out.

Helen. She wasn't my oldest sister, but she was the bossiest. She spent most of her time poking her nose and her opinion into the lives of all of us. She loved to ask questions and dig around sore spots until she found the pain, like she was testing your weakness against her own. And then she'd laugh, as if her bites were okay as long as she ended them with a chuckle. I was seldom in the mood for her.

We climbed the stairs into the kitchen. She and Mother stood side by side at the counter. Taller than the rest of us, Helen was thin and lean and took only the barest care of her appearance. She wore her dirty blonde hair in a braid down her back and dressed in a loose-fitting shirtwaist nearly every day of her life.

"Say hello to Grandma," I said.

"Hi, Grandma," the children said in unison.

"Hello, children," Mother said, "the toys are out in the front room."

"What about me?" Helen asked, an awkward scowl on her face. Barry grabbed my hand.

"Hello, Auntie Helen," I said for all of us.

"Hello, Auntie Helen," Carol echoed. Then she grabbed Barry's hand and they ran off into the living room.

"Don't make a mess!" Mother hollered after them. Another Sunday dinner at Mother's, ordinary as ever, even if I felt like the whole world had changed its color from rose to gray. I held up the brown paper sack I'd brought. Mother raised her eyebrow.

"Tomatoes," I said. "From Roger's garden."

"They'll be nice with dinner," she answered with a nod.

"Yes." I set the sack on the counter and pulled a glass from the cupboard. "Boy, this heat is a doozy." I ran the tap to get myself a cool drink.

"Summertime in the city," Mother said. "It's never as nice as it is back up north."

"I s'pose," I said. "Seems to me I'm feeling it more than in summers past."

"It *is* August, Eleanor," said Helen dryly. She opened the icebox.

"Well, thank you for the news, Helen," I said, giving her a nudge. "Maybe you ought to cool off inside there."

"Ha-ha. Sounds like you're the one who needs it."

I ignored her and swallowed a long gulp of water, ran the tap once more, and took another long guzzle.

"I guess you were thirsty," Helen said, bugging her eyes. I didn't reply, deciding instead to just pull the tomatoes one by one from the small brown bag. They were beautiful, a smooth, deep red with the sort of orange cast that makes you know there's a sweet ripeness inside. Each one had a good heft in my hand. Roger did have a nice touch in the garden.

Jean and Faye showed up not too long after and we slipped into our seats around Mother's table. We passed the dishes, a light summertime meal: cold Spam, potato salad, bean salad, tomatoes and cucumbers. Not a bite of it felt welcome on my lips.

"Strange with no man at all around, isn't it?" Faye said.

"The table does feel empty," I said, pouring iced tea.

"It's so quiet."

"I think we can manage," Helen chimed in, pushing a tomato slice between her teeth.

"I was just noticing...." Faye said. She shot a look my way. I rolled my eyes.

"Guess Helen'll be wearing the pants for us now," Jean said. "What with her job in the factory and all."

"I do work hard," replied Helen. "Hard as any man, eight hours a day. I'd even say they're lucky to have me." She laughed, and it seemed like she was laughing at herself.

"Oh, I'm sure they are, Helen," Jean teased.

"I don't suppose *you'd* even know." She dropped a pile of potato salad on her plate.

"I've been thinking about getting my own war work," Mother announced. "It's good money, and I'm as strong as the next lady."

"Ornery as the next lady," Jean muttered to me behind the potato salad bowl.

"But what about Mrs. Gaines?" Faye asked with quiet surprise. "She wouldn't want to let you go." Thin and bright-eyed, with a mane of deep auburn hair, Faye moved through the family like a friendly mouse, taking bits and crumbs as they dropped from the table. She was the sensitive one with a knack for knowing how other people might feel. She could mostly bring us around to understanding one another—when we took a minute to listen to her.

"She'd let me go for war work," Mother answered. "She said as much a few days ago."

"Who'll clean up the old battle axe's messes then?" Helen asked.

"Well, I don't think I took the time to check in about that," Mother said. "But I've got nothing against the woman. She's provided me a living. I just think maybe I could do a bit more with myself, is all." Mother looked pointedly at Helen.

"Okay, okay," she said, like she was writing it down. "I'll ask at the plant. But what about Jean?" She giggled. "She should ask at her place."

"I think we're full up at the moment," Jean shot Helen a glare. "But I'll ask." Jean worked in the hiring department at the Buick plant on Dort Highway, so she could easily get Mother a job. But that would be the day, Jean wanting Mother to work at the same place she did.

"Thank you, girls," Mother said, nodding.

"What about you, Eleanor?" Helen asked, turning her taunts on me. "Bet you could take on some work now, with Roger gone."

"Oh, you think so, do ya?" I shot back, my voice tight with irritation.

"We've all got to do our part," she said, flashing me her smug grin. "You know that." She shoved a chunk of Spam into her mouth.

"I think I am doing my part, with my husband gone to fight and two small children to see to."

"You're not the only one who sent her man off to war," Helen laughed, glancing Mother's way. Mother, bless her, kept her eyes fixed on scooping a mouthful of potato salad.

"Think what you want. I'm not about to go gallivanting off to get a job just to prove something to my bossy sister. I've got plenty to keep me busy right at home, and that is exactly where I am needed the most." I glared at her. She took an oversized chunk of Spam and cucumber and shoved it between her teeth.

"There you go, El," Jean cheered, but the whole thing was twisting my stomach up into a mess of knots. I swallowed a bite of potato salad, but that only made it worse.

"There's a gal down at the plant," Helen said, talking around her food. "She has four children, works every single day just like me, and she still gets dinner on the table every night." Pleased with herself, she smiled, a glob of mayonnaise clung to the corner of her mouth like it didn't want to go in.

"Oh," Jean said, her voice thick with a syrupy sarcasm, "isn't that nice?"

"Yes, isn't it?" I said, turning to Jean. "A right old workhorse down there at the plant. Bet she's carrying her groceries home on her back through two miles of snow, too, isn't she, Helen?"

"You don't have to get mad," Helen said.

"And you don't need to go around sizing me up against all the other women in town."

"Well, I..." Helen's face reddened.

"That is enough!" Mother barked suddenly from the end of the table. "More than enough. Lord, I thought the bickering was over once Jack and Mary went off, but I guess I was wrong."

Helen opened her mouth to say something, but Mother held a finger up. "Don't say another thing, now, Helen. There isn't a one of us here who wouldn't rather there wasn't a war on, but there is. And I expect that my daughters, each one, will be as brave and useful as the next girl." She glared at each of us in turn, then took her plate and marched into the kitchen. The children were looking from one to the other of us.

"Well," Jean spoke up. "I s'pose she told us." She laughed. Helen rolled her eyes and ran off after Mother.

"She's right, I guess," Faye said. "It isn't such an easy time."

I nodded, spooning a bite of potato into Barry's mouth. "No, it is not easy," I said, "but it sure isn't the same for all of us." Faye blinked, her doe-brown eyes surprised that I wasn't giving in.

"It's all fine and good for Helen to do her part at the factory. I do understand that. But does she understand there are some of us who have just said good-bye to a husband, not knowing if we'll ever see him again?" My throat tightened. I pushed a bite of tomato through my teeth. It dropped like a rock into my stomach.

Jean rubbed my back. "It'll be okay, El," she murmured.

"I hope so." I took a long swallow of tea. Roger'd been gone three days and I still wasn't finding that strength everybody was so sure I had. My stomach was a tumble of uncertainty, and everybody had ideas about what I ought to be doing next. "Don't you know there's a war on," and all that. I understood the need for it, but sometimes it felt like the whole gol-danged country was looking over my shoulder and tut-tutting.

"Hey, what about dessert?" Faye said, turning to Carol. "Didn't your mommy bring something yummy to eat?"

Carol clapped. "Yay! Dessert!"

Barry joined in. "Yay!"

"I'll be right back." Faye escaped into the kitchen. Jean cleared my plate.

With them all out of the room, the quiet fell heavily over me. I looked from Barry to Carol, bright blue eyes waiting for their mother to let them know it was okay. I smiled, putting on the happy face they were used to seeing in me.

"Eat up, little ones," I said. "We've gotta be strong for the fight." And I made a muscle like Roger would. Both kids took bites and made a muscle while they chewed, just like Daddy had taught them.

CHAPTER 8

ROGER

The rail journey itself was enough to make a man wonder if there was anyone truly in charge of this particular war or, if it wasn't all just the ends running the middle. Originally informed he was headed to Camp Robinson, Arkansas, Roger instead found himself climbing down off the train at Fort Sheridan, Illinois along with all the other new recruits. Kelly was long gone by then, having detrained in Grand Rapids, but this detour made Roger think of him and the general amusement he took in the Army's whims.

As it turned out, the stop was for enlistment, with all the demoralizing head shearing and nakedness that that process seemed to require. Processed in bunches, they exchanged their clothing for uniforms, sat for official Army photos, ate an unappetizing meal of beans and franks, and were, finally, herded onto a train bound for Arkansas, all within a few hours. In the fading light of dusk, Roger wondered what else a man might be subjected to in the concerted effort to make a soldier out of him. The other men, just as ready to speculate, chuckled and tossed around snide remarks about the simple nonsense in store for them. But it was just that: speculation. There was no longer a man among them who'd been anywhere near the raging conflict.

The southbound train chugged with a determined sense of delivery through the night. Roger snatched bits of uneasy sleep, his head jostling against the hard metal side at uneven intervals. Somewhere in the hours just past dawn, the train pulled into an empty station in the middle of a new town. Groggy and befuddled, the men filed onto a worn platform. They were in Little Rock, Arkansas, population 88,000, according to the sign posted on the station's brick wall. The train rolled away, leaving the group of them, about 200 in all, standing in the Arkansas night with nothing but the sharp buzz of insects for company.

"Looks like they pretty much roll up the streets after dark in this town," one of the men said. Roger flopped down heavily on his Army-issue knapsack and pulled at the stiff collar of his new uniform. His "civvies," as the enlistment soldiers called civilian clothes, had been packed into a box and shipped home to Eleanor hours ago, along with the photo they'd taken of him, freshly shaven and smart in his dress uniform. Roger could imagine Eleanor growing teary and maybe a little proud when she saw him all dressed up like a real soldier. It would have been nice to share that with her.

Sitting long enough on the empty train platform for it to seem they'd been forgotten, the men started complaining about hunger, boredom, and the terrible humidity. The sun rose slowly, but with a steady blaze over the horizon, adding heat to the mess of their predicament. Eventually, the louder fellas started talking about walking off and disappearing into the Arkansas wilderness, never to be seen again.

"Wouldn't even notice, I bet," said a short, swarthy man who sounded like he'd come from somewhere east of the Hudson. Dozing against his knapsack, Roger grunted his agreement, but kept his eyes closed, his hat tipped low. Wasn't a one of them going anywhere, and they all knew it.

The conversation slowed into sullen disgruntlement as four school buses painted deep Army green pulled up to the platform. A bellowing sergeant took charge.

"Hustle your sorry asses up on that bus now, gentlemen! This here's the Army and we're making soldiers down here!" He didn't crack a smile or catch an eye but kept hollering until the slow-moving bunch filed onto the buses. "Gentlemen" was a word he used only once.

Roger found a seat in the middle of the bus next to a chunky pink fellow. The heat seemed to be getting the better of him already. His cheeks were reddened, and droplets of sweat dripped from his hairline. Even his eyeglasses were fogged, as if his body were creating its own steam cloud.

"It's gonna be a hot one," Roger remarked.

"Oh my word, yes," the man answered breathlessly. "It is so hot. Can't imagine they'll expect us to do any training out in this heat. Do you think?" he asked, his eyes wide with genuine concern.

"Maybe they'll keep the heavy stuff to early morning or dusk when it's cooler," Roger offered.

"Oh, I do hope," the worried man went on. "A man I sat next to on the train ride down here told me they work you in the heat on purpose. 'To toughen you up,' he said." The man fussed at the buckles on his duffle.

"I s'pose we'll manage," said Roger, thinking it didn't seem they'd have much choice either way.

"Oh, not me. I'm terrible in the heat, just terrible," the pudgy man said, as if the worry was a never-ending loop playing on a phonograph record in his head. The last fella must have spent his train ride amusing himself with the porky man's concerns.

"Even when I was a child, oh, Mother would never let me out in the heat," the man went on. "No, it gave me rashes. Heat rashes. I'm not one for the heat."

Long since weary from the journey, Roger decided not to say any more. Any man who expressed his consternation this much wasn't looking to be eased. It made Roger wonder about the wisdom of such blind recruiting as the draft. Couldn't be helped, he supposed, but a man like this would be nothing but a sitting duck anywhere close to the front. Roger hoped they found him a desk job somewhere far away from battle.

Less than half an hour later, the buses turned into Camp Robinson. It was a grouping of low-slung white buildings fronted by a grand reception center, the whole thing looking like a small town built in the middle of nowhere. The men climbed down off the buses, traipsed through the reception center, and dropped their bags on the other side. In a stroke of unexpected empathy, they were allowed into the mess hall for a late breakfast. "'Bout damn time," was the sentiment among the new recruits. Roger was grateful to be satisfying at least one of his creature comforts. Eggs, toast, and oatmeal were the offerings and Roger ate his fill, wistfully reminded of the day before, when he'd eaten the same meal surrounded by Eleanor and the kids.

"Better eggs, better company," Roger said to the slim man sitting next to him. The fellow recruit, hunched over his own plate, raised an eyebrow.

"Just yesterday I ate this same meal," he continued, "with my wife and little ones. Same meal, but damn spot tastier yesterday sharing it with them. No offense, of course."

"None taken," responded the man. "Had some bacon along with my eggs yesterday, at my Pap's table. So, I'll see your 'better food, better company,' and raise you half a slab of salt-cured pork." He smiled.

Roger laughed. "Seems you got the winning food, but my young ones win the hand."

"'Magine they do," the man conceded.

They settled into an easy silence. Roger's thoughts turned again to the marked shift in his life. It seemed like weeks had passed since he'd seen Eleanor, but in fact it had been only a day. He wondered how long he'd be able to recall the comfort, the ease of his previous life. How long before Army life began to seem normal, and his life with Eleanor a faded dream? How long before he dared not recall his life with Eleanor, for fear he'd turn into a sniveler like the fat man on the bus?

After breakfast, bunks were assigned: forty men to a hot and crowded barrack. Roger was in the center of the open room with a bed, a footlocker, and one lone hook that hung from the rafter's edge.

"Hang your dress uniform there, soldiers, and get those fatigues on," the sergeant's voice boomed. "Then fall out." They did as they were told, halfway reluctant and halfway curious to find out what training was all about.

It didn't take long. Gathering into an ill-formed clump in the blazing heat, the sergeant wasted no time ordering them into rows. Pushing and pointing, he fashioned a formation out of the mass.

"Now stay that way," he hollered. Basic training became all of the ugly business promised: lengthy runs through dirt and mud (the heat of the day was indeed a prime time for such drills, just as the fat man had feared), endless calisthenics, exacting rifle training, late-night recon missions, marching, shooting, obstacle courses, hand-to-hand combat, and then some. Every command was communicated in deep bellows and sharp shouts— embarrassment and belittling were the favored methods of discipline. What little consideration any of the commissioned men showed to the newbies was punctuated by reminders of the point of all their efforts.

"You lazy bastards will be thanking me for this when you're chasing Nazis through the Ardennes," was a favorite refrain of the chiseled drill sergeant.

"Wherever the hell that is," groused one old boy, beads of sweat dripping off his chin like a running faucet.

"I'm sure we'll learn soon enough," Roger said. In the midst of the mosquito-thick heat of deepest Arkansas, he couldn't imagine the day he might find himself across an ocean chasing an enemy (or running from one), and he didn't particularly want to.

Along with adjusting to the relentless training, a man had to adapt to a complete lack of privacy. Everything was subject to the eyes, ears and nose of any other man walking by. For a married man used to sharing a bedroom with a sweet-smelling woman, being privy to the variety of noises, odors, and general animal tendencies of thirty-nine other men took some getting used to.

As promised, Roger wrote Eleanor every night with the details, dreary and drab though they were. That first letter was the hardest to write, as it was a true acknowledgement of their being apart.

Dearest Eleanor, he began, the pen scratching too lightly across the coarse Army paper for how much those words meant to him. *How are you?*

In his head he could almost hear her reply, "I'm fine, fine, honey. How are you?" It was what she answered every day when he walked in from the factory.

And how have the children been for you? he wrote, just as if she were sitting there in the room with

— 64 —

him, as if he could take her in his arms any time he wanted to. His throat tightened. He brushed a finger gently over her name and whispered, "I miss you with all my heart, Eleanor, but I will be brave, that I promise you, I will be brave."

He continued his letter more easily after that. *Today we ran five miles through the Arkansas swamps. And I've got umpteen mosquito bites to prove it!* He went on about the endless drills and exercises and his notes on the other men and where they were from. Likely she gave hardly a hoot about any of it, but he was committed to writing daily, and he felt sure she'd at least appreciate the length of his letters, if not a single thing more.

While he wrote, he kept her in his mind's eye, small and tender, smiling, her arms open and welcoming. In those moments he sometimes felt overcome by a primal longing for her, a physical ache; yes, the desire was sexual, but more than that, it was a longing for a deep connection with her. A feeling that if he could only just slip back into the safety of her arms, he might never let go again. Along the bottom of each of his letters he included his promise to return.

"I'll be back" he wrote, drawing a heart underneath. Whether he included it as a comfort to her or to himself, he couldn't be sure, but it had the ring of reassurance when everything else was so out of his control.

CHAPTER 9

ELEANOR

S pending time with my sisters was fine for the most part, but not one of them had near as much at stake in this war as I did. So, I was relieved to run into my friend, Rita, at the playground the next morning. Her husband, Ralph, had shipped out just a month or so before, so she was exactly the kind of company I needed. Like me, Rita was staying home, raising her children and trying to keep up some kind of normalcy with her husband gone. She lived around the corner and had three little ones. The oldest, a boy, was school-aged, but the other two matched up with my Carol and Barry perfectly. I invited her to my place for the following day, but she insisted I come to her.

"I know how strange it is in those first few weeks with the empty house," she said. "So, come over and I'll take care of you." I laughed and agreed. Truth be told, I was still feeling less than myself, so getting taken care of sounded pretty good right about then.

The children and I walked over after breakfast. Rita met us at the door, with Marjorie and Patrick standing alongside her. A thin woman with a thick brunette bob and a smile that always seemed ready to break into a laugh, Rita welcomed us into her home. Marjorie was the spitting image of her mother, petite and thin, her brown eyes round and bright. Little Patrick seemed to take more after his father, a thick-shouldered boy with dark hair and a burly disposition for a young boy. The oldest, Ralph Junior, was off at school. But, from all I'd seen of him, he was a kind boy who helped with his sister and brother and managed to be nice to my own children when he saw them, too. They were a dear family, and I was glad to know them.

"C'mon in," Rita said, waving her arm. "I've got coffee cake, and I made a whole pitcher of iced tea to beat this heat." The children ran off to the playroom, and Rita and I went into the kitchen to chat. She had a lovely home; her kitchen was painted a pale blue and she had it decorated with copper baking molds and flowered trivets. It was cool and bright, just right for a summer morning.

We sat at her kitchen table. She poured us each a glass of iced tea and I told her a little about Roger's send-off. She told me Ralph was still in training somewhere in Pennsylvania.

"I hear some of the wives are following their men around wherever they are stationed. But with the children, none of us can go anywhere too far." She flipped her hair off her forehead like it was a bother.

"And I've got Ralph Junior in school besides. So, I'm staying put, but I do miss him."

"I guess I hadn't realized wives were doing that."

"Apparently it's frowned upon, taking up spaces on the trains that are meant for soldiers, but women are doing it anyway."

"Well, like you say, it'd be hard with the children and all," I agreed. "What about war work? Have you thought about going into one of the factories?"

"It's the same thing. What would I do with the children? I know some women are doing it, but that's mostly women with children in school. It's just not that easy when they are so small."

"That's what I thought, too. I think I'll do better for the war effort if I stay at home with mine, at least for now."

She cut me a slice of her coffee cake and slid the plate across the table. "It's made with molasses and oat flour, but I think it tastes fine."

I took a thin bite and it did taste fine, as fine as a wartime cake could—better, even, dense and sweet. Then I swallowed it and my poor stomach sent out a protest the likes of which I hadn't felt in years. I couldn't hold back my grimace. Rita stopped right in the middle of her sentence.

"Are you all right, Eleanor?" she asked, her eyes wide.

"Oh, I'm fine," I said, trying to cover. "Just my stomach's been a bundle of nerves since Roger left. I can't eat a thing."

Rita pulled her chin in. "Just since he left?"

"Well, a little before, I guess. I'm sure it's just worry." I took a long pull of iced tea. That was another bad idea. Next thing I knew, my stomach lurched, my brow broke out in a sweat. Embarrassing as it was, I excused myself, and hurried upstairs to the bathroom just before the whole mess came back up.

"You okay?" Rita called from the other side of the door.

"Yes, yes, out in a minute," I answered. I wiped the place clean, rinsed my mouth, and opened the door.

"I don't know what's come over me," I said. "Maybe it was something I ate."

Rita eyed me. "How long did you say you've been feeling like this?"

"Oh, I don't know. A week or so." I dabbed at my brow with a handkerchief.

"Are you sure it's Roger being gone, or is it the saying goodbye?"

I hadn't an idea what she meant.

She leaned toward me, rested a hand on my arm. "What I mean, El, is you might need to get to the doctor and see if you're eating for two again."

"For two? Oh my word," I said in disbelief. Rita laughed and, just like that, I knew she was right. I'd felt this way only two other times in my life, and I had Carol and Barry to show for it. A flush went through my body. Rita got me a glass of water.

"Just sip at this. Morning sickness doesn't last forever."

"But I can't have a baby without Roger."

Rita shook her head. "Let's hope you don't have to," she said.

"Oh, Rita," I sighed, feeling like a fool.

"Just get to the doctor," she replied gently, "then we'll take it one day at a time."

Sure enough, the doctor confirmed it: the baby was due in late April.

CHAPTER 10

ROGER

"Well, how about that," said Roger as his eyes scanned through the first lines of El's letter. His voice was so thick with wonder that his buddy, Hendricks, craned his gangly neck for a peek at the pages.

"Good news, Mitch?" he asked. They stood in the dirt outside the mess hall. The air had the unsettled feeling of a storm brewing.

"I'll say. I'm gonna be a father again, third time over." Roger took off his hat and ran a hand over his shorn hair, the bristly nap still a surprise to his fingertips.

"Well, hell, congratulations there, Pop." Hendricks clapped him on the back.

"Yeah, thanks," Roger said, his tone a little bittersweet. Hendricks looked at him sideways. Roger shrugged. "Just doesn't feel right, me so far away down here. She's already taking care of the two we have."

Hendricks nodded. "Can't be helped, really. My own missus was none too happy that I was leaving

— 71 —

her with four boys." He laughed. "But it looks like things are working out okay." He beamed and held his letter up. "The two older boys have taken on neighborhood mowing and yard work. She says they're doing it because dad has gone to do his own duty, but I imagine they were looking for the extra pocket money I used to slip to them on a Friday payday." He chuckled lightly. "Either way, they're out of her hair and putting themselves to good use." Hendricks leaned back on his heels. All four of his boys were school-aged, his youngest older than Carol by three years.

Roger smiled. "You're raising a nice bunch of young men there, sounds like." But his mind was busy tangling with the possibility that he might get a leave to help Eleanor, even if only for a day or two. He knew the early weeks of a pregnancy were the difficult ones for her. Both times before, she'd had a hard time holding down more than saltines and ginger ale until she started to show. He hated the thought of her having to manage alone, but there was little he could do about it.

The storm Mother Nature had promised fell hard and heavy in the middle of afternoon operations. The sergeant kept them out in it. "They won't stop the fighting for a little bit of rain over there, now will they, gentlemen?" he said.

Roger slogged through it, barely listening to the sergeant. Rain was rain. Dirt was dirt. And all Roger could think about was the promise of a new life on its way, and how desperately he would have liked to get back home. He called Eleanor after chow that evening.

"How you feeling, darlin'?" he asked the second he heard her voice.

She laughed. "I guess you got my letter."

"Got it this morning. This is the first chance I had to call. We are gonna have us a big family, you and me." He grinned and hoped she could hear his joy through the phone.

"Seems so," she said. He could hear a touch of fatigue under her contentment.

"But how are you feeling, honey?" he asked.

"Oh, I'm all right," she replied. "A little tired and not much is agreeing with me, but I'm all right."

"Any help from those sisters?"

"Jean and Faye, of course. Helen didn't have anything nice to say about it, as you can guess. She seemed to think I had a choice in the timing."

"Don't let her bother you too much," Roger said.

"Oh, she does and she doesn't, depends on my mood."

"I'm sorry I couldn't be there so you might put your feet up from time to time."

"I'm just sorry you're not here period, whether I could put my feet up or not. I miss you."

Roger kicked at a tiny stone on the worn wooden floor, sending it pinging off a pipe across the commissary hall.

"I miss you, too, honey. I'm talking to the CO tomorrow, see if I might get a leave."

"Oh Rog, that'd be wonderful."

"Not much hope of it, the sergeant says, seeing as I just got down here. But I'm gonna ask anyway."

"Well, I'll cross my fingers, like I shoulda crossed my legs, I suppose," she quipped, and they laughed together. "Oh, it's a mess, isn't it? You there, me here, and now a baby on the way."

"We'll get through it. I promise we will. And we'll be stronger for it."

"Yeah, strong, that's all anybody talks about these days. I, for one, cannot wait to be weak again." This time she laughed alone, softly.

"I'll be strong enough for the both of us when this is over," declared Roger, meaning it more than mere words could really convey. They murmured a few more words of love and longing, then hung up.

Roger let his hand rest on the telephone receiver, its smooth enamel hot from where he'd held it tight. The quiet dark of the empty commissary settled around him and his thoughts turned to the young soldier on the recruitment train.

"You're doing the right thing," Kelly had said, "for the little ones you got." This baby was just one more reason Roger needed to do the right thing. And so he would, he resolved. No more pining for home. He'd do his duty here and he'd go where they sent him and do what needed to be done there, too. Then he'd come back home and see to raising the children and loving his wife like a good husband and father should.

CHAPTER 11

ELEANOR

We went on through the fall and into the holidays in pretty much our usual fashion. Jean and Faye came by a good bit. I'm not sure I could have done it without them. I wrote Roger every day and got a letter from him every day, too. The children drew pictures and scribbled and were tickled when Daddy sent letters back to them. They seemed to get bigger by the minute, and they were happy most of the time. My pregnant belly grew rounder.

Then Christmas blew in, blustery and bitter, a perfect match for my mood. The war wasn't over, and Roger wasn't home. He wasn't overseas in the fight yet, but he wasn't with me either, so I couldn't have cared less about celebrating anything. I'd kept myself brave and well-behaved for Thanksgiving, just like they said the war wives were supposed to. I'd baked pies and mashed potatoes, set a nice table, and managed to say I was thankful for something even when I didn't feel it. But Christmas demanded more, what with all its ribbons and good cheer, and I was in no mood for it. Still, I did my best to make some kind of holiday, for the children mostly. We hung decorations and baked up until the last minute. It wasn't the same sort of baking as in ordinary times, but by then I was used to making do with molasses, oat flour, and shortening.

Soon enough, it was Christmas Eve, the children were napping, and Jean was coming by around two o'clock to cart us to Mother's for dinner. I had just put a curl to the green ribbon I tied around a pie box when I felt a draft blowing up from the side door. It crept in, wrapping itself around my ankles like a thin, hungry cat. At first, I rubbed at my ankle with the edge of my other foot, registering it like an itch. Then it climbed up to around my waist, my back. I rubbed at my arms. When the fresh scent of cool air met my nose, I finally realized the problem.

"That danged door," I groaned out loud to no one. It was a little warped and had to be locked tight, or a hard wind could make it swing like a church bell. I wiped my hands on my apron and spun around to get it closed up again. As I rounded the corner, there, just inside the door, stood a man. My heart jumped. My mouth fell open. I screamed my fool head off.

"Whoa, whoa," the man said, a grin spreading across his lips. "Now, what kind of way is that to greet your old soldier husband come home for a visit?" He opened his arms.

"Roger?" I blurted.

He laughed. "You'd better believe it," he said, the grin on his face suddenly familiar. I reached a hand to touch him; his Army uniform felt stiff and official against my fingertips. I looked up and he came into full relief. Tall and smart, his hair trimmed to a brush, a bundle of red roses in one hand, it was my Roger. I thought I might faint. He wrapped his arms around me and pulled me into a hug. I let myself fall against him, and there he was, as real as the day I'd let him go. Tears welled in my eyes. I pressed my face to his chest. He was muscly against me, firmer, like a thickened tree. But his scent was the one I knew, musky and warm. I breathed him in.

"Oh, Roger," I whispered. I took hold of his smooth cheeks and pulled his face to mine, pressing my lips against his, hard and hungry. Rich, salty, and familiar, his tongue against mine confirmed it: my Roger had come home to me. He held me tight, kissing me as hard as I kissed him. I never will forget the strength I felt in his arms wrapped around my body, his hands pressed firm against my back. I could have melted into him and stayed forever.

He pulled out of our kiss only to say, "Now, there's the kind of welcome I was looking for." And we went right back to our mouths getting reacquainted, the roses a discarded jumble of red at our feet.

After a while, we pulled back and took a look at one another.

"I can't believe it's really you," I said, holding tight to his upper arms, his hands resting easy around my waist.

"How come you're kissing me like that, then?" he chuckled.

"Oh, stop it." I nudged him. "You could have sent a person a note or something."

"And miss all this?"

I kissed him again, slower this time, a kiss of comfort, of real welcome.

"Don't you look handsome in that fancy uniform," I remarked, smoothing his lapel. "'Course, I barely recognized you with the haircut. Looks like they took every single curl."

"Cleans up easy," he said, rubbing his hand over the stubble. "Looks to me like you added a little something extra while I was gone." He tenderly cupped the curve of my pregnant belly.

"That's what you left me with," I replied. "Oh Roger, I've missed you awful."

"Me too, El."

"Let's get your coat off and maybe you'll stay a while."

"Don't mind if I do. Where are the children?"

"Napping." I paused for a moment and listened. Nobody seemed to be stirring. "I'm surprised Carol hasn't stumbled down the steps with that scream I let loose." I took Roger's coat and hung it by the door, wishing I could have touched up my makeup, straightened the house, made things perfect to welcome him home. But there hadn't been an ounce of warning.

"I can make you something to eat," I offered, walking back into the kitchen. The roses were laying on the cupboard, but Roger was nowhere to be seen. My heart skipped a beat.

"Rog?" I called.

"No tree?" he answered from the front room. A wave of relief washed over me. I went in and there he stood, hands on his hips, his back wide and strong under his Army shirt.

"I'm gone a minute or two and the whole place falls apart," he said, swinging around to grab hold of me, a teasing smile curving across his face.

"Oh, I don't think skipping a Christmas tree qualifies as the whole place falling apart," I said, kissing him. "And you have been gone for more than a minute, my good soldier." He twirled me around. "Ooo," I said, laughing, "you built some muscles down there in Arkansas, I see."

"Told 'em I had a wife I needed to impress when I got back home."

"Just you being here is all the impression I need." A part of me wanted to take him by the hand and lead him up to bed, love him and keep him all to myself for as long as I could. But, next thing we knew, Carol was pattering down the stairs. She came around the corner of the bannister. When her eyes fell on Roger, they lit up like Christmas lights.

"Daddy!" she screamed and made a beeline straight for him. Roger pulled her up into his arms.

"Daddy, you're home!" Carol cried.

"For a few days, anyway, sunshine," he said.

"So, this is just a leave, then?" I asked.

Roger looked at me over Carol's curls. "Just for the holiday," he admitted. I wished I hadn't asked, wished I hadn't made him say it. Of course it was a leave; the war wasn't over yet.

I took a deep breath like I had every morning he'd been away and said, "Well, we'd better make the most of it, then!" I wrapped my arms around them and joined in their reunion dance. Roger was home, and we were gonna have a family holiday, the war be damned.

Barry appeared a little later at the bottom of the steps, his cheeks flush with sleep, curls tangled. He had moved into his own big-boy bed not long after Daddy left.

"Hi, pumpkin," I said. He eyed me sideways, then threw a questioning glance toward Roger and Carol.

"C'mon, honey," I said, "Daddy's home." I reached out my arms to him. He sat hard on the bottom step and peeked through the bannister slats.

"Hey Butch, it's Daddy," Roger said. "I've come home for a couple of days."

His eyes flitted from me to Roger and back again.

"It's Daddy, honey. You remember Daddy," I said.

Carol screwed her face up into a twist. "That's silly, Mama." But there wasn't an ounce of recognition in Barry's face saying she was right. I went over and swung him onto my hip.

"It's Daddy," I whispered into his ear, and carried him over to join us on the sofa.

"He remembers Daddy," Roger said. "Just remembers me without all these funny clothes." Roger pulled at his Army shirt. Barry sat with his head pressed into me but his eyes on Roger.

"Hello, Barry," he said in his silly Popeye voice. "You remember me, don't ya?" he said pounding his chest. Barry grinned. "Why, it's your ol' Pa come to visit from the Army." He pulled his mouth wide with his fingers. Barry smiled.

"Carol knows me, here, don't ya, Carol?" He grabbed her into a hug. "You know your ol' Pa." He tickled her neck. Carol giggled, slapping at Roger's arm.

"Maybe you don't recognize me 'cause the Army cut my hair to smithereens." Roger rubbed his hand over his brush cut. "Mind if I borrow this a minute?" he said, reaching for Barry's blanket. Barry, a curious grin in his eyes, handed the blanket over. Roger curled it into a ball, plopped it on his own head. "There, that's better! Now I have some hair. Just right," he said, nodding hard until the blanket slid onto his lap. "Oh, no!" he cried. "My hair!" Giggling, Barry leaned over, Roger pulled him onto his lap, and that was that. We were a family again, at least for a little while.

☆   ☆   ☆

Within the hour, Jean rolled up the drive. At the sound of her beep, I went to the door and waved her in.

"C'mon in for a second."

"No, you c'mon," she said. "Mother's bound to be burning something. We gotta go!"

"Just come in for a minute," I called.

"Eleanor," she huffed, turning the car off, "we have got to get over there." She marched across the driveway. "I am not eating another dry Christmas turkey. And I'm not letting Helen make the gravy, either. Last time I had lumps of flour stuck in my throat 'til New Year's."

"Just come inside." I grabbed her hand and pulled her into the living room. Roger was still on the couch with the children. He popped up and grinned when Jean walked in.

"Oh my word," she gasped, pressing a hand to her chest. "Roger?"

He smiled. "In the flesh." He pulled at his shirt as if to prove it.

"I thought I'd seen a ghost!" She fanned herself.

"Christmas leave," he said, that big smile still plastered on his face.

"Well, isn't that just the best Christmas present ever!" She gave him a big hug.

"I'm glad you think so. I'm pretty happy about it myself."

My eyes once again brimmed with happy tears, the kind I hadn't known for several months.

"All right, let's get to celebrating, then!" I said, handing each of them a load of goodies to carry out to the car.

"Yay! Christmas!" Carol shouted, and we all piled into Jean's red Caddy.

☆   ☆   ☆

Everybody was thrilled to see Roger. Even Mother managed a crooked little smile when he came into the room. Of course, he'd thought ahead and brought her a box of sweets, so that helped some.

As it turned out, Roger's visiting wasn't the only gift for Christmas; Earl, our oldest brother, showed up, too. We were just finishing dinner when the doorbell rang, and Helen went to answer, complaining as she went about who thought they could come around on Christmas Eve, blah, blah, blah. Then she swung the door open and hollered, "Land sakes, if it isn't Earl!" She pulled him in, and we all came running.

But Earl had been overseas for well more than a year by then, and he looked every bit of it. Thin and gray, his uniform hung on him like he was nothing but bones underneath. His eyes were bloodshot, his chin grizzled, and the distinct odor of whiskey wafted off him. Big brother Earl had always liked to drink, but this seemed like he was marinating his very soul in the stuff. None of us said a word. We just welcomed him home and loaded up a plate full of Christmas food for him, a whopping pile of mashed potatoes and gravy at its center. He hardly ate a bite and managed not to offer much in the way of conversation, either, but we were glad to have him with us. My sisters and I tried every which way to draw him out, but he spent most of the meal keeping watch of us and nodding from time to time, almost as if he didn't quite believe he was here safe and warm again. Mother didn't say much either. She encouraged him to eat and asked after where he was staying. He managed not to answer, and she managed not to mind. She just smiled, and in that smile you could see every bit of the pleasure a mother felt in having her eldest at the table. Drunk or sober, lost or found, he was home again.

☆   ☆   ☆

After dinner, Earl and Roger went out back for a smoke and some war talk. Roger had a worried twist to his brow when they came back in. Later, after the children were in bed, he told me bits of Earl's tales. It seemed Earl had seen quite a lot of fighting—enough that the Army had sent him on a "nervous leave" nearly four months ago. He'd been back in the States at a Virginia hospital since early November. Before that, they'd looked after him somewhere in England.

"He's awful shook up," confessed Roger. "Won't say exactly what he saw and did, but he's not the Earl we used to know."

"I figured he was just in his cups."

"It's more than that. I've heard stories from some of the men who've been over. War changes a man, they say, in ways you can't explain."

I pressed my hand to his cheek. He kissed my palm. "Last thing I want is for you to change, Rog," I said.

"One thing'll never change, Eleanor Mitchell, and that is my love for you." He kissed me hard. "I will always love you. Always. No matter what this mess brings."

"Do you think you'll have to go to the fight?" I asked, knowing I shouldn't, knowing it wasn't fair.

"Can't say," he whispered in my ear. "Loose lips sink ships." He kissed my neck.

"Oh, Rog," was all I could think to say.

He wrapped me in his arms. "Shhh," he said, and he pressed his mouth over mine, lifted me into his arms, and carried me to bed.

After that, there were no words, just love, long-missed and aching love between us. I knew his touch, his hands strong but gentle, and that desperation again, our need to know each other, one more time, to have each other, remember each other as best we could in all the days ahead.

We only had three days together, but we made the most of them, laughing, loving, and celebrating. I would have preferred not to share him, but we did go over and see his sister, Bea, for the holiday afternoon. Roger called his folks from her place to wish them a Merry Christmas.

When the time came for him to leave, he arranged a ride to the station with an Army pal of his.

"You stay here out of the cold," he insisted. So we said our good-byes there in the kitchen. I was steadier about it than I had been the first time; I didn't cry or ask him to stay. My eyes welled with tears, my throat tightened all over again, but I'd grown stronger in the last four months. Handling the household and the children by myself had forced me to come into my own.

Later, after it all played out, I sometimes looked back on that good-bye and wished I hadn't been so brave. Sometimes I wish I'd put up such a fuss he couldn't have gone, but that wouldn't have done either of us a bit of good.

I do remember watching him as he walked away down the drive, his stride familiar but those Army clothes making him different, too. He stood taller in them, more determined, his shoulders straight with resolve. He was a soldier now, and he was ready for the fight.

CHAPTER 12

ROGER

Leaving Eleanor and the children the first time had been difficult, but the Christmas good-bye was miles harder for Roger. He hadn't said a word of it to Eleanor, but rumor was that his platoon would be shipping overseas just as soon as they returned to camp.

"From what I heard, we'll be boarding that transport with our bellies still full from Christmas dinner," Murphy told them just before they lit out for home. So Roger held Eleanor just a little closer as they kissed good-bye. He committed the warm press of her body to his memory as best as he could, the curve of her pregnant belly a firm reminder of all he had to fight for, all he was meant to return to.

True to the gossip, ten days after the new year, the orders came for Roger Mitchell, PFC, and the men of his unit to pack their duffels and climb aboard a train bound for Maryland. From there, it was presumed they would ship out to Europe. Roger's heart dropped at the news. He waited, unhearing, through the rest of the sergeant's orders. Then, as soon as they were released, he hightailed it to the phones and dialed Eleanor. It had been two weeks since they parted. Those had been difficult weeks for him, his mind drifting back over and over again to the comfort of Eleanor's loving arms around him, the warmth of her body against his, the gentle powdery scent of her. He fed the coins into the slot, dialed with shaky fingers, and pressed the phone hard against his ear as if it might bring her closer to him.

"Hello?" she answered.

"It's me, darlin'," he spoke shakily. His stomach a pit of dark nerves, he swallowed hard so she wouldn't catch the fear in his voice.

"Oh, Rog. It's good to hear your voice, I've been missing you like crazy." Roger could hear her smile through the phone line. His shoulders eased.

"Me, too, honey, how are you?"

"Oh, I'm fine, you know, bored and lonely without you, but fine."

"And the children?"

"Oh, they miss you awful. All the talk around here is about Daddy and what we're gonna do when you get home again. Here, Carol, say hello to Daddy." Roger listened like a man who couldn't be sure he'd ever hear these voices again.

"Hi, Daddy!" came Carol's voice, bright and smart across the line. "I made a slush pie for lunch."

"Did you?" Roger's eyes welled with tears. "How'd it taste?" he asked, and bit his lip against the tightness in his throat.

"I didn't eat it!" she cried. "But Barry took a bite."

"What?" Eleanor hollered in the background.

"Mama, I'm just teasing," Carol said, then whispered into the phone, "He did have a little bite." Roger laughed, bathed in the relief of joy through tears.

"How *is* that brother of yours?" he asked.

"He's silly." Roger pictured Carol and the black receiver a size too big for her small hands pressed importantly against her cheek. With her little finger she might be twisting the telephone cord into knots.

"Carol!" Eleanor cried.

"Bye-bye, Daddy, love you! I'll send you a drawing of my slush pie."

"You do that. Bye-bye, sweet girl, Daddy loves you."

Eleanor came back on the line. "Oh my word, that girl. Barry's napping just now or I'd put him on, too."

"Sounds like she's as full of beans as when I left."

"More, I tell you," she laughed. "But how are *you*, honey?"

"Bored and lonely without my best girl." It was as true as any other thing he could think to say, but then he added, "I'm heading to Maryland in the morning," and it felt as if he was dropping a bomb of darkness into the middle of their easy joy.

"Maryland?" she echoed.

"Seems so." He wanted to offer some bit of hope or promise, or to soothe her. He wanted to say it would all be fine, but the outcome of war was never certain for any man. So, he did his best imitation.

"Just means we're all trained up," he said, swallowing hard. "How's that baby coming, anyway?"

"Well, he's coming along," she chuckled, as happy to change the subject as he was. "At least that's what my belly seems to be saying." He imagined El cupping a loving hand under the growing curve.

"It's a boy, then?" he asked.

"Only heaven knows," she said, "but either way will be fine."

"Yes, it will," he said quietly, knowing that no matter what happened in the next few months, he wouldn't be home for this child's birth. "Well, you make sure those sisters of yours are taking care of you."

"Oh, they are. Jean's been great. And you know, Helen, she'll take over as much as I'll let her, but she isn't any good at it." They laughed. Helen was an easy topic to lighten the mood. The phone line buzzed between them.

"So … you'll be going over?" Eleanor asked quietly, her hushed voice barely audible.

In her question Roger heard her vulnerability, her helplessness, and it renewed his sense of responsibility. He was to be brave for the both of them. Eleanor had enough to see to at home. So he stood tall, pushed his chest out, and tried to sound as honest and reassuring as he could be.

"Just Maryland is all we know for now," he answered. "But the guys say they don't bring you to the coast unless they plan on shipping you over."

"I had so hoped it would be over before now."

"I know, honey, but it'll be okay."

"Will it?"

"It will. I plan to make sure of it."

"Keep safe," she whispered, her voice thick. "Just keep safe."

"I'm coming home to you, El," he said. "Come what may." They both recognized it to be a promise a soldier couldn't keep.

"I love you, Roger."

"I love you, too, El." They listened to each other breathe. The operator poked in, asking for more money. Roger dropped two nickels into the slot.

"Thank you," the operator said and clicked off.

In the background, Roger heard Carol. "Momma, Barry's awake."

"I'll let you go, honey," Roger said.

"No, wait, I'll go get him, you talk to Carol. I want you to talk to him, too."

"Hi again, Daddy," Carol chimed over the line. "Barry's crying."

"Is that right?" he managed to say, then bit down hard on his knuckle to stem the thickness in his own throat.

"Yeah, he's still little. He cries. But *I* don't."

"You don't?" Roger asked.

"Only if I fall."

"What a big girl you are." Roger leaned against the rough-hewn canteen wall and closed his eyes so he could focus on his little girl's words.

"I'm almost four."

"You will be soon," he said.

"Here's Mommy. Bye, Daddy." Her words danced in his ears, delicate and happy. He wondered when he would hear her voice again.

"Here," El said, breathless through the line, "talk to Barry."

"Hey, Barry boy, it's Daddy. I just wanted to say a hel-*looooo* to you," Roger said in the voice he knew would make the boy smile. "I love you, my big boy."

Barry gurgled something then Eleanor said "Dada" and Barry repeated it, "Dada, Dada, Dada."

Roger's eyes welled with tears. "Hi, my boy."

Eleanor came back on the line. "We ought to have that mastered by the time you get home again."

"It's a fine family we have, El."

"A family to come home to," she remarked.

"It certainly is."

The operator broke in again. "Five cents for another two minutes."

"I s'pose we better hang up now," Roger said reluctantly.

"It'll have to be you, Roger," Eleanor said. "I'm gonna hold on here forever."

"Maybe if we do, they'll forget I'm supposed to go," he said with a laugh.

"Just hide there under the phone, why don't you?"

"Good idea," he said. "Tell the children I love them."

"I will."

"Every day."

"Every day."

"I'll call again, soon as I can," he said.

"And write every day."

"And write every day," he promised.

"I love you, Rog," she whispered.

"I love you, too, El. Now and forever."

Then, they counted one, two, three, and hung up together.

CHAPTER 13

ELEANOR

After Roger shipped out, the days turned cold and dark. There wasn't much to look forward to, the same day bleeding into the next all over again. So, when Rita called saying, "Let's get together," I jumped at the chance. Gabbing with her over a cup of tea seemed like just the thing. We made plans for the following morning, and I'm sure it would have been a lovely visit, if the war hadn't gotten in the way.

Shortly after breakfast, the children and I climbed Rita's porch steps. I let Carol ring the bell and we stepped back to wait. The three of us were a little giddy about getting together with our friends. But all that silly anticipation fell away when Rita creaked the door open and peeked around its edge. Her face was as pale as a ghost's, and she looked frightened.

"Rita?" I was unable to hide the surprise in my voice. A fake half-smile played across her lips, the sort of smile you'd give a traveling salesman you weren't ever intending to allow into your home.

"Rita, it's me, honey," I said, growing more concerned. "What's the matter?" She squinted hard, but I could see she didn't recognize me. "Rita," I repeated, firmer than before, and the light of recognition bloomed across her face.

"Oh, Eleanor," she moaned. "It's Ralph." And she burst into tears.

"Oh no." I rushed in and wrapped her in my arms. She leaned into me, and sobbed, her body heaving with despair.

"Momma?" Carol said.

"You and Barry go find Marjorie and Patrick," I said. "Rita's not feeling well."

Carol eyed me, unsure.

"Go!" I insisted.

She looked stricken, but she took Barry by the hand. "Come," she said, and Barry went right along with her toward the playroom.

"Let's sit, Rita," I suggested, guiding her toward the sofa. She flopped down and threw herself back against the sofa cushions. She closed her eyes, and the tears ran from under her long lashes. I took her hand. Her fingers were icy in mine. She felt fragile, like she might shatter at any moment. I didn't say anything, just let her weep. There wasn't really anything to say.

After a while, she turned toward me. "Oh, Eleanor, I'm so sorry. I forgot all about our plan for today."

"Don't you think a thing about it," I replied, laying a reassuring hand on her leg. "I'm here to help now. Whatever you need."

"I *had* remembered," she said, holding a finger up to clarify. "In fact, I was straightening the place up when the doorbell rang. I knew it was too early for you. I thought it was the milk man." She shook her head. "Can you imagine? I thought it was the milk man." She pressed a hand to her lips. "What a fool." She dropped back against the sofa again, trembling with her sobs.

"Oh, honey." I tried to pull her into an embrace. Her body was as limp as a worn-out rag doll. "I'm so, so sorry," I said, but they were weak words for such a monumental loss.

"Why would they send the Western Union man that early?" she said, thinking out loud. "Shouldn't they have certain times for that kind of thing? Something more civilized?" She tipped her head as if trying to work it out, her eyes fixed somewhere across the room.

"Seems like it," I answered quietly. But really, what did I know about when a Western Union man ought to come deliver his terrible news?

"Must have been before nine," she said, mostly to herself. "In fact, it had to be, because I'd just gotten Ralph Junior out the door."

"That is on the early side."

She swung her head around abruptly. "Eleanor! I'm so glad you're here," she said, as if seeing me for the first time.

Her confusion surprised me some; Rita was not the flakey sort. But who knew what awful news like this did to an ordinary woman's mind? I decided to ignore it. "I'm here as long as you need me,"

I reassured her. "Let me get you some water." I went into the kitchen. There on the counter lay the telegram, unfolded next to the telephone. She must have been calling people or getting ready to when I rang the bell. I left it where it lay. I was almost afraid to touch it, truthfully. I ran a cool glass of water for her.

She was there on the sofa where I'd left her, eyes closed, the trail of dried tears like a roadmap of grief on her pale cheeks.

"Rita, hon, here's the water." She popped her eyes open and drank the whole glass in heavy gulps.

"Did you need to make some calls or anything? I'm here now. I can keep an eye on the children."

She shook her head. "No, I called Mother. She said she'd call Ralph's folks."

"Then maybe you'd like to lie down here for a while?" I suggested.

"Oh, I couldn't rest," she insisted, shaking her head furiously. "My mind is whirling like a mad woman." And, as if to prove it, she pushed herself up from the sofa. "There's so much to be done. Mother's coming. I have to get ready." She scurried toward the kitchen.

I followed behind, not sure what else to do, or if there even was anything I could do. She buzzed around the kitchen, wiping at a phantom stain on her countertop, washing out her just-used water glass, folding a towel. She snatched the telegram up like it was a secret and set it on top of a pile of other papers on the edge of the counter. Then she rushed once more out of the kitchen.

"I have to see to the guest room. Mother likes it just so." She stopped at the bottom of the stairs.

"Rita—" I placed a firm grip on her arm, trying to slow her runaway thoughts.

"And the children," she continued, not seeming to hear me, "they have to eat. Ralph Junior will be back from school soon. He only goes a half day. He's five, you know. In kindergarten. Such a big boy." She skittered into the playroom. The children were busy, surrounded by dolls, blocks, trucks, and books. Carol glanced up, but the others played with the kind of concentration children use to ignore the world.

"S'okay," I mouthed to Carol, nodding reassurance. She looked down at the toy she was playing with and back up again, still unsure about what exactly was happening here in her friend's house.

"Oh, thank heavens you brought your children," Rita said suddenly. "I just cannot begin to imagine what I might do with Marjorie and Patrick." She turned and looked at me, a wide-eyed fear in her eyes.

"Rita, honey." I took her gently by the shoulders. "Let's go sit a spell. Just so you can catch your breath."

"Oh, good idea. Would you like some tea? I was about to have some myself. It's so nice to see you."

"Tea sounds perfect." And we went again into the kitchen. "Why don't you sit and I'll make it?" I offered.

"Oh no, oh no." She flipped the burner knob on. "Does me good to keep moving." She ran the water into the kettle, clattered the kettle onto the burner, pulled mugs from the cupboard, and slapped them on the table with a thud.

"I brought some cookies. I'll put them on a plate—"

"What am I going to do, Eleanor?" she blurted suddenly, her voice a tense whisper. "Without Ralph, what will I do?" Her eyes were round with fright.

"Oh, Rita …" I took a step toward her.

She grabbed the cookie tin from my hand. "Sit, Eleanor. Sit down," she snapped at me, as if speaking to a troublesome child. She turned toward the cupboard for a plate. I sat down, as instructed, and wondered if I should call Blanche, the neighbor lady, for reinforcements.

"You said your mother was coming?" I asked, hoping she'd find some reassurance in the idea of having her mother around.

Rita didn't answer. She just slapped the plate of cookies on the table, then stood next to the stove, hand perched on her thin hip, waiting for the kettle to boil. She blinked, straight smiled at me, but didn't say a word. And I, frankly, was a little afraid to say anything until the hot water was safely in the mugs. So, we waited in silence, the two of us, for the tea.

Rita looked off into the middle distance, the space between here and there, the space where a worried soul often looks for impossible answers. The steam built. The kettle began a slow whistle. Rita glanced absently toward the noise, then looked away again. Then the pot screamed full-out. She seemed not to notice. Its piercing cry was deafening. I stood up to see to it. She glanced my way, turned, and flicked off the burner. Her fingers wrapped tight in the hot pad, she grabbed the kettle's handle and carried it to the table, steam trailing behind like a chugging locomotive.

The water bubbled. Angry, popping and spitting, it soaked the tea bags, spattering droplets onto the table. Rita seemed pleased by the fury of its splash. She watched it intently. I sat back and kept my eyes on her, searching for something to say. Of course, there wasn't a word, a look, a hug that could change a thing. I knew that, but it didn't stop me from wanting to try. Rita set the kettle back on the stove and dropped herself heavily into the chair opposite me. She wrapped her hands around the hot mug, its heat seemed to soothe her. She sighed.

"I keep wondering, what if they're wrong?" She leaned into the tea's steam. "Millions of men over there, how do they know it's my Ralph? Lots of men are named Ralph. My own oldest child is named Ralph. How do they know for sure it's my husband? So sure that they send me a telegram? How do they know?" Tears wet her eyes. I reached a hand across the table. She stirred her tea.

"We had plans, you know, Ralph and me," she said. "Chicago, New York. Oh, he was gonna rule the world." She smiled, a proud wife. "He'd say, 'We'll drag the kids with us. It'll do 'em good.'" She shook her head. "'Life is gonna be grand,' he said. 'I promise,' he said."

"I'm so sorry, honey."

"Would you like to see a picture?" she asked. "I can't remember if you've ever met my Ralph."

"I met him a time or two," I said. "I'd love to see his picture."

She stepped into the other room and came back carrying a silver-framed Army photo of Ralph from his enlistment, just like the photo Roger had sent to me. Her photo was of a dark-haired man with a broad nose and piercing brown eyes.

"He is a handsome one, Rita," I said kindly. "You make a nice pair."

She laughed. "Doesn't half do him justice, if I do say so myself. He has just the thickest, dark hair, but they cut it all off." She traced a finger over his lips. "And I know his smile to be a good bit more mischievous than what you see here." She laughed again. "But he is shined up nice." She ran her finger along the edge of the frame. "Shame you haven't met him," she said, her eyes glossy again.

"I would have liked that," I said, choosing again to ignore her misunderstanding.

"He had so much to live for ..." She set the picture frame there at the head of the table. I imagined it had been Ralph's usual seat.

"It's a terrible thing."

"I'll tell you what it really is. It's a waste." She nodded, her mouth a bitter frown. "That's what it is. That damned Hitler. I'd strangle him with my bare hands if I could." She spit an angry laugh through her tears. "What he's done..." She slammed her fist on the table. "*Dammit!* Dammit to *hell!*" She stared at the picture. I kept an eye on her without trying to pry into her broken heart.

The children's chatter drifted in from the other room, lilting and bright, tea party talk or something. Ordinary stuff.

Rita heard it, her puffy, reddened eyes widening. "They've got no daddy now," she whispered.

"It's not right," was the only thing I could think to say.

Her eyes fell on my pregnant belly. "You'll have your hands full soon enough."

"Yes," I said, placing a hand on my roundness. "More to love."

"That's what I thought, too," she said. "When Patrick was born. More to love, what a happy life. I may have said those words out loud." She looked at me with a darkness in her eye. "Just be careful you don't count your blessings too soon," she warned.

I nodded, though her words stung me. I took a steadying sip of tea. A woman in her circumstances couldn't be held to account for all she might say or do. She stirred her tea, the spoon's clink ringing furiously throughout the kitchen.

"Well," I said, propping a protective hand under my troublesome belly and standing up, "why don't I get to work on that guest bedroom for you?"

She once again looked at me with that bewildered stare.

"The guest room," I repeated. "Maybe I could get that ready for your mother?"

"Oh, right, my mother. She's coming, all the way from Minnesota. Can't believe she even offered. Ha. I guess people surprise you sometimes." She sipped her tea.

"It'll be nice for you to have her help," I said.

She looked at me again. "I suppose."

"Someone who can take care of you and the children."

"Oh, she won't really, but that's okay. My mother isn't one for children and that, but at least I won't be alone."

"When will she be here?'

"She said as soon as she could. She was very nice about it. But I imagine it'll be a day or so."

"Well, I'm happy to stay and help until she gets here. Why don't I at least get lunch around for the children?"

"Lunch?" she asked, distracted again, looking out the kitchen window. "That's a good idea. There's tomato soup in the fridge." She stood up, nodding toward my belly again. "I am sorry, Eleanor," she said contritely, "I'm not myself today."

I smiled. "I know, honey, I know." But I turned my roundness away ever just so anyway.

"I'll just check the children," she said and left the room. I let her go, figuring that I'd take care of lunch and that would be one less thing to think about.

Poking around in her fridge, I found the soup, bottled milk, and leftovers—the provisions of an ordinary home. It brought a lump to my throat to see the homey goodness of peas and carrots in a porcelain bowl. They were just another ordinary family, made half and broken-hearted in an instant. Of course it wasn't lost on me that my own Roger was, at that very moment, in some similar sort of harm's way. I just wasn't going to think too much about that. I was here for Rita. That was that. I pulled a chunk of cheese from the fridge drawer. I found the pans in the cupboard and started warming lunch on the stove.

When it was ready, I went to the playroom to get the children. Rita was not with them. "Marjorie, has Mommy been through here?" I asked. She looked up, pushing her brown bangs out of her eyes.

"Mommy's in the kitchen," she said certainly.

"Okay. Well, little ones, it's lunchtime." I tried to sound cheery, but a feeling of unease was tickling my nerves. I led the children into the kitchen.

"Where's Mommy?" Marjorie asked, as if I hadn't just asked her the very same question.

"She's gone upstairs. She'll be down in a bit," I answered, setting bowls of warm soup and a couple of sandwich squares in front of each of them. They ate with the easeful patience of baby sloths. Not wanting to leave them alone for too long, but worried about Rita, I went to the bottom of the stairs and called for her.

"Rita? You up there? Lunch is ready." No answer. Part of me wanted to check on her, and another part thought she might just need some time alone. I went back into the kitchen and sat down with the children, moving Ralph's photo over to the counter as I did.

"That's my Daddy," Marjorie informed me. "He's in the Army now."

"My Daddy is, too," Carol said.

"Isn't that nice? Both Daddies in the Army," I said.

"That's silly," Carol said, smiling. Marjorie didn't say anything, just took a small bite of her sandwich and chewed absently, making me wonder how much she might already know.

After lunch, hands washed and faces wiped, the children settled back into the playroom. I cleared the table, then climbed the stairs to look for Rita.

At the top of the stairs, the bathroom door stood open, a tidy pale pink and white room. No Rita. The air hung sweet with the smell of fresh linens. The winter wind rattled at the windows some; otherwise, there was no other sound. I took several small, slow steps.

"Rita? You up here?" I called out, but not too loud. If she was resting, I'd let her rest. There was no reply. The first bedroom was dark inside. Heavy curtains were drawn against the midday light, but I could make out the foot of a full-size bed. It had to be Rita and Ralph's bedroom. I peeked around the doorjamb, expecting to find her napping in the middle of the bed, but it was empty, the bedspread pulled up tight and tucked in as tidy as a magazine photo.

"Rita?" I whispered. Still no answer. I stepped back into the hall. "Rita?" I said, a touch louder. Again nothing.

The next bedroom was just left of the first. Decorated in pale yellows and white, it was a bright, airy room with a bunk bed along the near wall and a twin with a pink bedspread along the far. The children's room. It was just as tidy as Rita and Ralph's room, beds made with tightly tucked corners, and all the books and toys in their spots on the shelves.

I went on around a small bend in the hallway. The door to the third bedroom was half-closed. I pushed it with one finger, and there sat Rita on a white coverlet-ed twin bed. She didn't look when the door creaked. She blinked slowly but kept her eyes fixed on the small, high-placed block of windows opposite the bed. Outside danced the bleak branches of February trees, leafless and barren against the winter sky.

"Rita? Rita, honey, you ok?"

She sighed, turning her head slowly. "This is the guest room," she said, her voice distant. "Mother'll stay here when she comes. She hates it in the winter when the branches are bare. 'Makes me think of old bones,' she says." Rita turned her head once more toward the window. "I hope she doesn't say that around the children."

I eased myself down next to her. "I'm sure she won't."

"It's the children," she continued in a hushed, weak voice, her eyes on the middle distance. "What to do about the children …" A chill ran through me at the way she said it—so hollow, so hopeless, that it sprouted goose bumps all up and down my arms.

"It'll work it out, Rita, one way or another." I patted her knee. She kept her eyes fixed on those barren tree branches. The room was dreary and cold in the dull midwinter light.

"They do look like bones, don't they?"

"Okay, Rita," I said, clapping my hands, hoping to break her out of her spell. "That's enough now." The handclapping hadn't done more than cause a blink in her eye, so I stood up and put myself between her and those branches. I took her icy hands in mine and gave them the gentlest tug. "Come. Let's get a little bit of lunch into you and we'll just see where we are."

She didn't move from where she sat. She just kept staring over my shoulder at those branches.

"Or maybe I could bring a tray up to you here?"

"Noooooooooooooo," she protested and fell back on the bed, her head narrowly missing a hard bang on the wall. "No food in the bedroom," her voice slurred, and she laughed, throwing a hand to her forehead and closing her eyes as if it were just the funniest thing in the world. My stomach did a leap. I caught hold of her by the shoulders and peered into her face. She'd gone pale, her eyes glassy and unfocused. I pressed the back of my hand to her forehead. She felt clammy and cool to the touch.

"What did you take, Rita?" I demanded, shaking her. "Tell me! Tell me right now!"

She smiled in her delirium. "You're a lovely mother," she said. "Would you take the children?"

Her eyes rolled back into her head. I slapped her cheek. "Rita, *Rita!*"

She was out cold. I looked desperately around on the floor, but there was no evidence of anything that might help me know what she'd taken. I raced to her bedroom—nothing. In the bathroom I found it, there on the sink next to the water glass: a pill bottle. I shook it. Empty. It was Veronal, a sleeping pill, that much I knew. The label said 30 pills. The fill date was from December. There was just no way to know how many she'd taken. I tore down the stairs to the phone in the kitchen and dialed an ambulance. Lucky for me, Rita had her emergency numbers there along the side of the phone.

Then I called Blanche, the neighbor lady from down the block. "Western Union came to Rita this morning and now she's swallowed a bottle of pills," I barked.

"I'll be right there," said Blanche without hesitation.

I raced back up the stairs. Rita was sprawled where I'd left her and still breathing. I pressed a wet cloth against her forehead and counted the seconds until I heard the sirens in the distance.

"Help is coming, Rita, dear," I whispered. "You stay with us." I ran down the stairs and got to the door just as the ambulance men pounded.

"She's upstairs, the room at the end of the hall." I handed the man at the door the pill bottle. "I don't know how many she took."

Blanche was coming up the walk just behind the men and I was about as grateful to see her as a person could be. Small, round and always sure what needed to be done, Blanche would help me get Rita through this.

"She's upstairs," I spoke frantically, and the both of us went up together.

As I reached the top step, Marjorie shrieked, "*MAMA!*" I hadn't even thought a minute about the children. I turned on my heel. Both girls stood round-eyed and frightened at the bottom of the stairs. Marjorie was on the verge of tears; Carol looked scared, but had a steadying arm on her friend's back.

"Blanche," I hollered, "tell them she's only had tea since ten thirty." And then I scurried back down the stairs to the children.

"Mommy's not feeling well," I told Marjorie, crouching down to her level and taking her hand. "The men are gonna make her all better."

Her lip quivered and she rubbed at her cheek. I gave her hand a gentle squeeze and led her to the dining room. "Come. Carol, you come, too, we are gonna wait here out of the way of the men."

"Ambulance," Patrick said. He and Barry were at the front window and all I could think was *thank God for that distraction.*

"Come, boys," I said. "Let's watch from here." I led them to the dining room window. Barry tucked himself up under my arm. Patrick curled in next to him. Carol and Marjorie were on my other side. Together, we watched the cherry-red light spin round and round on the roof of the long white vehicle. Above us, the men banged and barked, directing each other on how to save the life of my dear friend Rita. I held her children close and talked like a fool about ambulances and doctors and how they make people better, my own heart racing, and scared half to death, too.

Eventually, one of the men declared, "Stable. Let's move." Next, we heard the bump and heft of a stretcher coming down the stairs. I had Patrick under my arm already, so I turned to talk to Marjorie.

"Okay, now Marjorie, hon," I spoke gently, wrapping an arm around her middle. "Mommy is coming downstairs and she is gonna go for a ride in the ambulance. And we are gonna stay right here so she will know that we are safe and sound here at home."

Just then the men appeared, the stretcher between them heavy with poor Rita.

"Mommy!" Marjorie cried. She pulled against me, but I held her tight.

"Mommy will be fine, honey," I whispered into her ear. "She's just feeling a little sick, but the doctor will make her better." Marjorie looked up at me, her dark eyes not trusting me for a minute. They carried Rita right through her own front room and out into the icy February morning. Marjorie strained to get loose, but I kept my hold.

"The men are taking Mommy to the doctor," I said, more firmly this time, "and we must let them." She turned toward me. I think she might have wanted to slap me. The tears were brimming on the edge of her lashes.

"They'll make her all better," I repeated. "I promise, all better."

Marjorie looked out the window to see her mother being carried down the front steps and loaded into the back of the ambulance. She eased her fight against my grip, but the tears came full force.

"There, there," I cooed. "Mommy will be okay now. Mommy will be okay." I kissed her warm head.

"I'll call you," Blanche said, shutting the front door behind her. She climbed into the back of the ambulance and they were off, siren blaring, red lights spinning.

"Everything is gonna be just fine, now," I told the children. "Everything will be fine." Although I didn't have a single idea whether it would be or not.

☆   ☆   ☆

Around nine or so, Blanche called. Rita was stable. "They pumped her stomach. Have you spoken to her mother?"

"She'll be here by noon tomorrow."

"Thank the Lord. And the little ones?"

"My sisters came by and took mine home. Marjorie and Patrick are all tucked in bed. They went without too much trouble, although Marjorie cried most of the afternoon. Poor thing. Ralph Junior is brushing his teeth now. He had a lot of questions. I told him Mommy needed some rest. Wasn't my place to tell him anything more."

"You were right not to say too much," she said. "Let Rita tell him when she is ready."

"Yes," is all I said. And we were quiet on the line, not ready to hang up, yet too exhausted to have anything much more to say.

When first we moved into the neighborhood, I'd thought Blanche was a busybody. She seemed to know everyone and their business. But when the war came around, she was the one we came to rely on. She was a part of the civilian defense for our neighborhood, which made her privy to more war details than the rest of us, but it also meant we had someone who would handle all the news we were afraid to share. She was the natural choice for me to call when Rita faltered, and she would probably be the one to help Rita get back on her feet. She'd been through it before, her husband having fought in the Great War. He'd come back in one piece, but he wasn't ever the same, and she wasn't afraid to say so. They went on to have two children—a boy, Freddy, who was over in the fight now, and a daughter, Belinda Jean, who was finishing her last year of high school. I was glad for Blanche right then, her being there and knowing what to do.

"Boy, there's just no telling how a woman will react to news of this sort," I said.

"No, I s'pose not. But you did a fine job today, Eleanor, with Rita and the children."

"Well, thank you, Blanche. I can't say I wasn't a little afraid the whole time."

"We are all afraid from time to time, but it's the doing what needs to be done that gets us through. And you did that today." I might have blushed at her words, but I was alone in Rita's kitchen, so who was to know.

"I do hope she's okay."

"Yes, I hope so, too. It's always the women who get left to pick up the pieces in times like these," observed Blanche with a sigh. "I'll call you in the morning."

The quiet of Rita's house fell heavy upon me when I replaced the phone receiver. A clock ticked somewhere over my shoulder. I didn't bother to look. Instead, I carried my teacup to the sink, washed it clean, and set it to dry. It had been a very, very long day. I climbed the stairs to check on the children.

The young ones were sound asleep. Ralph Junior had just climbed into bed.

"I'll be downstairs," I whispered to him. "Mommy's doing fine." He nodded and rolled over. I pulled the covers up over his shoulders. I couldn't imagine what was running through that poor boy's mind right about then.

I made a bed for myself on the sofa, but sleep danced just outside my reach. I couldn't help but imagine how it all might have turned out if I hadn't gone to look for Rita, or if I had climbed those stairs a little later, when she might have looked like she was just sleeping. I shuddered to think about it.

I rolled onto my side and the baby kicked. I pressed a hand to the spot and thought about what Rita had said. *"Don't count your blessings too soon."* She hadn't meant it, not really. Still, I cupped an arm around my growing baby and, although I'd never been all that much of a religious woman, I crossed myself.

"God bless Rita. And please bring Roger home," I whispered into the quiet of my friend's house. In the darkness, without her here, it felt more like a stranger's.

CHAPTER 14

ROGER

After a week at sea, it was cattle trains that carried the men through the frigid cold to the front. Riding huddled in bunches with the others, trying to keep warm, Roger finally recognized that in this war, he was less a man—less a human being—than a commodity. Men were needed to fight and so men were called, suited up, deployed, and used, but they mattered only as a group, as a force. Any concern for them as individuals was left for the women and children, the mothers and fathers at home. It was a brutal but obvious truth, and one he could do little to change. He was just another one of the bunch, and there wasn't anything to do but what was expected.

Somewhere near the French border, the wheels of the cattle cars slowed, then stopped. The men shook themselves loose and dropped one-by-one onto the frozen ground. It was a jarring welcome. They had been planted squarely in the middle of one of the brutalized landscapes they'd all seen on the movie house newsreels back home: a burnt-out village with battered, collapsing buildings, soldiers in various states of disarray, jeeps and equipment moving about. But, unlike the newsreels, this was in full color, the sights grim, charred, and impossible to believe. The air was filled with an alternating mix of heavy silence and grinding machinery. Roger took a deep breath, and in its icy, sharp pinch, he accepted that he was here now and would soon be in the fight. He shoved his nagging fears deep inside himself. He was as ready for the battle as the next man, and he would execute the task with courage when it was upon him.

It wasn't long. Just two days later, he and the other men from his company made their first push into enemy territory. Roger charged as commanded and fought ferociously, firing his weapon with a kind of detached clarity, ducking and moving, taking cover when necessary.

In that first battle, his focus was strictly on survival for himself and his fellow soldiers. But the next day things changed. On a push deep behind enemy lines, Roger's righteous determination to win was triggered in a way he hadn't anticipated. Climbing a ridge in the midst of a German stronghold, Roger was accompanied by Porky, the pudgy, worried man from the basic training bus ride those many weeks ago. Porky had grown in the months since basic training. He was still often worried, but he took his role as soldier seriously and had every intention of returning to his mother as a hero. Despite the training, he hadn't lost the roll around his middle. Still, he managed to hup along just fine and had learned how to handle his weapon capably. So, when the captain picked out Roger and Porky for reconnoitering the ridge's rise, Roger had no qualms.

They moved out together in the shadowy half-light of early morning, slowly and with as little sound as possible. Porky volunteered to walk lead, three steps and a foot to the right of Roger. Lead position was the dangerous one, but Porky had insisted. They hadn't gone forty yards when a shot rang out from behind a thin tree. Porky was hit. He dropped, wordless, onto the snow-covered ground. Roger crouched behind a rock and spotted the enemy. Raising his rifle expertly, he fired just as the German felt safe to peer out from behind the skinny tree trunk. The German fell backward and disappeared from sight. As he did, another soldier rose behind him and aimed. Roger returned fire just as that man's bullet whirred past his ear. The forest fell quiet. Roger waited, the sound of his breath the only sign of life for miles, it seemed.

Knee-deep in the frigid snow, Roger waited until the wind in the trees was all he heard, then he crawled, combat-style, through the biting snow to where Porky lay. Splayed and unmoving, it was clear he had died instantly. The bullet had struck him through the bridge of his nose, shattering his glasses and cratering his face. His blood was a startling splatter of red across the dry snow. Still Roger shook his shoulder, "Porky?" he whispered. There was no reply. Roger was reminded of Ol'

Henry and the suddenness of death—one moment here, the next gone. Porky's death horrified him in a way Ol' Henry's hadn't. There was a peace in Henry's death, a certain kind of inevitability to it, maybe because Henry was older. But Porky was young, a very young man, a boy almost, well-loved, frightened but courageous, dead in an instant, in a snowy field somewhere in the middle of a foreign land. Such a terrible waste. Would his body ever go home again? What would his mother do without him? The poor kid had been so afraid to go to war.

Roger crossed himself and said a quiet prayer for the kid. Then he looked around. He was alone and not entirely sure what to do next. Already in these two short days he had stumbled across his fair share of fallen men, frozen and abandoned on the battleground to be collected, word was, when things settled down. But something in him wouldn't let that be Porky's fate. *Bad enough he's gone,* Roger thought. *I can't leave him.*

Were he not so desperate to do the right thing, his first attempts to lift the rotund young man might have been laughable. The kid had to weigh 200 pounds, most of it solidly concentrated, like a beach ball, in the middle of his 5-foot 9-inch frame. First, Roger tried to hoist Porky up and over his shoulder like he might a sack of potatoes. He bent down and grabbed an arm to pull over the opposite shoulder, then tugged. The kid barely moved. The whole of him was true deadweight. Roger, in his frustration, disbelief, and increasing fear, changed tactics. He lay down atop of Porky, pulled the kid's arms over his shoulders, rolled onto his knees and pushed himself to standing with Porky across his back. It was not easy, but Roger managed to turn and lift in such a way that he got the kid evenly situated. Then he curled himself low to the ground, knees bent, legs wide, and ran like a hunchback with the dead man lying over top him like a cape. He ducked and dodged as he went, zigzagging and trying to listen for the possibility of trouble. And all the while he hoped that he might, instead, hear Porky heave a whiny sigh and sputter back to life.

Of course, he never did, but when Roger ran into the camp with him across his back, the medics came running, everyone thinking that Porky was just wounded. But when Roger threw him onto the med stretcher, revealing his face—a bloody mess with a hole in the center—it was obvious to them all he had been killed instantly.

The medic looked up from the corpse at Roger. "You brought him back, knowing he was dead?"

Roger nodded, trying to catch his breath. The medic put him in a chair and gave him a tin cup of cold water.

"You could have left him. We go back for them."

Roger, still breathless, shook his head. "He has a mother."

"We all do."

"Yeah, but he's all she has."

The medic gave his shoulder a considerate squeeze. "Not anymore."

After that, Roger had no trouble steeling himself for battle, for killing, for maiming, for winning at any cost. Porky's death had flipped a switch in him. He did as was ordered, when ordered, without question. And the enemy became something less than human, something to be conquered. He didn't know himself anymore after that, as if an animal instinct had taken over and kept him alive. He kept thoughts of Eleanor and the children far from his mind. He dared not lose his resolve. Instead, he thought of Kelly and Kelly's brother, Colin.

"A better world when this is over," Kelly's words ran like a wartime refrain. That made Roger's actions worthy, if not easy.

CHAPTER 15

ELEANOR

This being my third, I knew a contraction when I felt it. But in my heart of hearts, I wanted Roger home before the baby came, so I pretended the squeezes and hitches running across my belly weren't anything but growing pains. Heck, I might have crossed my legs and held the baby in there if I'd thought it would work. As it was, I pressed on. I made breakfast for the children, folded a pile of clean diapers, even managed to get the breakfast dishes washed and put away. Then I went over to open the kitchen window a little. It was a beautiful spring morning, late April, not quite warm, but bright and new. I flipped the metal lock and pushed against the sash. It didn't budge. Stuck from the winter. I put a little muscle into it. And that was it; the window pushed open and the pains seized my back like a vice. They grabbed me up so tight, I wondered if I'd pulled something. But I held off hollering or making any kind of noise. Instead, I leaned hard against the window ledge and waited, breathing heavily and trying not to alarm the children. Outside, the birds sang easy as you please, and a cool spring breeze blew light and fresh through the screen. Inside, I was holding on for dear life against the pain. It was a pain I knew, but this time I was afraid of it some, because this time I was alone.

From behind me I heard, "You okay, Mama?" Carol never missed a trick. But all I could do was nod my head.

She put a hand on the spot where the pain was the worst, in the middle of my low back, and rubbed, as if she had a sixth sense for it.

"Mama?" she asked.

"I'm okay, baby," I said between heavy breaths. The pain was edging down a little now. "Seems like maybe the baby's ready to come."

"Today?" she asked, clapping her hands.

"Seems to be," I said.

"Barry, the baby's coming!" She squealed a little, but I could tell she wasn't quite sure how excited to be, with her Mama leaning hard on the windowsill and breathing like a heifer. Barry, still in his highchair, pounded the tray and squealed with her.

"Time to call Aunt Faye," I declared, and made my way to the phone. "I'll dial, honey, and you tell her."

"Okay, Mama," said Carol, her breath almost as ragged as mine. I dialed the number and handed her the black receiver. "Auntie Faye, the baby's coming!" she hollered, then handed the phone right back to me so she could run into the other room and work off some of her thrill.

I took a few breaths, then, when the pain eased, I pressed the phone to my ear.

"Faye?"

"It's Helen. What was that?" she barked.

"Oh, Helen. The baby's coming. Where's Faye?"

"She's still in bed."

"Well, could you please wake her and send her over?" I demanded. "I'm not sure how much time we are working with here."

"One of us will be along," she said, casual as you please. "Did you call Jean?"

I couldn't answer; the next wave of contractions had taken ahold of my back.

"Eleanor?" Helen's voice sounded weak through the line. Carol came scurrying back into the room. I held the phone out to her again.

"Mama's hurting 'cause the baby's coming," she called into the receiver, then danced off into the other room.

Helen's voice came small through the line. "Oh no, it's like that? Oh my word, we're coming," Helen said. I was well beyond speaking. "Okay, okay," she said, and her phone clattered into place. I put mine back on the hook and breathed out through my tightened lips. The phone rang just as the next contraction was taking hold. I groaned into the receiver.

"Helen called me," Jean said. "I'll be there in a heartbeat." She hung up. I put the phone back again, breathed again, and tried to steady myself. When this contraction subsided, I took Barry from his chair and wiped his face.

"You're gonna be a big brother," I whispered to him. He smiled, patted my shoulder, then wriggled down and went off to dance with his sister.

Another contraction came. I held tight to the table and took a deep breath. A certain kind of anger blew up into my throat as I waited through this one. Tears of frustration stung in the corners of my eyes. It wasn't bad enough the war had me worrying late into the night over Roger; now here I was without him and with our new baby coming. I pounded a fist on the table. Didn't help a whit. So, I steeled myself like I'd done a million times since Roger'd left, threw my coat over my back, and took a seat at the kitchen table to wait for the cavalry to arrive.

From the next room I could hear Carol and Barry's excitement.

"I'm the big sister," Carol told him. "And you're the big brother."

"Big brother," Barry repeated.

"But I'm the biggest," Carol insisted.

"Big!" Barry shouted.

"Biggest!" And back and forth they went until they both dropped off into giggles.

Listening to the two of them joke and play, I couldn't help but wonder what this new little one would add to our family. And what the world would look like for the three of them as they grew. The grand plans I'd had when Carol was born were a far cry from the ones I had now. *Just bring their Daddy home*, I thought. Then a contraction seized me again, and Jean ran in the door.

✮   ✮   ✮

Afterwards, alone in the hospital room, late in the evening, the anesthetic was wearing off in that drowsy way it does, and it hit me hard again. Since I was a girl of fifteen, I had shared everything in my life with Roger, all the milestones: marriage, babies, houses, and new jobs. We'd done every bit of it together, and that was the way I'd expected it always would be. Until the war came along. Now, here I was with a brand-new baby, our new baby, and Roger didn't even know he'd been born. Seemed like salt rubbed hard into an already open wound.

Looking out the hospital window into the dark night, I let myself wonder about Roger. How was he holding up? Was he okay? It wasn't a thought I'd let myself concentrate on too much while he was away. Never having an answer always drove me a little mad. But that night I wondered, was he sleeping just now? Resting somewhere warm and comfortable? Maybe a kind old woman had allowed a few soldiers to bed down in her home that night. Late as it was here, it must be close to morning for him. I hoped there might be something hot for him to drink, to warm him through. Maybe that same kind old woman offered him a cup of coffee.

"The baby's come, Roger," I whispered, tears forming in my eyes. "He's a beautiful boy, just like we thought." I hoped to heaven that somehow he knew; wherever he was, whatever he was doing, I hoped Roger could sense that he was a father of three now. I pressed a hand to my lips and threw a quiet kiss across the room toward the window. "Come home soon, darling," I whispered.

After a while, the nurse came in. She smiled, prim in her white uniform, dark hair slicked back under her stiff white cap. "Just checking your vitals, then you can rest," she advised softly.

She fussed around me, taking my temperature and checking my pulse. I moved and shifted as she needed, trying to be helpful. She knew exactly what she was doing and how to do it. I envied the simple certainty of her knowledge. I had that kind of certainty at home with my children, taking care of them and Roger. But now, in this hospital bed, I didn't have an ounce of certainty about any of it. Instead, it felt like the future, our future, our hopes and dreams, were full of question marks. It felt like taking the long view and finding a whole wide world of emptiness up ahead. I drew a sharp breath. The nurse looked at me.

"You all right, honey?" she asked, her eyes searching mine. "Can I get you some water?"

"Can you bring me the baby?" I asked. "I'd like to hold him another time before morning."

"Don't suppose a couple of minutes will hurt." She patted my arm, then disappeared out the door.

When she returned, she carried a bundle of blue. I gingerly took him in my arms. He blinked up at me with a silent curiosity, as wide awake as if it were noon. Our brand-new baby boy. John was the name we had decided on if he was a boy. Now here he was, born into this world with no father home to catch him. I pressed my lips to his dear head and burst into tears.

The poor nurse, she put a hand on my arm, warm and comforting, and whispered, "He'll be back before you know it." I hadn't told her about Roger's being off to war, but a woman didn't have to say it in those days for another to know.

She smiled. "And you'll just have the most precious gift to welcome him."

"From your lips to God's ears." I pressed a kiss to Johnny's head again.

The nurse stayed with me for a bit, the room quiet around us, the moonlight illuminating the edge of the bed. She had a way about her that soothed me, just her standing there with me, the aura of a wiser, older soul. Together, we looked baby Johnny over, marveling at his tiny features. My thumb caressed his fist, and I felt overwhelmed with wonder at the way something so tiny could be fully formed, with five fingers, fingernails, and tiny lines at the knuckles for bending. The fingers he would be using the whole rest of his life were right here now, brand new. It was like magic. I slid my pinkie under his fingertips, and he held it tight.

"A miracle," I cooed.

"Every time," she agreed. She tucked the edge of his blanket tighter under his chin.

"I wonder," I began. "If a man could bear a child, would he be so quick to send him off to war?"

The nurse, her hand cupping Johnny's delicate head, had a weary smile on her lips. "Not likely."

"No." I kissed Johnny's little fist.

She squeezed my hand. "You enjoy that baby, now," she said. "He's a perfect angel."

I smiled. "I will."

She left the room with her quiet grace. Alone together, I pulled him close and settled down to nurse. Johnny's face was turned to me, and in his eyes was a look that favored Roger.

"Your Daddy is handsome like you, Johnny boy," I spoke softly. "And strong and funny and sweet as the dickens. And you are going to love him when he gets back home again. Yes, you are, my darling boy."

CHAPTER 18

ROGER

When word came down in early May that the Germans had surrendered and Roger felt like he could believe it, he looked up at the pale, innocent sky and pulled the first long, full, deep breath he had swallowed in ages. He shook out his hunched shoulders, stood taller, loosed his grip on his rifle, and relaxed. The Pacific battle still raged, as far as anyone among them knew, but for the moment they were safe. So, for the first time, Roger felt free enough to look around at his surroundings, taking in the now-peaceful German countryside with the eyes of a man no longer scanning for danger. It was a beautiful place, green and lush. It reminded him of his boyhood home in Northern Michigan: vast farmlands, abundant with new growth, untamed and overgrown from the neglect of war but buzzing with new life. And here and there, small houses sat planted like stakes in a claim of the good earth. The houses themselves were fairy-tale-like, with thatched roofs and exposed rough-hewn beams. Michigan farmhouses were larger and more modern by comparison. These German homes were older and wiser, he guessed, for all they had silently witnessed.

Still, Roger was careful not to look too closely at any particular thing as he marched to his new landing place. Among the beauty of nature was sobering evidence of the recent conflict this landscape had witnessed: gaping craters, earth torn asunder. Discarded scraps of the means of destruction were strewn haphazardly: heavy chunks of metal blackened with ash, abandoned burnt-out vehicles, a single boot, shredded fatigues, battered helmets—and sometimes the men who'd worn them—shattered and ruined, rotting whole or in pieces. Roger kept his eyes to the middle distance, trained on the hopeful green of fresh-grown grass, the crops not tended yet still returning, the tidy houses. He nurtured the ease he felt in his war-tensed muscles with long breaths of tranquil air. He had survived. He was grateful but fully understood himself to be no more worthy than the men who'd been less fortunate.

Eventually, he and the company were stationed in the bombed-out German town of Wetzlar. They made themselves at home in the abandoned houses, sleeping four to a room and taking shifts on the beds. They never spoke about the people whose homes these had been, although there was ample evidence: photos, clothing, books, dishes, and towels. Acknowledging that they were interlopers seemed unnecessary after so much transgression against the rights and will of others. Instead, they tucked in and found a kind of contentment among the tattered remains. War, in Roger's opinion, created situations where otherwise normal, considerate, kind men found themselves making choices of survival and protection that in regular life would have been impossible to consider.

One afternoon, Roger looked up from his guard duty and saw two young children skipping alongside their mother. Breathtakingly thin, and dressed in worn, oversized clothes, the children jumped and danced, and the mother, who carried another small child in her arms, smiled, relief fresh in her eyes. Her face was young, but her cheeks were sunken, her forehead lined with permanent disquiet. Roger watched them approach, meandering but making steady progress. He imagined that this must be the first time in months, maybe years, that she wasn't hurrying her babies along as quickly as possible. She could allow them to dawdle, to play, to be children again. Chatting and singing, their exuberant voices ricocheted off the factory façade. They paid no attention to Roger. But their mother, a wary survivor, kept an eye half cast his way. When he smiled, her face eased somewhat, but she kept her distance.

"*Guten Tag,*" he said, exhausting his German.

"*Guten Tag,*" she echoed his greeting.

"Beautiful family," he said in English.

"*Danke,*" she replied, smiling a weary smile. She wiped at her forehead, the practiced swipe of a mother on a long journey home.

"I have three children at home," Roger said.

"*Danke*," repeated the mother. She hadn't understood, but she knew he was being kind. Roger nodded, smiled. The little girl pranced past her mother. She looked to be about six or seven.

"*Guten Tag*," Roger said to her. She eyed him with the cautious demeanor of one who had learned far too young not to trust anyone. He smiled, and she seemed to decide he meant well, a bashful grin curving her lips.

She tapped her brother's arm. "*Kommen*," she said and off they ran, ahead of their mother, who shouted something after them.

"Not too far," is what Roger imagined she said, what he imagined Eleanor might say if Carol and Barry were skipping away down a rubble-strewn, war-torn road. He thanked his lucky stars that his own wife and children would never know this deprivation—the devastation, the fear, the heartache. His thoughts shifted to wondering about the woman's husband, who was notably absent. Would he be returning to her? Or was she grieving as she walked her little ones along the road?

CHAPTER 17

ELEANOR

J ean called me. That was how I found out. It was early in the morning, August again, just over a year since Roger had left. I'd just finished changing the baby and was carrying him down the stairs when the phone rang.

"It's over, Eleanor!" cried my sister over the phone. "The blessed war is over! Turn on your radio!"

My heart immediately began to race. My hold on Johnny tightened. "What? Are you sure?"

"Turn on that radio, lady. It is over!"

"Hold on, hold on." I put the phone down and snapped on the radio.

"The Japanese have surrendered!" the announcer proclaimed. "I repeat: the Japanese have surrendered! Our last great enemy is defeated! The war is over!"

"Oh, thank God," I gasped, and started to cry. I've never known such relief in my whole entire life before or since that day. It was finally over.

Carol came dashing down the stairs. "What Mommy, what?" She pulled at my arm.

"The war's over, honey! The war's over and Daddy's coming home!" I spun Johnny around in a twirl. Joyful giggles bubbled out of his chubby baby cheeks.

"Spin me!" Carol called.

"Let me finish with Aunt Jean, then I'll spin you all day, sweetie." I picked the phone up again.

"Oh, Jean, I can't believe it. I just can't believe it."

"It's about time, is all I can say. Now you go on and celebrate, and I'll be by tonight."

Oh Lord, what a day that was. I grabbed Carol and twirled her around the living room. We danced and sang. "The war's done and Daddy's coming home! The war's done and Daddy's coming home!" Barry, the world's slowest waker, sat on the sofa, watching all the commotion without a peep. He just rubbed at his eyes and yawned a time or two.

"Barry! The war's over!" Carol told him, shaking him by the shoulders. He pushed her off, blinked, and pressed his blankie to his face. He wasn't the sort to let himself get riled up until he was darn good and ready. Carol danced over to me. I hadn't noticed until now, but outside a commotion was building.

"Hear that?" I said. We all went quiet for a minute. Car horns were blowing, people cheering and hollering.

"Sounds like a party!" I said.

"Yay, it's a party!" Carol cried.

"Well, we'd best get outside and join in!" I ran upstairs with Johnny, Carol right behind me. She dressed herself lickety-split while I got Johnny fixed up. We hurried back down and I dressed Barry right there in the living room. Poor boy still wasn't ready to greet the world, but we were going out to see what was happening anyway. I took a bottle for the baby and gave Carol and Barry each two cookies.

"You eat these now, and we'll have a regular breakfast in a little while." That woke Barry up. He bit into the cookie like he might never see another in his life.

Out front there were scads of people, all of them streaming down the boulevard. We walked over to the corner to watch them stroll by. Seemed like the whole city was walking down toward Chevrolet Avenue: men, women, children, soldiers, old folks, and every single kind of person in between. And everybody was happy, laughing and carrying on, streaming by like a jolly river. The air was thick with the noise of pure joy, and the sun shone bright and glad. It seemed as though even the sky was celebrating the end of so much heartache. It was beautiful.

An older man in shirtsleeves and a straw fedora stopped when he caught sight of us. He smiled, but never broke his stride. "Hey, little ones," he called, "the war's all done. Whyn't you come have some fun?" And he kept on walking with the crowd.

"Can we, Mommy? Can we go too?" Carol asked pointing the way the people were flowing.

"I don't know. It's so many people," I said, not sure it was such a good idea to take them into the thick of it.

"Please?!" Carol danced at my feet.

I hemmed and hawed for about a second before giving in. "Oh, all right. Let's go get the buggy."

We ran back to the house. I tucked Johnny into the buggy. At four months, he was still young enough not to realize he was missing his daddy. Now he wouldn't even have to know.

"All right, you two hold on tight to the handles. I don't want to lose one of you in the crowd." We went to the boulevard and joined the parade. We stayed near the edge, and people were kind in their joy. The children screamed and laughed every time someone tossed a bundle of newspaper shreds into the air. Must have been the whole city that came out that day to share the relief.

I overheard some men bragging about "the bomb." "Put an end to things quick now, didn't it?" they said, all proud like they'd built the thing themselves. I didn't care too much for talk about bombs. I was just glad to know the men were finally coming home again.

After a while, we happened on a short man wearing a red striped vest and standing behind a popcorn cart. "Free popcorn!" he called. "Who wants popcorn?" he asked. Both he and the children looked to me.

"Well, why not? It's a celebration, isn't it?" The children clapped and jumped up and down. I tried to offer him money, but he refused.

"It's free popcorn today," he said. "My son is coming home!"

"My daddy is coming home, too!" Carol shouted around a mouthful.

"A lucky girl!"

"We're all so lucky," I said. Oh, it was so hard to believe, and so wonderful at the same time. Until that day, I hadn't realized just how heavy the worry had weighed on me. I'd done what I had to do, but the whole time I'd been keeping my shoulders up by my ears and taking shallow breaths, afraid, afraid, afraid. Every bit of food I tried to eat barely wanted to slide past the anxious lump in my throat. And the nights were full of the most terrible dreams. Finally, now, the day had come when I could let my shoulders loose and take a full deep breath.

"Lord, oh Lord, we made it," I whispered.

CHAPTER 18

ROGER

F our months and some days after the Nazis laid down their arms in defeat, the Japanese followed suit. The Allies had won in a show of might never seen before. The world found a new peace. There was rejoicing among the men, and great, terrific relief. Talk turned easily and almost exclusively to the topic of home. That first night, a group of the men sat around a small fire in the dark, taking turns tossing around all their hopes and dreams for when they got stateside again.

"I'm looking forward to a cold American beer," Polk said.

"A warm bed," Turner suggested.

"Hell, a warm *girl*," Coleman said laughing. The group laughed with him.

"Yeah, a girl, warm and *soft,* smelling like the corn on my Pa's farm," Hamilton added.

"Jesus, Hammie, sounds like you're thinking of a lying down with a big ol' sow," teased Polk, laughing. "You a pig poker, farm boy?"

"I'm not saying that..." stammered Hamilton. But the runaway joking of the group forced the kid to fall silent and let them all carry on about his love for pigs. Roger chuckled and gave Hamilton a reassuring clap on the back.

"You know Polk's poked a few pigs in his day," he said, in an undertone. Hamilton shot Roger an appreciative look, but he walked away from the fire, the crunch of his footfalls disappearing into the blackness of the German night.

Polk turned his attention to Roger. "Who's waiting on you back home?"

"I've got a beautiful wife and three kids, one I haven't even met yet," said Roger proudly. "My wife tells me he's got my eyes."

Polk whistled. "Three kids? You best be gettin' on back, then. Them boys'll need a father around."

"My oldest is a little girl. Four years old, a real pistol." Roger choked up a little in opening up to these men about his children. He hadn't allowed himself to talk of them at all while he was in the fight. But now, finally, it seemed safe to let the other soldiers know what had been at stake for him in this war. Roger took a worn photo from inside the breast pocket of his shirt and handed it to the man next to him.

"Carried it mostly in my helmet 'til now," he said, glancing at the roughened edges, the faded likeness of Eleanor, Carol and Barry.

"Now, that's a nice family," declared Goss with a sharp nod. "They favor you." Goss passed it to the next man.

Roger watched his cherished picture make the rounds of the men, all of them nodding, making appreciative sounds as men do over another's family. "No photo yet of the baby, but my wife is sending one."

"Might be lucky enough to get home before the picture gets here," Polk said.

"That'd be it, wouldn't it?" Roger said, tucking the photo back into his pocket. The group went quiet, thoughts turning back to their own homes.

After a while, Roger made his way back to the house where he was billeted. He threw himself across the sagging bed and thought about Eleanor. He couldn't wait to get back home to her, to hold her, love her, even just have her sit alongside him, maybe watch a movie holding hands. The warm, powdery scent of her would be an elixir for all his worries, he just knew it.

And yet, since the war's end, he had found himself dogged by a new and nagging worry; an apprehension he hadn't felt in all his days marching around the ravaged landscape. Having survived the war, he had expected to feel only ease. Instead, his thoughts had become increasingly fitful and dark. His heart raced, his hands shook, his mind was a jumble of unanswerable questions. How could he possibly return to his family after all this? How he could wrap his war-hardened arms around Eleanor, around his children, and not wound them or destroy them in some unknowable way? After all he'd seen, all he'd done, how could he again become a loving husband, a gentle, guiding father? He was a man who had killed and nearly been killed. A man who had stumbled over the bodies of enemy soldiers, then kicked out at them, disgusted, horrified, frightened, when he realized what they were. A man who'd laughed along with his war buddies as they pulled weapons, flags, insignia from their bested combatants. How could a man like that, a man like him, go back to the warm, loving bosom of his family? How could a man who'd wrapped his battered feet in the cast-off belongings of civilians fleeing for their lives, who'd slept like an animal in a darkened burrow of the forest, who'd survived on wood grubs and pine needles, how could he expect to love another with any sort of tenderness, any sort of decency? How could he ever truly be a civilized man again, knowing what he had done?

He'd thought the war might make a man of him. Instead, it turned him into a kill-or-be-killed monster, and he wasn't so sure he could live with who he had become. He was no longer the man Eleanor had kissed goodbye. Not the man she'd shed tears for, not the man who had promised he'd return. He could not claim to be that man any longer. And he could not imagine Eleanor ever loving who he had become. He had seen the darkest side of himself, and it kindled in him a deep fear that his dark side might taint all that he loved.

CHAPTER 19

ELEANOR

That next morning, I awoke as giddy as a schoolgirl. At first, I couldn't recall why. Then I opened the medicine cabinet, and there on the top shelf was Roger's bottle of Aqua Velva. I'd looked at it in those first days and wondered how I was going to survive without him. Now, it stood like a joyful reminder that my man was coming home. Soon that shelf would be full again with a razor and a shaving brush, a styptic pencil and his comb. My lone toothbrush would have another to share its cup again. The gol-darn war had ended, and Roger was coming home. I laughed out loud, pulled the Aqua Velva bottle down from the shelf, uncapped it, and waved it under my nose. That familiar scent felt like a dose of Roger right there in my hand. I couldn't wait until it was splashed on him and I was burying my face in his neck. I put the bottle front and center of the shelf and gave it a little rub for good luck. It was August when he'd left and August when he'd return, or thereabouts.

Only one year without my man. Looked like I was one of the lucky ones.

Later that week, the week the war ended, I ran into Rita at the grocery store. It was Saturday, and Faye was staying with the children so I could do my shopping. I was walking down the coffee aisle and noticed a woman in heels and a trim black suit, a bright pink scarf knotted around her neck. She was clipping down the aisle toward me. She caught my eye because it was rare to see such a smartly dressed woman in the store on a Saturday morning. A small leather handbag hung from her arm and her hair was pulled up off her face. She looked familiar, but I didn't have any inkling at all that it was Rita. Then she stopped to look at the shelf, and there was something in the way she tipped her head that made me pause.

"Rita?" I said.

She turned sharply and her face broke into a huge smile. "Eleanor!" She pulled me into a hug, and her perfume wrapped a cloud of bright citrus around me. "How are you?" she asked.

"I'm fine, just fine. How are you? You look like a million bucks." And I meant it—she was so put-together I was almost jealous.

She smoothed her suit. "Well, I'm a lot better than when you saw me last." She laughed. "Thank you for that, by the way." She put her hand on my arm. "Truly."

This was the first I'd seen Rita since the incident. It wasn't that I hadn't tried, but once her mother took charge, she refused to tell anyone anything. "Rita is just fine and doing well, thank you," was just about all either Blanche or I could get out of her. The best we knew was that they'd kept Rita in the psych ward for close to a month and no visitors were allowed. I called a time or two after I heard she was home again, but Rita never picked up—it was always either her mother with the same stiff answer or no one home at all. After Johnny came along, I just got caught up in taking care of him and hadn't the time to try again.

"I'm just so glad to see you doing better," I said.

"I'm so glad to see you had the baby." She laughed again. It was a charming little laugh, but not as boisterous as I remembered.

"I did. Baby boy. He came in late April and he's just starting to roll himself over."

"Oh, how wonderful!"

"Yeah, thanks. But how are things with you? You look just great."

"Oh, I'm doing as well as can be expected. I'm working now. Real estate. Mostly I handle the office work, but sometimes I get to get out and show a house or two. I'm taking night classes to get my license, so it keeps me busy."

"Real estate? That's fantastic, Rita. And how are the children?"

"Oh, they've adjusted. I have a woman who comes in and sits them. My mother up and announced her child rearing days were over about a month ago, so she didn't leave me much choice." She rolled her eyes.

"Well, looks like you've landed on your feet," I remarked.

She tipped her head when I said it, like she wasn't too sure about whether or not she had. "I s'pose," she said finally. "But I'd much rather be welcoming my soldier home like everybody else." She swept a hand over her suit. "But we do what we must."

"Yes. I am sorry, Rita."

"Thanks, hon." She looked back toward the shelf and grabbed a can. "Listen, I've got to run. I was just buying coffee for a showing we've got this morning. These soldiers are coming home and they want places to live." She laughed. "But let's get together one day soon. I'd love to meet that new baby."

"Yes, let's," I agreed.

"Take good care," she said, and clipped away the same way she'd come. And all I could think was just how hard it had to be for her. The whole world was celebrating, and her man wouldn't ever be coming home.

CHAPTER 20

ROGER

Fleming swerved the jeep up in a flurry of dust and rattle. Krakowski nearly toppled from the passenger seat when Fleming hit the brakes. Roger took a few steps back, shouldered his rifle, and waited for the dust to settle.

"This guy," Krakowski said, poking a thumb back toward Fleming. "He's more dangerous than the whole damn war." He laughed.

"Hey Mitch, jump in," Fleming said, ignoring Krakowski.

"Thanks, I'll walk," Roger answered with a wave.

"Smart man," Krakowski laughed.

"Suit yourself." Fleming shrugged and pulled away in the same bat-out-of-hell way he had arrived.

Krakowski, a brawny man from outside Detroit, offered Roger a smoke. Roger declined. "I'm laying off them now," he said. "They've got my nerves in a rattle." Krakowski shrugged and slipped the Camel back into the pack without a word.

"All quiet on the western front?" Krakowski asked, his eyes scanning the horizon; once a soldier, always a soldier, at least until they got back home.

"Has been since seven this morning," Roger answered. They'd been assigned guard duty outside a camera factory, which amounted to little more than watching officers traipse into the factory and out again, sometimes with boxes or bags, sometimes not. Compared to what a soldier saw during combat, this wasn't work at all.

"Good enough," remarked Krakowski, resting his gun against the building wall. "Still up for a little baseball when we get back home again?"

"I am if you are. It'll be nice to catch a game after all this time."

"Let's hope the Tigers have got some kind of game to give us."

"Ha. Yeah. I'll see you later." Roger raised a hand and set off down the dusty road toward the town. It would have been a jolting but quick ride back with Fleming, but Roger preferred walking. There was no hurry anymore, no more night exercises or recon missions, no humping through the rain, almost no orders, and no more fighting. The war had ended the world over, as Army radio repeated day in and day out, and Roger aimed to savor it. That, and figure out a way to ease his nagging sense of doom. It had been five days since the Japanese surrender.

The afternoon was warm and dry, dust kicking up around his feet. There was a music to his journey: his footfalls, thudding and crunching in the dry earth, the buzz of insects, and the intermittent calls of happy birds. It reminded him of summer days back in Michigan when he was a boy, before he had a thought for war or death or what came after. The simple sounds of nature soothed him. He allowed his mind to drift.

Without fail, his thoughts always turned to Eleanor and the children. He thought of them daily now. Before, in the midst of the fight, he might go for days without allowing them to cross his mind. Afraid the brutality of war would taint his memories, he had kept them tucked deep in the recesses of his heart, hidden away from the man he'd had to become in order to fight. But now, he could freely think of them. And he did, often and with great love, imagining long summer days at the lake, cold winters building snowmen and warming by the fire, and Eleanor, loving Eleanor with all of himself again. It would be grand to be a father and a husband again.

Around a gentle curve in the road, the town appeared in the short distance. Rubbly walls intermingled with untouched buildings gave the place a look of teeth in an ill-kept mouth. Still, the sight of it was a comfort, a way station between war and home. It allowed Roger to believe the end was in sight. He was a high-pointer in the Army parlance—a man who had seen serious action and had a wife and kids to provide for at home. It meant he was to be among the early returners when shipping back home began in earnest. He was grateful to be on that short list, but he did hope to solve his nervousness before he wrapped his love-starved arms around Eleanor again. It just wouldn't do to present this shaky man to the woman he loved.

Ambling into town, he found the other soldiers gathered, as usual, in an easy circle, leaning and sitting on cast-off objects, passing the time until chow. There was a collegial sense of relief among the men now. Out of danger but heavy with horrific memory, they found comfort in their camaraderie, and spent most of their time together, even if it was no longer strictly demanded of them. Roger moved toward the group, looking for that very sense of belonging. He did make certain to stuff one unsteady hand into his pocket and wrap the other firmly around the barrel of his gun. He had no interest in the men taking notice of his jitters.

"Hey, Mitch."

"Hi, Mitch."

"Ahoy, Mitch." The men greeted him in round-robin fashion.

"That factory still standing?" Bryant, a small man from Seattle, asked.

"It was when I left, that's all I can tell you," Roger answered.

The men chuckled and shifted sideways to let him in the circle. There were about ten of them, give or take.

"As much as those officers manage to cart out of there in a day, you're probably guarding an empty building by now," Halliday said. The men laughed. Halliday wasn't known for holding back on his opinions.

"You should have gone to West Point," Bryant countered. "Then you'd be in on the looting, too."

"Sure as shit should have," Halliday laughed, "but I doubt they could handle an ol' Brooklyn boy like me."

Roger pulled a crate up underneath himself and sat, giving his full weight to the thin wood. His gun he leaned against the low stone wall behind him.

"Hey," Slim said, pointing toward where Roger had propped his gun. "That there is one of those guard rifles, ain't it?" Slim was a friendly guy from the woods near Nashville.

Roger nodded. "It is." Not all of the men billeted in Wetzlar were on guard duty, and so they weren't all issued the same guns.

"Mind if I have a look?" Slim tucked his cigarette in the corner of his mouth.

"Go right ahead." To Roger it was a gun, same as any other, but Slim was a curious kind of guy.

He handed it across the circle. And somewhere in the passing of the weapon, a failure occurred. The gun slipped. Slim cried out. Both men reached for it— too late. It landed hard on its butt-end and went off.

The other men hollered, but Roger heard only the bullet. It whirred and buzzed like a mosquito on a humid August night. He cocked his head, and the bullet pierced the thin vulnerable flesh on the underside of his chin. Had he not reached forward, the bullet would have struck him square in the forehead. It was meant for him; not in a malicious way or from the deliberate human intent that had already claimed so many millions of lives in this war, but rather in a divine, preordained way. His number was up. He was not meant to return from the war. He was not meant for anything more, not meant to be a father to his three small children, not meant to grow old with his beloved wife. The simple truth of the matter was that his life would end as a Private First Class in the US Infantry assigned to guard duty in Wetzlar, Germany awaiting transport back to the United States in the aftermath of the Second Great War of the world.

In the final moments between the bullet puncture and the furious bleeding out of his life, Roger conjured Eleanor. He found her at the sink in their tidy, bright kitchen. Small-framed and delicate, her fine dark hair was pulled back away from her face, with stubborn little wisps curling at her temples. She was wearing a yellow housedress. Yellow looked beautiful on her; it pulled the glints of gold from her dark hair and added light to her deep blue eyes. He could see her as if he were there with her in the kitchen, by her side one last time. She looked weary but peaceful, seeing to their small family on yet another ordinary afternoon.

"I'm sorry, El," he said.

She looked up, seeming to hear his words. Her face twisted into confusion.

"I love you." Her eyes went round with fright. She tipped her head as if waiting for something, anything more. There was so much more he needed to say, but his visit ended as quickly as it had begun, and he was left only to hope that today had been an easy day for her—that the children had all been in terrific moods, playing in the yard and going down easy for naps. And that she had been able to find a little respite for herself while the children slumbered. That was his final wish for her: a pleasant, ordinary, forgettable sort of day, because soon enough, August 20, 1945 would become forever a dark day on her calendar, and he was so very sorry for that.

He exited the earth in a tumult of light and peace. Like in a dream, he was whisked away from all the chaos of his parting: the shocked gasps of the other men, the mad scramble to save his life, Slim's anguished regrets. Roger missed all of it, but not one of the men ever forgot him. All of them, Bryant and Halliday, Slim and Krakowski, Fleming and the others remembered him: Roger Mitchell, PFC, a thin, easy-going man from Flint, Michigan who'd done his duty and still ended up buried in France, victim of a stupid accident, another pointless loss in a world full of them, and just days after the full surrender had been won. Down to a man, it seemed a particularly cruel twist of fate.

CHAPTER 21

ELEANOR

I remember that morning, the morning they say Roger died. You wouldn't think I would, one day blending into the next like it does while you're waiting for something better, but I remember it. I don't think I'll ever forget it. It was exactly five days after the war ended.

The day started out ordinarily enough. We'd had our oatmeal breakfast as usual. I remember that because when the storm came, I was standing at the kitchen sink, scrubbing the last bits of stuck-on oats from the pan. I had left it in the sink to soak, like I generally did, planning to see to it when the children were napping. But after lunch that day, the children, Baby John included, were refusing the very idea of a nap. That was the first unusual thing. My children were always good about naps, going down without a fuss and falling off for an hour or two. But that day, not a one of them could settle. They were tired, fussy, and out of sorts, but none of them would nap. I blamed it on the weather.

The air had shifted from the morning. A storm was brewing. Everything felt unsettled and agitated, like it does when thunder and lightning are moving toward you. Had me a little cranky, too. So, I went into the kitchen to get a minute's break. In the sink there sat the morning's oatmeal pan, filled with water, a beige goo floating on top. I set to work on it. Wasn't long that I was scrubbing when, outside the kitchen window, it started getting dark and windy. Large, grey thunderclouds were gathering, filling my bright yellow kitchen with gloomy shadows. I remember looking outside and thinking, *finally we'll have this storm and get it over with.* That's what I was telling myself, but a part of me was feeling heavy, those dark clouds stirring a worrisome feeling in me. Made me wonder if I ought to get the children down into the basement in case a tornado was coming. I rinsed the oatmeal pan one last time, wiped the counter, and glanced out the window again. It was so dark; all I could see was my own reflection in the glass. Seeing myself didn't help me feel any better. I looked a fright—dark circles sagging under my eyes, my hair pulled back tight but pieces still falling out all around my face. I was going to have to fix myself up some before Roger returned from the war.

Just as that last thought crossed my mind, a thick bolt of lightning came shooting straight down, dead center from the sky. The sudden, blinding burst of light cut the sky's darkness right in two. And, just as quick, an image of Roger flashed in my head. And I heard him. I swear I heard him.

"I'm sorry, El," he said. That's all he said. Then his voice, his face, it was all gone, as quick as it came. He was there in my head and then he wasn't—a flash—just like the lightning in the sky.

Right on the heels of the lightning bolt's disappearance, a thunderclap boomed so loud, so close, it rattled the dishes. Carol screamed. Then the crying began. I didn't have a second to think. I ran like the dickens into the living room. The children were a sobbing, frightened mess when I got there. Carol made a beeline for me and I grabbed her up.

"There, there, baby," I said, smoothing her hair. Poor Barry was so frozen with fright, he couldn't move. He sat there on the floor stock-still, his eyes round as two moons. I pulled him in with Carol. Baby John didn't seem to know what to do. His blue eyes were wide, watching every bit of the commotion. Then he saw me, and he busted out crying harder than the other two. I grabbed him up as best I could and plopped us all on the sofa. Crowded onto my lap, not a one of them complained about the other's being on top of them.

"Shhh, shhh," I soothed. "It's just a big, big storm. Shhhh." Then I heard the rain splashing on the glass. Lord, it was summertime and I think I had every single window in the house wide open. I pushed myself up from among the children.

"Mommy, don't go," Carol whimpered.

"I've got to close the windows. You stay there. Mommy'll be right back. Carol, you hold Johnny." That started them all in wailing again, but it had to be done. I raced around the downstairs, slamming windows tight.

"Almost done!" I hollered, running up the stairs two at a time. "I'll be down in a second."

I closed the children's window first, then raced into our bedroom. The curtains flapped and fluttered against the window glass, a puddle of rain collecting on the floor. I slammed the window closed and turned toward the bathroom for a towel. And there he was again, in the medicine chest mirror, Roger, like a filmy image from an old photograph, his hair short like it was cut for the Army, his blue eyes looking sad.

"I love you," I heard in my head. I stared at the mirror, but he was gone again. In his place was the same raggedy image I'd seen of myself in the dark kitchen window, only this woman looked frightened.

"MOMMY!" Carol screamed from downstairs. I tore away from the mirror, half wondering if I was losing my mind.

"Be right there," I called weakly and threw a towel on the sopping wet floor. I did not look at the mirror again.

Downstairs, I pulled the children back onto my lap and took a deep breath. I had no idea what I was seeing and hearing, but as I settled in to calm them, a dark feeling of fear built a nest inside my heart. The storm battered the house for a very long while.

☆   ☆   ☆

Around five or so in the afternoon, Jean rolled in. "Yoo-hoo," she called. Her voice roused me. The children and I had fallen asleep like a pile of puppies there on the sofa. I heard her skip up the stairs, and then her tiny little bleached-blonde head peered around the corner.

"Well, Lord in heaven what is going on here? I come home from a long day at work and find you all sleeping? What on earth?"

"We had a hard time getting down for our naps today," I said, rubbing the sleep out of my eye.

"Well, I guess you got there. Look at the lazy bunch of you." She pulled baby Johnny off my lap. "I sure don't know what kind of house your mother is running here," Jean said, nuzzling Johnny's neck. My housedress was a damp mess from the sweat of sleeping boys.

"Let me go change," I said.

"Okay, hon, take your time. You still look exhausted." She winked.

"Well, thanks a bunch."

"Anytime." We laughed and she took over with the children while I went upstairs to change.

Warm and shadowy like a hug, the bedroom seemed to be welcoming me to keep on napping. But there was dinner to make. I slipped out of my sweat-dampened housedress and pulled a fresh one over my head. I went into the bathroom, splashed a little water, and pressed the towel hard against my face without so much as a glance in the mirror. I refused to look. It didn't have to be true. It could just be the worry of a war wife, the same worry I'd carried around inside me all these months. But another part of my mind, the part attached directly to my heart, knew more than the rest was willing to admit.

☆   ☆   ☆

Later, with the children tucked in, Jean and I settled ourselves out on the front porch. It was a beautiful night. The moon hung thin, a tiny curve in the sky. The humidity of the day had been broken by the afternoon's storm, so the night was comfortably cool and dark.

We started out talking about nothing much. Jean always brought some gossip from work that we generally had a laugh about, or she'd tell me stories of her dates. We complained about Mother and Helen, and that night we wondered out loud what life would be like now that the war was over.

"How long you think before Roger gets home?" she asked, and my heart seized just a little, afraid to even think about it.

"Don't know," I said, "but I wish I did." That was all I felt safe to say right then. We sat side by side in the quiet. I looked off across the street.

There was an alley there between the Whitter house and the Eaton's. Narrower than usual, it was a funny little sliver of concrete and dark. The older neighborhood kids used it as a shortcut to get to the playground on the next block. Some afternoons I'd catch a glimpse of one of them ducking through that gap, and something about the shadows of the late day sun made it seem as though they disappeared when they went in. One minute they'd be there and the next gone, like they'd never been. Not a stray leg nor a loose arm trailing behind. It was always the whole kid and then no kid. It gave me a chill whenever I watched them go. I felt that same chill run through me now, but it had nothing to do with neighborhood children.

Of course, Jean being Jean, she picked up on my nerves. "You all right tonight, El?"

"Lost in my thoughts," I answered, laughing a little.

"You been lost in your thoughts most of the evening. Something heavy on your mind?" She looked over at me.

"I s'pose I'm tired. That storm had the children and me in a tizzy for a while." I tipped my head back against the chair and closed my eyes a second.

"What storm?" she asked sipping her coffee.

"This afternoon, the thunderstorm."

"I didn't see any storm."

"What?" I looked over at her, my head still resting against the back of the chair. "Sure you did. It was raining cats and dogs, thunder, lightning, the whole thing. At about two or so."

"Two o'clock? No, I didn't see any storm, and I would have. I had a meeting in the big boss's office. He has windows the size of your front porch here," she spoke candidly. "Wasn't sunny, but there wasn't any rain, either."

"Surely the roads were wet when you drove over." Now I was sitting upright in my chair, my feet planted.

"Not so as I noticed." She shrugged.

"Jean, I am telling you, it rained like the dickens here today," I insisted, sounding like I was trying to convince the both of us.

"Well, okay, honey," she conceded. "Okay. Sometimes a storm can crop up just in one spot. I've seen it before."

"But this storm was a big one and went on and on. I can't tell you the commotion."

"Well, maybe it was later than you thought. Maybe it was more like 3 or so. I'd have been back at my desk by then. They haven't yet let me have a window all my own."

"Maybe," I said, "but you would have heard this storm. Thunder and lightning, loud and banging. It had the children twisted into a sobbing mess. That's how we all ended up napping on the sofa. Before it rolled in, not a one of 'em would go down for a nap. Then the storm came and scared the daylights out of us all. Once it passed, we fell asleep where we sat."

"I did wonder why I found you all there."

I looked out across the street to that empty place. "The strangest thing happened during the storm," I said, surprising myself that I was telling her. But I suddenly felt like I needed someone to help me try to make sense of things.

"I always thought storms could be a little spooky." She sipped her coffee. "Dark clouds and all."

"This was spooky, all right," I said. "You're gonna think I'm crazy, but I was at the kitchen sink. And I was thinking about Roger, his coming home and all. Then, I caught sight of myself in the kitchen window. I started thinking about how badly I needed to fix up my hair some, start wearing makeup again, you know, for my husband." A chill rolled through my body as I told her. I wrapped my arms tight around myself. "Then, all of a sudden, Roger's face was in my head, like a picture or something. He just appeared. 'I'm sorry, El,' he said. And that's all he said. 'I'm sorry, El.' Then he was gone as quick as he came. Before I had a minute to think, the thunder crashed, and all heck broke loose with the children."

"Sorry for what?" Jean asked, looking puzzled.

"Well, I don't know," I said. "But I think maybe..." My voice became a whisper. "Oh, I don't even want to say it out loud." I ran a hand over my mouth, thinking hard about what I was going to say next. "It's just... I think maybe something happened, Jean. I think that's what he was saying, 'I'm sorry,' 'cause something went wrong."

"Like what?"

"I don't know. I just think maybe something happened," I said, watching the outline of her face in the dark.

"What kind of something?" she pressed, still not as serious about the whole thing as I thought she ought to be.

"Well, I don't know exactly, but something bad. That's what I think. Something terrible." I nodded.

"Oh, c'mon, El," she groaned, not having it. "The war's over. Roger's coming home. Sooner than most, probably. You know that."

"I know he's supposed to. But why would he say he's sorry? It doesn't make sense any other way."

"You know what I think? I think you just can't believe that he is finally coming home." She dipped her head like she was giving the very last word on the subject. And something about that dip of the head, that dot at the end of her sentence, made me regret saying anything at all.

"I don't know," was all I could murmur, hoping to just drop the subject.

"Think about it," she went on. "You've been nothing but a ball of worry, trying so hard to keep strong, to carry on like a good wife, a good mother. And you're having a hard time believing it's gonna be okay again."

"Well, I have worried. What war wife doesn't worry? But I never believed any other thing than Roger coming home again to me. This whole time I've not done one single thing but believe," I said.

"Okay, all right. I'm not saying otherwise. I'm just suggesting that maybe you're having a hard time getting used to the notion of Roger finally coming home again."

"I don't know why that would be so awfully hard to get used to," I snapped. "It's all I've been celebrating for the last week." I could feel my ears getting hot.

"I'm not saying you don't want him to come home, or you're not happy he's coming home."

"No, you're saying I don't believe he will, maybe I didn't ever believe he would."

"Ellie, for God's sake I'm not saying that at all."

"Sounds like it to me."

"I'm just saying sometimes a person's mind gets to playing tricks on them when they get too much happening, too much to think about. That's all I'm saying, El, truthfully."

And she might have meant just that, but her words were putting me into a corner of having to argue for the one thing I definitely did not want to be true. I put my coffee cup down on the small table between us. The air throbbed with the chirp of summer crickets telling their tales.

"It isn't my mind playing tricks, Jean. As much as I might want it to be, it isn't. Something has happened to Roger. I just know it. I don't want to know it, but I do. I just plain do." I heard her twist in her chair, but I kept my eyes on that dark hidden place across the street.

"Eleanor," she said firmly. "The war is over."

"I know the fool thing is over."

"C'mon," she said. I could feel her eyes on me.

"Look," I said. "Look over there across the street between those houses." I pointed. She kept her eyes on me.

"Look!" I demanded, shaking my finger.

"All right, all right." Jean's eyes followed my finger, but I could tell she thought I was putting on a show or something.

"You can't see a thing, can you? It's just plain dark over there, a little bit scary from here, right?"

"El, I don't see what this has to do with anything." She looked at me again, but I kept my eyes over there on the alley, my finger pointed.

"It's just dark now. But in the morning when the sun comes up there will be three rubbish cans sitting over there alongside the Whitter house. I know that even if I can't see them right now. Who says we can't know other things we can't see? Who says?" I asked her, jutting my chin out a touch. She looked away, shaking her head.

"Ellie, it's different." My sister's voice was hushed, as if she were scared for me.

"It's only different because we think it is."

"No, it's different because just like the sun comes up on rubbish cans, your husband will be coming home, too."

"Well, think about this. I also know there's a trellis over there waiting for Tommy Eaton to get home from the war and put it up for his mother. Mrs. Eaton bought it a month or so before he left, but he never got around to it. Now, if you go on over there tomorrow and you ask Mrs. Eaton about her trellis, she'll tell you she's having Tommy put it up because she's 'always loved a trellis.' But I know, and everybody in the neighborhood knows, that she thinks those three Whitter boys are a bunch of wild things. But, being generally a polite and kind woman, she wouldn't dare say anything of the sort. Still, she thinks it and we all, including Mrs. Whitter, know it. And not a single word has been said out loud about any of it. But every one of us on this block knows and maybe one or two houses behind know it, too."

"That's neighborhood gossip. We all know about our neighbors."

"And we can know about other things, too, is all I'm saying."

We fell to an awkward silence. I didn't have a single idea what Jean was thinking, but I knew my mind was racing and exhausted at the same time. For as much as I was arguing here with Jean about what I thought I knew, I sure would rather have been entirely wrong, and to say so wrapped up in Roger's arms here on our own front porch.

"Ellie," she whispered. "You really think so?" She reached out and grabbed my hand. Her fingers were small in mine.

"I'm just afraid it is," I admitted.

"Let's just wait and see," she said, squeezing my hand.

"Only time will tell, won't it?" We looked at each other. She gave one more squeeze of my hand.

"We'll just wait," she said. And I knew then she still thought I was just worn thin with worry. I pulled my hand out of hers and took the coffee cups into the house. She followed me.

"I hope you're not mad," she said.

"Mad? No. I'm not mad," I said. "I just hope you're right and I'm just a damned worrywart. That's what I hope." She hugged me, and I wrapped my arms around her as well, but I didn't feel much of anything.

"It'll be all right," she promised softly. I latched the screen door and watched her climb into her big red car. She drove slowly off into the night.

★ ★ ★

I went around the downstairs locking doors and turning off lights, then climbed the stairs with a heavy foot. The children's room was thick with the sweet scent of little ones sleeping. Just enough of the sliver moon shone in the window that I could make out their restful faces. Carol was curled up, fists tucked under her chin. She was my good sleeper. From the time she was a baby, I could put her down just a little drowsy and she'd fall right off to sleep for the night. She looked like an angel, her curls a golden halo on the pillow. I pulled a light cotton blanket up over her back.

"Sleep tight, my girl," I whispered, pressing a kiss to her forehead.

As usual, Barry's arms and legs were splayed wide like a flying squirrel jumping from the highest tree. His small body seemed to cover the whole mattress. He slept like he played—busy, busy, busy. Tonight, he was warm and sweaty like any other night, and sleeping heavy.

"Sleep well, my angel," I whispered, and kissed his forehead. I pulled his baby blue blanket to his shoulders, knowing it would surely be back under him in less than half an hour.

In our room, Baby John slept in the small crib alongside the bed. A mix of Carol and Barry, he slept with his little baby fists stretched over his head, but his legs curled up tight to his belly. The blanket I covered him with when he went down was still tucked around him. I placed the palm of my hand lightly on his little chest just to be sure he was breathing. He'd been sleeping through the night for about a month now.

"Sleep tight," I whispered, pressing a kiss to my fingers and touching them to his forehead.

Without turning on the bathroom light, I washed up quickly, pulled my blue nightgown over my head, and slipped into bed. I reached over to Roger's side, trying to remember what it felt like to have his weight occupy the space next to me. I'd spent all those months trying not to think about that empty side of our bed. That night, trembling from the afternoon, more afraid than I thought I could truly be, I threw my arm around Roger's pillow, pulled it tight to me, and pretended it was him. Cold comfort for sure, but I couldn't think of any other way. Still, I held back the tears. I would not cry. I would *not* cry. I swallowed hard, pushed the ache down in my throat, and waited for sleep to help me forget what I was sure I already knew.

CHAPTER 22

CHAPTER 22

ELEANOR

all came early, bringing an unexpected chill to the air. I shut the bedroom windows tight and dressed the children in long sleeves. It had been a month since the storm. I'd gotten one letter from Roger, but he'd written it in early July. Late mail from the Army wasn't so unusual, but it provided no salve to my worries, either. I tried not to think about the storm or what I thought I heard in the middle of it. There wasn't proof until there was proof, I told myself. And, if I kept busy, most of the time that worked.

That morning, I set myself the project of changing out the summer clothes for winter. The children were quiet, the new chill taming them like summer fireflies, and I was up to my ears in heaps of dresses and cotton rompers when the knock came. With the house all shut up tight, I hadn't heard a thing until the banging.

"Good Lord, who is that?" I said out loud. The children hadn't noticed. Barry sat in the corner building block towers. Carol had her toy kittens involved in a tea party, and Johnny was on his belly, kicking in an effort to get himself to a crawl.

"Okay, Johnny, come with me," I said, grabbing him up. To Carol and Barry, I said, "You two stay here. I'll be right back." The banging came again. I started down the stairs with half a mind to tell whoever was pounding at my door not to break the darn glass.

In my snit, I didn't bother to try to see who it was until I pulled the inside door open. Then I looked, and there stood the Western Union man just on the step outside the front porch. I stopped dead. I sucked in my breath. My heart started to race. But everything else ground to a halt. The Western Union man was standing on *my* front doorstep.

I moved toward the outer door, but it felt like I was moving through molasses. Every one of my steps across that porch seemed slower and more impossible than the one before. My ears were ringing. My head was spinning. I thought I might faint dead away. But I had Johnny in my arms. I hugged him tighter against me. Then I watched my own hand reach for the lock. It turned, but I didn't feel the metal of it in my fingers.

The Western Union man looked up when he heard the lock unlatch. I say man, but he was just a boy, really, fresh-faced and nervous. His eyes went wide when he saw me, I think because I had the baby in my arms. Or maybe he was just afraid for what he had to tell me. Maybe my own face looked frightened to death and that was what scared him.

Either way, I could see he was as anxious to get this over with as I was to not to have it happen at all.

I pulled the outer door. It stuck. It had been swollen against the frame since the day of the storm. I yanked, even though I didn't at all want what this boy was bringing to my home. The door popped open. Now, only the screen door was between us.

"Morning, ma'am," the young man said, tipping the brim of his too-big hat. Through the gray screen, I peered down at him in his brown uniform. He had a thin face, bright eyes. A bead of sweat was winding its slow way down from his hairline, although the weather was far too chilly for perspiring. His neck was as thin as the rest of him, lined with blue veins like trails of forgotten ink and as pale as his face. His collar was too big around his neck by an inch, and the shoulders of his stiff brown uniform made him look like a child playing dress-up in his father's coat. *This is who they've sent?* I thought. He was just a boy, a boy like the one I was holding in my arms. Where was this boy's father? Had he gone off to war? Was he coming back? Maybe this young man in his smart brown uniform had had his own Western Union visit, months before. Maybe his own mother was a widow. Maybe he, the son of a war widow, was earning the living for his family now. Just like my own Johnny was about to become the son of a war widow, right here, right now. Would he have to go work too soon? Deliver terrible news to worried wives and their children just to help keep his family fed?

The boy held a light brown envelope up to the screen. "Western Union, ma'am. For Mrs. Roger C.

Mitchell." He spoke in a matter-of-fact way, his voice deeper and more sure of itself than I expected.

I didn't open the screen door. The boy blinked, waiting, his hand holding the envelope out in front of him. And there I stood, for the very life of me unable to open the door. I looked at him, irritation and fear spinning up a frenzy inside me. I just couldn't open that door.

He reached for the handle. I suppose he was used to women acting strangely. His bosses must have told him how to handle it. Probably told him something like "If the lady of the house won't let you in, go ahead and open the door yourself. You have to step in and be a brave soldier." The boy did just that; he reached up and grabbed hold of the cold metal handle. He didn't pull the door open, just held the handle. My breath caught in my throat. It felt as if the Grim Reaper himself had a bony grip on that knob.

"Ma'am?" said the boy. He rattled the door just a touch. It was hooked from inside. But the noise annoyed me. How dare he? Maybe that widow mother of his ought to have worked on his manners before she sent him off to talk to agitated women in their very own homes. Quick as a flash, I flipped the hook off and shoved the door open. It barely missed him when it swung wide, but I felt I'd made my point about who would be doing all the demanding about opening doors and the like. I propped the door with my foot and held my hand out toward him.

"Give it to me," I demanded. "Give it." I shook my hand at him like he'd shaken the door handle.

I leaned out the door, little Johnny grabbing tight onto my shoulder. "The telegram. Give it to me."

"Sorry, ma'am," he said, and held the envelope out.

"Yes, I s'pose you are." I grabbed the envelope, yanked it from his hand, and let the screen door slam. I pushed the storm door closed, too, and didn't bother with a fare-thee-well to the kid. Later I felt bad about that, but at the time, I had no use at all for that boy and his troubles anymore.

And so, there it was: a War Department telegram right there in my shaky hand. I carried it into the living room. The room was shadowy in the late afternoon; I hadn't put any lights on yet. Didn't think I would now. The dark felt like just the kind of quiet, lonely place to meet with the worst news of my whole life. I put Johnny on the floor near the toy corner. He looked up at me with those blue eyes, eyes just like his Daddy's.

"S'okay," I whispered.

He didn't look as if he half believed me, but he smiled encouragingly anyway.

I dropped onto the sofa and turned the envelope over and over in my hands. It looked official, with my name typed out: Mrs. Roger Mitchell. I held it there, my hand quivering, and I was afraid. I didn't know what to do. I couldn't read it, but I had to. It seemed I already knew what news was folded up inside there, but what if I was wrong? What if Roger was still alive, recuperating in a hospital somewhere, terribly injured, but alive? Or maybe he was coming home, and this little envelope was about to make all my wishes come true. It still seemed possible, in spite of all that I thought I knew.

So, there I was, my whole life's dreams resting on a thin piece of yellow paper inside a rough brown envelope. With the deepest fear I'd ever felt, I slid my trembling finger under the edge of the envelope and pulled the telegram from inside. Sure enough, the words I dreaded more than death itself were spelled out on the page before me:

"It is with deep regret I inform you that your husband Roger C. Mitchell Private First Class has been killed by accidental gunshot on Twenty August Nineteen Forty-Five in Wetzlar, Germany. The Secretary of War asks that I express his deepest sympathy on the loss of your husband. Letter to follow."

I held that slip of paper, thin and mean, in my fingertips and read those words over and over again. They made sense, but it wasn't real. Wasn't possible. Or maybe I just didn't want to believe this dull yellow piece of paper with its serious black type could change my whole life. I flung the telegram away from me like it was a message from the devil.

"No!" I cried. "No, no, no, no!" I slapped at the sofa cushions; I stomped my foot. My head started spinning, my heart thumping. A flush came into my face that spread all over my body. I turned and threw myself against the sofa pillow and screamed right into it. I bit it hard, wanted to rip it with my teeth like I was tearing the very flesh from whoever'd stolen my Roger. I punched and pounded the sofa arm, kicked and slammed my heels against the floor. I didn't feel a thing. I can't say for certain I even knew what I was doing. The tears came, giant wracking sobs of them, all the waiting, all the worrying that had lived curled up inside me for months let loose like a tidal wave.

Then, just as quick, I stopped myself. Like a faucet or a light switch I went from on to off. There was no getting away from it now. No matter the fit I threw, no matter the tears I cried, Roger wasn't coming home to me. The room took on a dark, hollow feeling, the air emptied of sound. I thought of Rita. I thought of Mother. I was one of them now. Another woman alone. *Oh, God, why?* I thought. But there just wasn't an answer. To this day there is no answer, and I don't believe there ever will be for any war widow throughout time.

I looked up through my tears and my shredded heart. There sat Johnny, innocent and confused. His eyes were fixed on me, but he sat stock-still, his round face a mask of worry. He would never know his father.

"S'okay, Johnny," I whimpered. His eyes said he believed me less than before. "S'okay," I repeated, but I couldn't move from where I sat. Not even to soothe my own baby boy.

CHAPTER 23

CHAPTER 23

ELEANOR

As the next of kin, the notice had come to me, and that meant I had to be the one to tell. I had to call people with the terrible news. I was to be brave and smart and know exactly how to say it. I was to comfort and accept condolences at the same time, and I was probably supposed to do it right now. But all I could do was sit and wish for a mistake, for another knock at my door taking this fool telegram away. "Very sorry, ma'am," that skinny-necked kid would say, and place in my hand a letter from Roger telling me he'd be home on the next train.

But that wasn't going to happen, so it would be left to me to tell everyone. The thought of it made me go cold. It seemed the cruelest twist. We'd all been so happy; the war's done, the men are coming home. It was just not to be believed, to never see him again, to not hold him or kiss him or touch him. Tears ran down my face. Maybe I couldn't tell anyone. Maybe I hadn't the nerve. Maybe my bravery had been all used up. I'd been working so hard at being good, doing what they said I ought, and look where it had gotten me. I was damned if I would do one more thing according to the rules.

I flung myself back on the sofa. Carol came down the stairs. Watching her bound around the bannister, I wondered what on earth a mother was supposed to say to a child at a terrible time like this. Was I supposed to tell her and Barry and Johnny? Was I to keep it a secret until they were older? How, then, would I explain Daddy never coming home? The ladies' magazines didn't offer one bit of advice about how a mother ought to tell her children their father had been killed.

Carol slowed when she came into the living room. She could see the evidence of tears all over my face. She eased her way over to me.

"Mommy?"

I smiled, but the thickness in my throat wouldn't let me talk. I shook my head.

"It's okay," she said. She climbed up next to me on the sofa and placed a comforting hand on my knee. We sat together, neither of us saying a word. I put my hand on her back and rubbed it. I would tell her, tell them, in time. Knowing Carol, she'd figure it out on her own long before I found the words.

Maybe it was an hour, must have been closer to two, and I heard Jean push the side door open. She would be the first I'd tell. Her pumps clacked on the linoleum, and my heart churned up a nervous flutter.

"Evening, family!" she called. Carol, who'd been reading books to me, slipped off the sofa and ran to meet her.

"Hello, darlin'," said Jean, bright and cheery. "Where's the rest of the crew?"

"Mommy's in there," Carol said. Jean came around the living room corner, Carol beside her. I can only imagine the sight I was to her, because she paused and her face immediately twisted up into worry.

"El?" she said. "You okay?"

I grabbed the telegram from where it lay on the coffee table and held it up like a flag of surrender. "It's Roger," I moaned. "They say he's been killed."

"*What?!*" She dropped down onto the sofa next to me and read the crumpled paper.

"Oh no, Ellie, oh no," she said, shaking her head. She wrapped me up in her arms. "No, no, no," she said over and over again in my ear. I let her hold me. I held her tight, too. Heartache and comfort fell over me in even amounts.

"Oh, Jean," I whispered, "this is terrible. The war is over. How on earth does a man get killed after it's over?"

"After?" she asked.

"Yes, look. August 20th. The whole thing was over."

She looked again at the telegram. "When did it end? I don't even remember now."

"August 15th. I remember because I was counting the days."

"But how can that be? What does accidental gunshot mean?"

— 176 —

I shook my head. "I don't know. It doesn't make a bit of sense."

"Not a bit," Jean said, quietly.

"I just can't understand." I broke into tears again, but they had no use. No amount of crying would bring him home. The war had won.

She grabbed hold of my hand, squeezed it. "I'm so sorry, El."

"It's not right," I sobbed.

She shook her head. Wasn't anything else to be said.

"Have you called Roger's folks?" she asked after a moment.

"Haven't called anyone yet. You're the first to know."

She laid a cool hand over mine. "Want me to?"

"Ought to be me," I responded.

"Later, then." She patted my hand and turned to the children. They were gathered in a knot in the toy corner, pretending to play, not saying a word.

"Well," she said, forcing a smile. "How are my darlings, then?" She walked over to where they sat and threw her arms open. Carol and Barry, released from the strange afternoon, jostled themselves into her. She picked Johnny up and hugged all three of them tight, planting warm kisses on each head.

"Did you call Mother and them?" she asked, looking over their heads.

I sank deeper into the sofa cushions.

"Soon enough," she said. The afternoon was growing long, and the sun was nearly done shedding any light on this terrible day.

"I can't do this," I said, shaking my head. "Not without him." My tears ran again.

"Oh, honey." Jean held the children near her while I cried.

"But seriously," I whispered, swiping away the tears as fast as they came, "what am I going to do?" The question was as sincere as any I had ever asked in my whole life.

"I don't know, but we'll figure it out. We will figure it out." She said it firmly, with real conviction. And it sounded reassuring. It was also all anybody could say, but nowhere near the answer I needed. It was just all the answer I was ever gonna get.

"I'd better call Mother," I said, without moving.

"I'll keep an eye on the kids," she said.

I gave a long sigh, snuffled, and pushed myself up off the sofa. In the hall, I picked up the phone and dialed Mother's number, every twist of the rotary like a step closer to the end of my life as I knew it. The more people I told, the more real it would become, and I still didn't want to believe it. Faye answered on the first ring.

"Hi, Faye, it's me."

"Hey, big sister," she said, but something in my tone must have told her. "Everything okay?" At those words, my throat seized up and I couldn't speak.

"El?" Faye said through the line. "El, honey, what?"

"It's Roger," I said, my voice barely a squeak. "He's been killed."

"What?"

"Western Union was here." The sobs overtook me. "Nooooo, oh, El," she cried, and then she was bawling along with me. Jean came and put her arm around me. I handed her the receiver.

"Faye, hang on," Jean said into the phone, then set it there on the table. She took me by the hand, led me to the sofa, and tucked a blanket over my trembling shoulders.

I listened to bits of their conversation. "Notice." "Accident." I closed my eyes. My sisters had loved him. They had lost him, too.

Jean came back around the corner, her eyes red. "Faye'll bring dinner," she said. "Mother's not home yet, so she's gonna wait for her."

"Oh, Jean, I can't."

"I know, honey." She perched on the edge of the sofa cushion. "I know. But I'm here. Me and Faye and all of us. We'll do it as best we can together." She laid a gentle hand on my leg and I closed my eyes. "Why don't you take a little rest right now? I'm here. You rest, and when you wake, we'll just take it one minute at a time." I leaned myself back.

Jean went and got a cool compress, placing it gently across my aching forehead. "S'alright," she soothed. And I drifted off to a fitful sleep there on the sofa. It was a welcome respite from my new truth.

★　　★　　★

Sometime later, I woke to the sound of Faye coming in the door. I hadn't any idea what time it was, but the room was shadowy and dark. Faye's face was hard to make out, but I had no interest in turning on a light. She sat next to me on the edge of the sofa and wrapped me in a strong hug.

"El, I am so very sorry, honey," she said into my ear.

I shrugged. I didn't have a tear left, but my mouth sagged like it might be permanently broken.

"Maybe you should go upstairs and rest a little more," she suggested.

"I'll be fine here," I said, reminded of that terrible day with Rita and not at all sure I could trust myself. "Better I'm with you all than alone."

Faye frowned. "We'll be here as long as you need."

"You told Mother?" I asked.

"I did. She said she'd be by. She's as heartbroken as any of us. 'I loved that boy like he was my very own,' she said when I told her."

"She did not say that."

"She did." Faye smiled. "Surprised me, too."

I had to laugh. "Lord, just when you think you know her …" It was a relief to laugh over some Mother nonsense. Faye squeezed my hand, and I tipped my head back against the pillow.

Faye sighed. "I better help Jean with dinner."

"I s'pose," I said. "Let me come with you."

"You sure?"

"Can't lay here forever." I shrugged and lifted myself up off the sofa. Faye walked with me into the kitchen. Jean was busy at the stovetop and the counter, moving from here to there. She had the children working at things, too. It looked very much like they were spreading oleo on saltines.

"Mommy, look," Carol said. "I'm making the appetizer." She held up a cracker. "Want one?"

"Don't mind if I do." I plopped down next to Carol and took a bite of the heavily oleo-ed cracker. The simple, greasy salt taste was a comfort in my mouth.

"Delicious," I declared, and Carol buttered me another one.

Jean winked. "She's a good cook, that one."

"Yes, she is," I agreed, munching the next cracker. Then we heard the side door open.

"Eleanor, it's Mother," she called from the door. The sound of her voice brought a shaky kind of surrender over me.

"In here," I called. Mother came into the room.

"We're just getting dinner around," said Jean.

"I didn't know the whole bunch of you were here," said Mother, that pinched look of consternation on her brow. She dropped her bag on the stool by the door.

"Not a bunch, just me and Faye."

"Come sit, Mother," I said. "Faye and Jean are on the job."

"I came to see you, dear," she said, looking pointedly at me.

"Okay," I said, and wiped the oleo from my lips.

"Can we go into the other room?"

I nodded and followed her into the living room. She sat on the sofa, patting the cushion next to her. I sat and she took my hand.

"Honey, I'm so sorry about Roger," she said. "He was a good man."

"He was good to me," I said, just above a whisper.

"I know he was. I am sorry for you." She looked me in the eye, direct but gentle. "But it's in times like these we learn who we are, Eleanor. Now, you've got three children to raise, and it won't be easy. But you are good with them and you will find a way. That is what we all do in this life. We find a way. I know you know what that means, even if you don't have the answer quite yet."

"Yes, okay." I nodded.

"Your sisters and I are here to help, but if I can do it, you surely can." She smiled, a soft, encouraging kind of smile, and I saw a side of Mother I had never taken the time to notice before. She could be cold, and she could be cranky, but she was also brave and strong. I understood now that it was that combination of qualities that had seen her through her own dark times. We were different, but we were the same in a lot of ways.

"We do what we must," she said, standing.

"Thank you, Mother," I whispered. She hugged me and I hugged her back gratefully.

"Okay, then." She patted my back. I followed her into the kitchen.

"Sit here, Mother," I said, offering her my chair. We shared Faye's tuna casserole, not saying too much, just the women and the children around the table. Because someone had to cook, and someone had to clean, and someone had to look after the children. Someone had to make sure the world kept moving along, no matter the awfulness of it all.

Late in the evening, I sent them all home. I decided my first night as a widow would best be spent alone. I climbed the stairs, both familiar and different now with no promise of Roger's return. In the bathroom, I looked in the mirror and was reminded of the storm. "I love you," he'd said to me that day. "I'll always love you." I opened the medicine cabinet. There stood the half-full Aqua Velva bottle. I took it down, untwisted the cap and waved the bottle slowly under my nose just like the day I thought he was coming home to me. But now, knowing I'd never see him again, I let my mind conjure him through the scent. I let myself slip into thoughts of his arms wrapped around me. In the pit of my belly a thrill seized me, just as it had when he'd last held me in his arms. How could it be that I'd no longer hold him? No longer hear his easy laugh, see his gentle smile? How could it be that he would no longer wipe my cares away?

"Oh, Roger," I whispered. "How am I going to live without you?" I took a final sniff of his aftershave, then twisted the cap tight again, put it back on the shelf, closed the cabinet, and splashed my weary face with cold water. Yes, being strong was one thing, but what about all the memories? How was I supposed to live with those?

CHAPTER 24

CHAPTER 24

ELEANOR

The next morning dawned bright and sunny, as if all was right with the world. It wasn't—wouldn't ever be again. If I'd had my druthers, the weather would have been rain—heavy, pounding rain that poured buckets so dense they'd run gullies through the streets until every last one of us was drowning. Not really, of course, but I would have felt better if at least the skies were cloudy and gray.

I lay under the tent of our marriage blankets and thought about the morning before, how I'd awoken ignorant as a child of the coming change to my life. What bliss it had been to only be missing my man. Now I was mourning him. *Forever without him,* I kept thinking, then dropping off into sobs and slow tears. And what about Roger? He'd never meet his new child. He'd miss all the growing up of Carol, Barry, and John. He'd gone through all that war, made it, survived, and still he lost. It seemed terrifically unfair. And there wasn't a single thing I could do about it. I threw the covers back, angry and sad, just as Carol poked her head around the doorjamb.

"Morning, Mommy," she whispered. Johnny still slept in the crib along our bedroom wall, and she knew well enough not to wake him.

"Morning, princess," I whispered back. I held my arms out to her. She pressed up against me for a morning hug. "Hungry?"

"A little."

"Let me wash up and we'll put the oatmeal on." She nodded and plopped into the blue chair in the corner of our room.

I washed my face, brushed my teeth, and changed into a faded blue housedress. I didn't think, just went through the motions. I refused to look at that Aqua Velva bottle in the medicine chest, I refused to think about my lone toothbrush. It wasn't easy, but I wasn't ready yet to cry over every danged thing that wanted me to. I wiped my mouth and went back into the bedroom.

"Ready?"

Carol nodded. She slipped her hand in mine. I peeked over at the crib. Johnny was still fast asleep. I checked up on Barry in the next room. He was still slumbering, too. So, Carol and I went down the stairs hand-in-hand, just the two of us, which was a rare event most days. She didn't say much, which wasn't typical of her, but I let her be. She'd get around to it, I figured.

The kitchen was warm and sunny. I pulled the pan from under the counter. "Want to help?" I held the measuring cup out to her.

"Sure." She took the cup, and I grabbed a chair for her to stand on.

"Measure two cups for us, hon." She dug the cup deep into the oat bin. I leveled it with a knife. "Now, dump it in the pan and scoop another." She scooped and leveled it herself, spilling a smidgen of oats onto the counter.

"Uh oh, Mommy."

"Don't worry, every cook spills a little now and then." She dumped the other scoop into the pan. I turned on the tap. "Now, four cups of water," I instructed. She put the cup under, filled it, and dumped it into the pan four times in a row. I watched her careful efforts, comforted by the simple ease of teaching my young daughter to make oatmeal. "Good girl. Now, we stir." I handed her a wooden spoon and turned on the burner. We stood side-by-side at the stove, wrapped in the morning quiet.

"You're making breakfast, princess," I said, kissing her head.

"I could make breakfast for Daddy, when he comes home," she said, and looked at me sideways, a finger on her lips. And there it was, the question that had likely been weighing on her since yesterday.

"Daddy would have liked that, Carol," I said, turning the burner to low. It wasn't a surprise to me that my sharp-eyed first-born was looking for answers, I just wished I didn't have to tell her. But what would be the point of that, lying to a child who, as she grew, would figure it out anyway? And how would I answer her questions then, if I kept the truth from her now?

"Come with me," I said, "we'll let the oatmeal simmer." I picked her up and carried her over to the table. I sat her on my lap and chose my words slowly and carefully. "There's been some trouble with Daddy... he won't be coming home anymore."

She chewed on her finger, trying to work out what I meant. "Ever?" She searched my eyes, looking for truth. I nodded. "But I want Daddy to come home." She pressed a finger against the button of my housedress.

"Something terrible has happened, and now Daddy can't come home."

A smile worked at the corners of her mouth, as if she hoped I was fooling around. I shook my head.

"But..." She slumped into my arms. I kissed her curls, wrapping her tight against me. "I want Daddy." She sounded choked up, but she did not cry.

"I know, honey, I know." She lay there against me, not speaking, not crying, but I was sure her little brain was working overtime.

Finally, she said, "It's not fair." She said it quietly, no fight in it. Surrender wasn't like my little pistol at all, but I think she was coming to understand the meaning of futility at far too young an age. It made me want to cry all over again.

"I know," I said instead. It was the best I had, but it broke my already shattered heart into even tinier pieces.

Barry shuffled into the kitchen. "Morning, Butch," I said.

Carol slipped off my lap. "Can I put the oatmeal in the bowls?" she asked. I nodded, and on we went, just like any other morning. The two of them sat at the table with oatmeal and the sugar bowl, and I went up for Johnny.

He was awake, but not fussing. A ray of sun blazed across his crib. He seemed to be looking at something off in the middle of the room, a baby grin on his lips. I put my hand on his round baby belly.

"Whatcha looking at, Johnny boy?" He glanced at me, then looked back toward the middle of the room. His eyes lit up and he giggled. I turned around, but I didn't see a thing.

CHAPTER 25

ELEANOR

It wasn't just me who had lost Roger, of course; there was his family—his dear mother, Evelyn, and his pa, Charles. They had always been good to me. The day we married, young and barely out of high school, they were nothing but welcoming.

"You're family now, dear," Evelyn said, taking my hands in hers that day. "You call me 'Ma'." And that was it. I became her daughter-in-law and part of the Mitchell family. Now, I had to call and break her heart. My stomach seized at the very idea. But it was just another in a long series of bucking up I was gonna have to do.

I ran a glass of cool water and pulled a chair up to the phone table in the hall. I flattened the telegram open on top of its envelope and pulled that cold black receiver to my ear. As I was dialing the number for the Mitchell house up north in Kalkaska, I tried to figure the right way to break the news. Should I blurt it out? Should I let Roger's mother comb through the bits of her own life first? Let the woman have one last conversation as the same person she was before she answered the phone?

The phone rang, once, twice. I could picture her hurrying to pick it up, a small woman with a round build and a sweet careworn smile.

"Hel-looo." Her high-pitched lilt sang familiarly through the line.

"Hi, Ma, it's Eleanor," I said, a sob building in my throat. I swallowed against it and remembered Mother's firm advice: *We do what we must.*

"Oh, Eleanor," she began. "So good to hear from you, dear." Through the phone came a long, pleased sigh. She must have settled herself at the kitchen table for our chat. Now that the war was over, talking on the phone wasn't the hurry-up affair it had once been.

"How are you now, honey?" she asked. I started to say I was all right, but then out of my mouth it tumbled.

"Ma, there's been some news." Then I was crying like a blubbering fool.

"Oh, Lord, is it Roger?" She sounded breathless.

I swallowed my tears hard and straightened my shoulders.

"It is." I told her. "Roger." I had to press my hand over my mouth once more before I could say it. "They say he's been killed."

"Oh no!" she cried then I heard the phone clatter to the table. I pressed the receiver hard against my ear.

"Ma? Are you there?" I said, in a panic. I heard nothing. "Ma?"

Then, far away in the background, I heard Ma calling. "Charles! Charles! Come quick!"

I gripped the warming receiver like a lifeline, straining to hear what was happening up on the farm that had been Roger's childhood home. I felt like I could hear the breeze through the kitchen windows, then footsteps; a door squeaked wide, then slammed shut again. I could picture the house. Pa would be coming in the back door. Ma would deliver the awful news right there in their cozy farmhouse kitchen. I heard murmuring, then more footsteps. I imagined Pa striding across the floor to the phone. The voices grew louder. Still, I couldn't make out what they were saying. Someone picked up the phone from where it lay.

Roger's father's voice, deep and thick, came through the line. "Eleanor, are you there, dear?"

"I'm here," I answered, sitting up straight.

"What is this now about our Roger?"

"I received the notice yesterday. The man was here. Says Roger's been killed. Accidentally. It says accidentally."

"Well," was all he said. In the background I could make out Ma crying.

"I just can't believe it," I said finally.

"No. It can't be, can it?" Pa said. "The damn war's a month over, and now this."

"Can it not be?" I wondered aloud. "Could they make a mistake?"

"I don't think we can hope for that." He cleared his throat. I could hear Ma's breath hitching.

"I suppose not," I answered, my shoulders sinking nearly into my stomach. I was just so tired all of a sudden.

"Came by Western Union, then?" he asked. "The notice."

"Yes, a young man, Western Union."

"Lord, I thought we'd seen the end of that." His voice broke.

"Do you want me to read it to you?"

"What?" he asked through a sorrow thickened voice.

"The telegram. Do you want me to read it?"

"Well, no. I don't suppose..." and through the line I could hear their tears. I cried with them, sharing silent tears with the two people in the world who loved Roger as much as I did.

The next voice was Ma's. "Are you okay, dear? One of your sisters there with you?"

"They'll be by soon."

"I hate for you to be alone."

"It's fine. They're coming."

"Should we come down there and be with you for a while?" she asked.

"I have my sisters and my mother," I said.

"Yes, I s'pose you do. How are the children? Everyone okay?"

"Yes, the children are good. Napping now."

"Oh, dear. And we haven't even seen the baby yet. Here I thought we'd drive down when Roger came home, see him and the baby at one time."

"Yes..." was all I could say.

"Oh, it is just terrible," Ma said. "I can't even think what to do." The poor woman was just as lost as I was.

"Why don't we talk again in a few days?"
I suggested. "It's hard to think too far ahead after
this kind of news."

"Yes. Well, that is true. But will you be okay?"

"As okay as any of us, I s'pose."

"Yes," Ma said, her voice sounding distant. The
line went quiet, nothing more for either of us to say.
I waited.

"Well, all right," Ma said, snapping back into
herself. "You take care. We'll be calling you in a few
days. We love you, dear."

"Okay," I said. "Ma?"

"Yes, dear?"

"I'm so sorry."

"Oh, honey, me too. Now, you call your sisters."

"I will."

"Bye, now."

The phone rattled back into its cradle on her
end. The disinterested dial tone buzzed in my ear.
I placed the receiver down softly. There it was—
another bunch of hearts broken together.

In the silence, I looked around. This house, our
house, had at one time seemed like the beginning
of all my dreams. Tidy and just right for a family,
I saw us growing old together here. Now, the old
brown runner under my feet looked as tired and
hopeless as I felt. We'd planned to replace it, Roger
and me; we talked of pulling it up, refinishing the
floor underneath and laying something new. Green,
maybe, or a lighter brown again. I never thought
to ask him what color he'd like, figuring we'd make
that decision together. All those simple things you

count on when you marry the one you love, those conversations you expect to have.

I ran my hand over the telephone table. I remembered Roger's brother, Wesley, hefting it in through the front door one humid June afternoon. A hand-me-down from the Mitchells, its surface was smooth, marred only by one deep nick along the front edge. My fingers worried at that dent, imagining that maybe Roger'd been the one to put it there as a young boy. Maybe he'd come running down the farmhouse hall and banged into the table with a stick or a stone. And maybe he'd gotten a lickin' for being careless. Or maybe Ma had seen the whole thing happen, seen him smack hard into the table and maybe it was his front tooth he hit on that table and she'd come running to comfort him. Or maybe one of his brothers or his sisters made that mark, and Roger had no idea what happened. I'd never thought to ask how that dent got there in that table. Now, I'd never find out.

CHAPTER 26

ELEANOR

Ma and Pa did come to visit me and the children for a few days. During the war, long-distance driving was forbidden except in emergencies, but the rules had loosened since then, so they drove down. Roger's sister, Bea, lived in Flint, so the folks stayed over there, but they came by most days. We had dinner over at Bea's, Ma insisting she didn't want me doing any extra work on account of them. It was a comfort to see them. They looked the same as I remembered: Ma, a tidy round homestead woman who favored a certain shade of cornflower blue, and Pa, a thin, leathery man of the field who generally wore deep green work shirts. They were dressed in their visiting clothes when we had dinner at Bea's, Pa in a dark pants and an ironed cotton dress shirt, Ma in a neat print dress. We were careful and kind to each other.

They were tickled with the children, marveling at how they'd grown. We all agreed Johnny was the spitting image of his father. Ma promised to send a baby photo of Roger when she got home. All of us were a little melancholy when the visit finally ended. It had been nice to spend the time, but Roger's absence was sorely apparent. I was grateful they'd thought to come for a visit at all, but a part of me expected it was as much to say goodbye as anything. We hadn't spoken of it, but it seemed like seeing their son's family without their son might prove more difficult as time went on.

When there wasn't any more to be said or done, Ma and Pa decided to head back up north. They were planning an early start, so I invited them over for breakfast before they got on the road. I made the coffee cake I knew Pa loved, along with eggs, bacon, toast, oatmeal, and coffee. We ate and the children went off to play. Pa, Ma, and I lingered around the table, sipping on the last of our coffee.

"Looks like we've got a cold winter ahead, if this morning is any inkling." I pulled my sweater a little tighter around my shoulders and gave a shiver.

"You're right about that," Pa agreed. I stood to clear the table and Ma put a hand on my wrist.

"Sit, honey," she said gently. "Just sit." That was none too hard for me; I hadn't yet found my usual vim since the day of the telegram. Ma brought the pot of coffee over and refilled each of our cups. Pa cleared his throat as I took a sip of the weak brown liquid.

"Eleanor, Ma and I have been talking, now," Pa said. I could hear a thread of nerves in his voice. Whatever he was about to say, it was something more than talk about the weather. My stomach started to churn. I set my coffee cup down, trying to replace it in the ring it had just left on the table.

I looked up at Pa. His blue eyes met mine, the same pale shade as Roger's. I was sure they were about to tell me good-bye: that with Roger gone, there was nothing to hold us together, no need to stay in touch with what was left of us. And who could blame them? The children and I would just be a terrible reminder of Roger and all they'd lost.

"We've talked over your situation," Pa said, "with the news about Roger." He stopped, shook his head, looked down at the table.

"Yes, dear," Ma said. "We've talked it over." She reached for Pa's hand. "We were wondering if you and the children might think about moving up to Kalkaska with us." She smiled that soft, easy smile she had, her own blue eyes gentle and welcoming.

"Move?" I echoed, like some foolish myna bird. I was so surprised. I didn't have half an idea what to say.

"We thought with the farm and all, well, there's lots of space for the children. And we'd help with whatever you need." Ma's eyes flitted around as she spoke, her hand fussing at the top button of her dress. I didn't know if she was nervous about asking me, or nervous about my answer. I looked over at Pa and he, too, looked a little tense, his shoulders raised up near his ears.

It was kind of them to offer. It brought tears to my eyes that they cared enough to ask. But moving up to Kalkaska wasn't something I was ready to do. Not now, probably not ever. Roger and I had planned for this life long before all this war mess. We planned to live in the city, go up north for summer vacations. I couldn't see changing any of that now. It was enough that there was no hope of his return, but to change the whole plan wasn't something I was ready to think about.

"Well, I have the house," I said, grasping. "And my sisters all live near."

"Yes, dear," Ma said.

"'Course, it's none of our business," Pa said too loud, then cleared his throat again. "But that's a little what we were thinking. With the house and all, how will you manage?" He took a deep breath, worried, I think, that he was prying.

"We aren't trying to meddle, dear, but we worry for you and the children without Roger's earnings," Ma explained.

"It's likely to be hard for you, Eleanor," said Pa. I nodded, and the tight fist of money worry churned up in my belly, as it had on and off for all these awful days. I didn't have a plan and I knew it, so I told them what I'd been telling myself for the last little while.

"I've got the insurance money. From the War Department. They say that comes eventually." I said it as strong as I could and managed a smile to go along with it.

"That's good," Pa said.

"And I've been taking in some sewing for a few of the ladies in the neighborhood," I threw in. There was only the slimmest bit of truth to it, but it sounded okay. They looked at one another and Pa gave a little nod.

"That's a nice idea, isn't it, Charles?" Ma said, a lift of encouragement in her voice.

Pa nodded. "That it is," he said. "But..."

"I know it's not what Roger earned, but I'll figure it out," I said, sounding more confident than I felt. "Somehow," I added.

"Just so long as you think you'll be all right." Ma looked expectantly at me.

"I aim to be," I said.

She moved her hand from the button to a teaspoon on the table. She straightened it ever so slightly, then reached for her coffee cup.

"We can help," Pa offered. "With the war over, things are getting back to normal. We can help you, dear. Send you a little something from time to time."

"Yes," Ma echoed. "And you are always welcome with us, Eleanor, if things change, or you just want to come for a visit. We do love seeing those grandchildren."

"Oh, sure, of course. I'd love to bring the children for a stay next summer."

Ma stood up and came around the table to wrap me in a hug. "That would be wonderful, Eleanor. Really wonderful." She kissed the top of my head and gave my shoulders an extra squeeze. I patted her hand.

"You're family, Eleanor. To us, you'll always be family."

Tears came to my eyes. I couldn't speak. I just nodded and hugged her tight.

Pa stood. "Yes," was all he said. Slipping an envelope under the sugar bowl, he left the room.

They said their good-byes to the children and climbed into their Studebaker. We stood inside the side door, watching Pa back the car down the drive. He curved it onto the asphalt. Ma waved, Pa beeped the horn, and they were gone.

I closed the door, turned toward my permanently half-empty house, and all I could think was, *Well, you've gone and done it now, Eleanor. Sent those lovely people on their way, declaring yourself able to handle this whole life—three children and a house and bills and a car and whatever else—all by yourself.*

I leaned my back hard against the door, its thickness holding me up. I was probably crazy. I'd probably end up throwing myself on their mercy—or someone else's—before it was all said and done. But for now, I was going to try. What exactly I was going to try, I didn't half know, but I'd figure it out. Life would go on, whether I wanted it to or not, and I would go on with it. I pushed myself to standing and took my very first real step into this new life—a life that looked a lot like the old one, only emptier, less magical, less perfect, but life nevertheless. And whatever it had in store for me, the Widow Mitchell and her three fatherless children, I'd face it head-on.

PART
TWO

CHAPTER 27

ROGER

R oger sat on the floor at the foot of Carol's bed. Carol sat near the bedroom door. Between them lay her cloth dolls. Eleanor had made them for her, a family of four—the family they'd had before the war crept in. Roger guessed there hadn't been time to make a baby Johnny yet.

Carol stood the mother doll at the edge of the circle. "Joyce, you keep your dress from wrinkling, now," she said in a perfect imitation of Eleanor's serious voice. "And Jimmy, you come on over and let me wipe your hands and face." Roger chuckled. She was her mother's daughter.

"Here, Daddy," she said, handing him a doll dressed in a navy blue suit, complete with tiny tie and black cloth shoes. "You be the daddy and wait downstairs for everyone." She held the doll out to Roger. He reached for it, but when she let it go, the doll fell through his filmy fingers onto the floor just in front of his crossed legs. She shrugged but didn't say anything.

The ease she had with his presence thrilled him, and it had been that way from his very first visit. It was just after his folks left town. He'd been watching Eleanor and the children for a few days, silent and unseen. He watched the rhythms of the home he'd been forced to leave behind, the waking and the sleeping, the meals and the cleaning. He felt the sadness that threaded through Eleanor's day and heard her plaintive cries late in the night. He ached to console her, but knew he must wait until the time was right, the time her grief would crack enough to let him in. He was back now; not the same, but back nonetheless, just like he had promised, and she would never have to be alone again.

When Eleanor declined Ma and Pa's offer to move in with them, Roger saw his opportunity to restart their life together. Eleanor wasn't ready to give up, and neither was he. And so he appeared, first to the children, but with the ambitious plan to one day win Eleanor over to a new kind of love.

The first time he appeared, Carol was just waking from her nap. Roger stood at the foot of her bed, smiling.

"Daddy!" she cried in a canned whisper. Barry was still asleep in the bed next to her. "I drew you so many pictures." Her eyes grinning with excitement, she threw her blanket back, climbed onto the floor, and pulled a pile of drawings from under the bed. "Mommy said we couldn't send them to you anymore." She patted a place next to her on the floor for him to sit.

"Well, now you can show them to me yourself," he told her. She tried to lean into him, but there was nothing for her to cuddle against. She caught herself with one hand, looking up at him.

"It's different now, sunshine," Roger explained. "Daddy's not all the way real anymore, but we can still talk and play together."

She frowned, looked at him sideways, then shrugged. "Okay, Daddy, look at my picture of the trees." And, as simple as that, they were father and daughter again.

It had been same ever since. "Hi, Daddy," she'd say, easy as you please, and pull him into whatever she was doing. She was neither bothered nor particularly curious about his shortcomings. And Roger was just grateful to have a relationship with his daughter, even if it was from the other side.

Still playing the role of mother doll, she said, "Let's wipe your face," and leaned it toward the smallest doll. Then she pressed the two doll faces together and made a kiss noise.

"C'mon, little ones," she called in a sing-song voice. "Daddy's waiting." She bounced the dolls, clustered in her fist, along the floor toward Roger. Carol gathered up the daddy doll in her free hand.

"Let me have a look at you," she said in gruff imitation of a man. "What a nice family."

"Come now, honey, we're going to be late," Carol said in the mother's voice.

"Daddy, hold my hand," called the daughter doll. Pairing father and daughter in one hand, mother and son in the other, Carol moved them gently across the wooden floor and around the corner of the bed to "church".

Watching her, Roger was filled with a bittersweet mix of admiration and ache. She had grown so much since he'd left. Everything about her was a size or two bigger than before, such a confident bundle of her little-girl self. He had missed so much.

From around the edge of the bed, she called to him, "Daddy, c'mon. Come over here to the church." She patted a spot on the floor near her. He hesitated, uncertain if she meant him or the father doll in her imaginary world. Her second pat and "Daddy, come over," made him sure that he was the one being summoned. Roger moved in beside his daughter. What he wouldn't have given to plant a kiss on her forehead, breathe in the sweet scent of her curls. But there were limitations in this new existence, limitations he accepted just to be with his family again. In the choice between this or nothing, he'd happily take this. They could see each other and hear one another; the words between them passed from his mind into hers. When Carol spoke, he heard it in his head, and she "heard" him the same way. He wasn't physical anymore, so there was no physicalness, no hugging or holding. Still, here he was. And that was better than nothing.

Eleanor peeked into the room, her arms full of folded linens. "Whatcha up to, sweetie?"

Carol didn't answer but handed the father doll to Roger, along with the boy doll.

"You be the boys, Daddy. I'll be the girls." Again, the dolls fell to the floor in what would have been

Roger's lap. A puzzled look flashed across Eleanor's face. She waited, watched. But Carol, busy with the girl dolls, offered no explanation. Eleanor watched a moment longer, then shrugged and moved down the hall to put the linens away. Roger heard the closet door open, then close. On her return, Eleanor stopped again in the doorway, her arms empty now, her brow wrinkled. She took two steps into the room.

"What're you playing, honey?" Eleanor asked.

Carol glanced up, brushing a curl out of her eye. "Dolls. With Daddy," she said matter-of-factly.

"With Daddy?" Eleanor asked gently.

"Yeah, but he's not very good. I have to do all the walking."

Roger laughed. Eleanor grinned but looked around the room with a searching eye. Carol had spoken of Daddy more and more often lately, and Eleanor had evidently taken notice. At first, she had chalked it up to all the conversation of Roger since the telegram, but now she was starting to suspect something more.

"We're at church," Carol said, placing the father and son doll alongside the mother and daughter.

Eleanor crouched next to Carol. "Honey, does Daddy play with you a lot?"

"Sometimes. He plays with Barry, too."

"Is Daddy here now?"

Roger's heart quickened. Carol pointed directly at him. "He's right there, Mommy. He likes to sit on the floor. I showed him all my drawings."

Eleanor squinted into the empty space that was him. He looked directly into her eyes. For a split second, she seemed to meet his gaze. Roger knew she could feel something. He knew she wanted to feel something; the air seemed thick with possibility. Then she blinked as if to clear her eyes and gave up. Her heart was too broken to believe in magic. She shook her head roughly and stood up.

"I'm going back downstairs, sweetie," she said. "Call me if you need me."

"Okay, Mommy."

Roger tried to speak to her in her mind, tried to convince her to come back and look again. She took a few steps down the hall, then paused. He could feel her considering, loosening; she wanted to see him and she could, he knew, if she'd just let herself. Instead, she shook her head again, as if rattling the idea from her mind, and carried on downstairs. Roger stayed with Carol, watching her play and biding his time. Eleanor had seen him once before on the day he died; she had it in her to see him again. And he had the patience to wait until she could.

CHAPTER 28

ELEANOR

I n the weeks that followed the terrible news,
I leaned on my usual routine to see me through.
What else could I do? The bright promise of my
life had been snatched away from me, and still
my children needed meals and baths and bedtime
and diaper changes and what-all. Laundry had to
be done, dishes washed and dried. I did it because
I had to, but I wasn't the same anymore. I was
broken, truth be told. In the space of a trip down the
stairs I'd gone from war wife, giddy and optimistic,
to war widow, frightened and alone. Seeing to the
dull routines of life seemed like the only way I was
gonna get by. I hardly slept. Food didn't taste like
much to me. One or another of my sisters generally
came by to help most evenings, same as before. But
we didn't laugh like we used to, we didn't kid and
joke. I'm not sure they knew what else to do, either.
We ate Sunday dinner at Mother's just like always.
No one went near the mention of soldiers returning,
never mind we were still waiting for our brothers—

Jack, Bill, and Perry—to get back across the water. And our sister, Mary, had come back from her Red Cross work, but she'd gone right away to California— something about more work to be done, but we thought it had more to do with a man.

Brother Earl had gotten a clean bill of health from the Army doctors for his nervous disorder, but he stayed lost to the demons of war. We hardly saw him, and when we did, it seemed he wasn't sure who we were. He was thin and hollow around the eyes; his cheeks were sunken, and he generally smelled of alcohol. Mostly, he came around because he needed money, so Mother or one of us would put a few bills together. We didn't want him drinking, but it seemed better to give him what he needed than to worry what he might do to get it. Mother told him, "You come by anytime," which was just her way of trying to keep tabs on him. It was hard to watch her during those pop-in visits from Earl. We knew Mother to be as stoic as anyone we'd ever known, but every time she laid eyes on Earl, a sadness came over her whole face, one even she couldn't hide. She'd fuss around and get him food, ask him if he'd like to wash up or take a nap. Fussing had never been Mother's way, but what the war had done to Earl changed that, even in her.

Other than that, the five of us did and said all of the same things, ate the same mix of foods, had the same kinds of tiffs and tattles. Every one of us pressing on as best we could. Except Helen. She was like a bull in a china shop, never having the good sense to leave well enough alone.

"Hello, Eleanor," she said, clomping into my kitchen one late afternoon. "I've got loads of goodies for you and the children. It's day-old, but there's nothing wrong with that, is there?" She dropped a paper sack on the table. She'd taken a cashiering job at the Hamady's up on Chevrolet Avenue by then because the war jobs for women had ended along with the war. Jean was lucky enough to keep hers because she worked secretarial, but the rest of the work was earmarked for the men returning. In fairness, Helen was disappointed to have to leave the factory job and the money it paid, but I was sure that being privy to every darn grocery a person might decide to buy kept her in gossip and good cheer all day long.

"Let's see," she said, taking things from the bag. "There's bread and cinnamon rolls, oh and look, two packages of oatmeal cookies, too." She clapped her hands together. "I told Mr. Langford, my manager, that I was bringing this here for you. 'Course he knows you're a war widow, so he added some extras. What a sweet man." She smiled, and in it was both pity for me and excitement at the "extras."

"Helen Osborn? Are you sweet on Mr. Langford?" I asked, winking.

She swung her head around quick, and I swear I saw a blush in her cheeks. "Lord, no, Eleanor! He is quite happily married, I'm sure."

"You're sure, or you know?" I grinned.

She fussed at folding the paper sack into a neat rectangle. "Maybe I should just take all this back, then," she said, jutting her chin out.

"Maybe you should." I shrugged. Her face went red.

"And how would I do that?" she huffed. "Have me looking like an ungrateful fool?" She gathered the packages and put them on the counter. "I'm sure the children will be glad of them, even if you aren't."

"I never said I wasn't grateful. I just asked about your boss."

She rolled her eyes and shoved the grocery sack in the bin.

"Dinner will be ready in twenty minutes," I said, turning back to the counter. She didn't say anything, so I looked over my shoulder. And there she stood, hands on her hips, giving my kitchen the once-over like the place was going to ruin right there in front of her very eyes. A pitiful sigh slipped out from her lips, and I knew just where she was headed. Helen had been on the trail of my life and how I didn't stand a chance of an iceberg in August of surviving on my own. I was in no mood for it that night. She opened her mouth to say something, but I cut her off.

"Would you mind checking the children, please?" I asked, before she could speak. "The boys are in the front room, but Carol might be upstairs. She was thrilled you were coming over tonight." Of course, Carol was nothing of the sort, but I had to nip Helen in the bud somehow.

Helen grinned. "She was? Oh, what a darling! I'll go see what she's up to." I breathed a sigh of relief, but I was sure Helen would have more to say later.

We got settled at the dinner table, all of us tucked in, and we had barely taken our first bite when

Helen began. "Oh, Eleanor, what *are* we going to do with you and the children now?" Her words were muffled around the food she had just stuffed in her mouth, but they were still laced with a thick dose of pity. I couldn't say it surprised me, what with all her carrying on earlier, but I'd hoped she had better sense than to say it in front of my little ones. I turned to Carol. Sure enough, her baby blue eyes had gone round as saucers.

So, I swooped in. "What are you gonna do with us?" I laughed. "Why do you have to do anything with us at all? We're just fine." I winked at Carol. She smiled, but her eyes were watching me carefully.

"But it's just so sad, isn't it?" Helen went on.

"Good Lord, Helen," I groaned, rolling my eyes.

"Reminds me of Mother," she said.

I blew on a spoonful for Johnny and tested the food against my lip. "Good bite, Johnny. You're a hungry boy," I said cheerily. But in my head, I kept repeating, *Shut up, Helen, shut up,* over and over. But like a dog with a bone, she was gonna gnaw after the topic.

"... A whole handful of children to raise and no way to provide..." she persisted.

"Oh, Helen, it's dinner time, isn't it?" I said, using my best mother voice to cut her off. "And look at your plate, you've barely touched a thing. No dessert without a clean plate," I said. "Isn't that right, Carol?"

"That's the rule," Carol declared, and took a big bite of potato. Helen glanced down at her plate, then looked hard at me. I bugged my eyes. She bugged hers back, but she picked up her fork and shoveled in a giant bite.

"Carol," I said. "Tell Aunt Helen what we have for dessert today."

"Apple pie!" she called.

"Yay!" hollered Barry.

"Can we have it now, Mommy?" Carol pleaded.

"Clean your plates," I instructed. They downed those last few bites in seconds. But there was my next mistake; the children's full mouths cleared a space for Helen to shove her way in again.

"I know you don't want to talk about Roger's being gone, but you are going to have to do something about your predicament. I don't believe that waiting until the lot of you are banging on the door of the home for widows and children is the proper time to start talking about it." She humphed, nodded her head firmly, and folded her arms across her chest, a satisfied curl to her pursed lips.

"But Auntie Helen," Carol said, earnest and certain, "Daddy isn't gone anymore. He's home now." She smiled. "So nobody has to do a thing with us."

Helen narrowed her eyes. "Oh, Daddy's home, is he?" She looked first at Carol and then at me. "Good Lord, Eleanor."

"He's sitting right beside you," Carol declared, pointing a pudgy finger at the chair next to Helen, Roger's usual chair. Of course, there wasn't a thing to be seen in it.

"Right beside me, I am sure." She glared at me. "Very funny, Eleanor."

I just shrugged.

Then Carol asked, "Can we have pie now, Mama? Daddy says Helen can have his piece." This she said as sweet as could be, without a glimmer of teasing. I laughed. I couldn't help myself. Helen glared harder at me, but I just went over to the counter and cut the pie without a word. She shoved away from the table and stomped over.

"Eleanor," she whispered, hot and sharp in my ear. "Do you think it's wise to let your children believe Roger is home again? How will they ever come to terms with his passing if you don't tell them outright?" But I didn't give a hoot what Helen thought was a good idea. I let her words fall all around me as if they were less than rain. I handed her a plate of pie.

"Here's your piece," I said. "Courtesy of Daddy," I added, winking at Carol. I glanced over at Roger's chair, and I could swear it almost seemed like there was a glint of some kind coming from over there.

☆ ☆ ☆

Over the dishes, Helen broached the topic again, shaking her head. "I know you'd rather not talk about it," she resumed, all high and mighty, "but your life has become strangely like Mother's, hasn't it? Have you ever thought about that?"

"My husband was taken from me in a terrible war. You do remember that, don't you?"

"I don't think that matters much, do you?" Helen returned, wiping a dinner plate. "Alone is alone."

I snapped. "Helen, how on earth are you saying these things to me? You don't think I know I'm a woman alone with three small children without half an idea how I'm going to provide? Do you honestly think I don't know what is going on in my life?"

She stood there gaping at me, her face flushed, looking like she might actually be embarrassed by her behavior for the first time in her life. I marched over to the sink. She took a step back. I turned the hot water on full blast and rinsed the dishrag under it. I wrung it as if it were the neck of a chicken and turned back to look hard at Helen. She tried to look hard back at me, but this was my house and my life—and she had crossed a line.

"You don't have to be so mean," she muttered, her sharp tongue finally dulled.

"Neither do you." I scrubbed at the kitchen counter as if the thing hadn't been cleaned in a year.

"I'm sorry, El," Helen said. I didn't for a minute believe her. "But I've been thinking a lot about how you'll manage money-wise and all. So even if Roger was doing his duty..."

"He would have come home," I interrupted, my throat growing thick. "If he could have."

"... Doesn't change you're all alone now, just like Mother. And, if you don't mind me saying, you don't seem as ready for it as Mother was." She put a hand on my shoulder. "I'm worried about you, Eleanor."

"*This* is worry, Helen?" I said whirling around. "Telling me I'm not prepared to make it on my own? Wringing your hands and saying, 'what *will* we do with you?' And saying it all in front of my children? Well, thanks very kindly, but I don't need it. I've been on my own for a good while now and I am managing things just fine."

"This is more of a permanent thing," she said softly, but she managed to look down her nose at me at the same time.

"So now I'm a fool who doesn't know my husband has been killed? You've got to be kidding me." I threw the dishrag onto the counter. "Let me tell you something, Helen." I gritted my teeth. "I am aware that my husband, who I loved more than life, is not coming home. But thank you very much for reminding me. Again. I also know that everyone from the butcher to ol' Mr. Callahan next door has made it a point to assure me that my life is going to be hard without him. I do know this, and I have known it for longer than the lot of you." She opened her mouth to say something, but I wasn't having anything more. I held my hand up in front of her face.

"I also know that I have made my way this year—with some help, surely—but without Roger. I have scrimped and saved and budgeted and rationed and done what every other war wife has done. All the while I was hoping against hope, praying and begging, that he would come home to me."

My tears started to run, but I had more to say. "I loved Roger, Helen. I loved him, and I still love him." I swiped at the tears, betraying me as they were. "There's part of me who still hopes the Army got it wrong, made the biggest mistake that could be made. I wouldn't mind one bit if they did, because that would mean Roger would walk through that door. And if he did, and I know it's a fantasy, but if he did, I'd throw my arms around him and never let go, not for a second." I stared hard at her, my eyes wet and angry. Her face was a puffed balloon of shock. She didn't say a word.

"Now, if you'll get the hell out of here, maybe I can get on with things without any more of your 'good advice'." With that, I put my hand on her left hip and turned her right toward the door. She was sputtering and spewing like an old car that didn't know whether it could make it to the end of the block. But I made sure she found the door.

Handing her the ugly beige wool coat she favored and her purse, I finished my speech. "Thank you *very* much for all your help tonight. I believe I can get things in order for my new life now." Finally, I shut the door and locked it. I knew I was being rude—maybe even unappreciative and downright ungrateful—but I'd had enough of being everybody's favorite charity case. Telling Helen to get a move on was my next solid step toward making my own way in the world. I'd stood up for myself, instead of getting pushed around one more cotton-picking time.

When I turned around, there were my babies, all three of them lined up in a haphazard row, unsure what to make of me now.

"Oh, that old Aunt Helen, she needed to get on home," I said with a laugh. "Who wants more apple pie?"

"Me!" Carol cried.

"And how about a little ice cream to go along with it?" I offered.

"Yay!" they all sang. Then I went to the Frigidaire to find we hadn't a scoop. So, I bundled them up, and we set off on an evening stroll. Brisk, but not too cold, the night air cleared my head. We spotted the moon making its way up into the sky, and we held hands at the corners. Didn't matter I ought to be running a tub and getting the children to bed, didn't matter we were lonely orphans on a mission for sweets, didn't matter we had a future as uncertain as the war itself had once been. We could go get ice cream any old time we wanted. Wasn't anybody here to tell us otherwise.

The fight with Helen carried over into my sleep that night. 'Long about three o'clock, I nearly jumped awake. My heart pounding, my breath short, I was sweating like I'd just run downtown and back. It was a terrible dream. My sisters had taken the children off somewhere and returned without them. Not one of them, even Jean, would answer me about where they'd gone. Instead, they turned their backs on me, linked arms, and went skipping down the road. I was chasing after them out on some old country road, calling, "Where are the children?" Up ahead of me, the three of them sang a song I couldn't make out, but the tune was teasing and mean, *"na na na-na na."*

Finally, Helen, seeming to be the leader, turned to me and said, "It's for the best, Ellie." Then she giggled and hooked her arm back through Faye's, and off they went without me. I woke in a flush of anxiety. The dark room came into shape, and I realized it was a dream. I threw the covers back and hurried to check on the children. Everybody was fine, sleeping peacefully.

I climbed back into my bed, wound up like a cuckoo clock. Sleep had no hope of visiting me again that night. Instead, I tossed and turned, covers weighing me down, then not covering me up enough. I started to worry that maybe Helen was right, that I wasn't prepared to live without Roger. Maybe I couldn't make my own way in the world. How on earth was I going to make it without him? What was the point of even trying without him? Then I turned, and there was baby Johnny, sleeping the sleep of angels in his little crib. And he was counting on me. It was then I understood my true responsibility. The children were the reason to go on, to try to make a good life for them, no matter how much my heart was hurting.

In that very moment I made up my mind not to be afraid anymore. I couldn't afford to be afraid if I was going set my three little ones off on a decent course. It was all up to me, and I was surely going to try.

CHAPTER 29

ROGER

A quiet came over the house after Eleanor sent Helen packing. She had, again, declared her independence and was as determined as ever to press on alone. She had no idea how just yet, but she was committed to figuring it out. Worry sometimes got the best of her, and in those times, Roger would hear her whisper, "If I can be nothing else, I can be brave." The words provided a balm for her jangled nerves. And she was brave—brave in the face of tantrum-throwing toddlers, brave in the face of bossy big sisters, brave in the face of household disrepair. She kept her chin up and her resolve strong, even as she sometimes cried herself to sleep.

Roger wanted so much to help her. He didn't come with any easy answers either, but he could at least offer support, be her confidant, let her know she was not alone. So he remained present and aware, checking her feelings, reading her emotions in a way he never could in life. Now, he knew when she was worried or happy or feeling a little bit carefree. It was in those moments he tried to reach her, tried to show himself. She hadn't seen him since the day of the storm, but her curiosity was heightened. She listened closely to the stories the children told, asked questions, and wondered what it was they all felt so sure about.

One bright morning, Barry was singing a familiar tune, and it instantly perked Eleanor's ears.

"Honey, what song is that you're singing?" she asked.

"'Sunshine'," he answered proudly. "Daddy taught me."

"Daddy taught you?" Roger felt his widow's interest rise.

"Yes, Daddy did," he answered in that precise way of his. "He sings it to me at night." He dipped his head shyly. "When I can't sleep."

"When you can't sleep?" she repeated.

"Yes, Mommy," Barry went on, nodding seriously. "Daddy comes when I wake up at night. He says 'Don't wake Mommy, she needs her rest. Let's sing a while.'"

"And you sing 'Sunshine'?"

"Daddy says it's his favorite."

Eleanor knew that Roger liked that song; he'd sung it to the children from the day they were born. "What else does Daddy do?" she asked.

Barry shrugged. "Sometimes he plays trucks with me."

"Do you see Daddy every day?"

He shrugged again. Eleanor looked around the room as if hoping to catch a glimpse of something. Roger sat in his usual chair, waiting and listening.

"Do you fall asleep when Daddy sings?"

"Mostly."

"Every night?"

"Every night when I wake up. Some nights I don't wake up." Barry took a contented bite of his toast. "Daddy sings with me whenever I want. But we never wake Carol."

"Well, that's good, isn't it?" Eleanor said, standing. "That's good not to wake your sister." She kissed his curls.

"Or you," he added with a nod. "We don't wake you either."

"No, you don't." She kissed him again. "You never wake me."

Roger could feel that Eleanor was taken with Barry's story. She knew Barry believed Daddy would sing him to sleep now and forever, if he needed it. Just like how Carol believed Daddy was home now. The children were privy to something she only wished could be true. Roger could feel her reach this understanding, could see her open up to the possibility of it. In fact, he knew that she wanted it to be true, but she was afraid to believe. She had believed with all her heart that Roger would return from the war and look where that had left her. But Roger had faith enough for both of them. Her heart would open, she would see. He would help her see the world beyond the physical. More than anything, he wanted her to know she was not alone. He was with her and he could be there for her. And, together, they could make some kind of new family again.

CHAPTER 30

ELEANOR

ot long after I kicked Helen out, Rita turned up on my doorstep tapping at the side door, a knock so gentle I wasn't sure I'd even heard it. Then she called my name in a quiet voice, so uncertain and shaky I couldn't immediately make out who it belonged to. I walked over to the door and there she stood, tired and shy-looking in dungarees and a wool coat, with Marjorie and Patrick shoring up her sides.

"Rita? Oh, goodness," I said. "What a surprise!"

"Sorry I didn't call first," she shrugged. "I'm just never sure when I'll have the spunk for getting out the door, so I don't like to make plans too much." She smiled weakly and shrugged again, letting her head drop into her shoulders like she was shrinking from something.

"Well, come on in!" I said, holding the door wide. "It's been so long."

She let the children through the door first, then slipped in after them. "Too long, I'm afraid. I'm so sorry about Roger."

"Aw, thanks, honey," I said and wrapped her in a hug. She was slight and thin in my arms.

"I should have come by sooner."

"S'all right. Let me put some tea on. I'm just so happy to see you." And I was. After sending Helen on her way and foregoing Ma and Pa's offer, well, I was beginning to wonder who on earth might be willing to put up with me.

"Before we do that, where is that new baby boy of yours? I haven't even met him yet."

"Oh my gosh, that's right. C'mon, he's in the other room with the kids." And there he certainly was, my precious little cherub sitting up and proudly able to crawl. Rita swooped him up into her arms.

"He's so big."

"Nearly six months now."

"Goodness, it has been a while," she remarked. She kissed Johnny's head and put him back on the floor, and together we made our way into the kitchen while the big kids settled in to play with one another.

I clattered the teakettle onto the burner and put some cookies on a plate. "How's your bunch, then?" I asked.

"Oh, they're fine. We're getting on with things. I'm still working at the real estate job, although I don't know for how much longer. So many women are getting pushed out to make room for the men. I'm not sure what I'll do if that happens to me."

"That's just the thing my sister, Helen, went through. She was working in the factory and as soon as the surrender came through, they let her go. 'Back to the kitchen,' they said, 'your husband will be needing a job when he gets home.' Not that my sister has a husband, but they didn't care a bit. She even offered to switch to office or cafeteria work, but there was no conversation about it."

The teakettle screamed and I got up to see to it. Rita didn't say anything in the quiet of me pulling it from the stove, and I didn't bother either, just poured the bubbling water off into the cups. It reminded me of the day we'd sat at her kitchen table, only now we were both widows.

When I sat again, I must have let out a weighty kind of sigh, because Rita looked up at me.

"It's like that, isn't it?" she said. "Everything covered with a shade of gray now, don't you think?"

"What's that?" I asked.

She rubbed at her forehead like she had a headache coming on. "When you sat down, you sighed. I find myself doing that a hundred times a day if I do it once."

"I s'pose I hadn't noticed."

"Might just be me..." She trailed off.

"I guess I am a little heavier in my heart."

"Don't have to tell me," she said. I looked at her and I could see the weariness in the melancholy curve of her lips, the dark circles cupped under her eyes. She looked like the image of burden itself, hollowed and heavy.

"You've been at this longer than me," I said.

"Doesn't get better, doesn't get worse. Just the same old dull horror every time you think about it." She fiddled with her teaspoon, forcing a half-smile over those saddened lips.

A quiet settled between us, and I felt overcome by the words Rita was putting to my feelings, feelings I couldn't quite put a finger on in those early days. We sipped at our tea. The chatter of the children bubbled through.

"I am sorry for that day," she said after a time. "That first day, when I…"

"Hey now, I'm just glad you pulled through."

"I can't say whether I have or not," she said quietly, shaking her head and purposefully not looking my way. "It was touch and go there for a while. That's why they kept me so long."

"Oh, Rita. That must have been hard," I said consolingly.

"It was and it wasn't. To tell the truth, I would have liked to join him, wherever he went."

"You don't mean that…" I countered.

"I do," she said. "It frightens people to hear that. My own mother nearly slapped my face when I said it to her." She shook her head. "But sometimes I wonder if it wouldn't have been better if I'd completed the job, so to speak."

"But the children…"

She looked at me over the rim of her teacup, took a considered sip, and said, "It's always that, isn't it? 'The children, what about the children?' But I'm not sure what use I am to them now anyway." She tipped her head, as if listening for the tinkle of her little ones' voices. "I'm not half the mother I was."

I let that sit, allowing her whatever time she needed to gather the thoughts she'd been keeping to herself. It wasn't my place to judge anyone's reaction to losing the man they loved—didn't want to be judged myself.

"Oh, if I could do it again..." she went on. "If I'd known what I know now, I would have waited to have children." She twisted her cup in its place on the painted table, then looked up at me, a wide blink in her eye. "Do you think of that?" she asked suddenly.

"Think of what? No children? Oh my word, no. I fairly think the children are just about the only thing that is getting me through these days," I said, meaning it in a way I hadn't known until I said it.

"Yes," she nodded, looking down. "There is some truth to carrying on for the children's sake—some honor in it, even. I just can't help but wonder how it all would have gone for me if I hadn't had children, if I'd known that life could get so uncertain."

"Wasn't any way to know," I said. "We had every right to think we could have a regular life."

"Did we?"

"Oh, I don't know if we did or we didn't," I said, "but I do know it's not such an awful thing to want to share a life with the man you love and bring babies into it, too. Even if the world decides to go mad. Can't blame yourself for the mess others make; you just gotta do what you can to help clean it up sometimes. At least that's what I tell myself."

She smiled. "Maybe," she said, "but I do wonder."

"For me, the children are a little bit of Roger I can keep hold of," I said. "Sometimes Barry or Carol will have a hint of him in their eyes. And John is practically the spitting image of him, so I'm glad of it, something to hold on to."

"Ralph Junior does favor his father," she said with a wistful grin. "But I find that just makes me ache for Ralph all the more." She looked off, out the window.

I shrugged. Two ways of looking at it, I supposed, and who was I to say mine was better than hers?

"Still working on your real estate license, then?" I asked after a while.

She pulled her eyes away from the window. "Oh, yes, my license." She smiled weakly. "I'm still working at that. But I can't say I have the same enthusiasm for it that I started out with. It all just seems a little like a fool's errand. I've got these three children and no husband. And all the damnable jobs out there, seems like every single one of them is meant for the 'men returning.' That's what they are all saying. 'Give it to the men returning.' Well, doggone, some of the men are not returning, and what about that?" She ran a hand roughly through her hair, tears of frustration brimming in her eyes. "Oh, Eleanor, ignore me," she said. "I think I've been too caught up in my own worries and consternation to make sense anymore." She shook her head. "I came here for you," she said, "and here I am going on about myself."

"It's not easy for any of us, I don't think," I responded.

She reached a hand across the table, rested comforting fingers on my forearm, and smiled. "How *are* you?" she asked, but her heart wasn't in it. She was pushing herself to be kind, to be thoughtful, to be there for me, but she was having enough trouble understanding her own predicament to have much left for mine. The tank was dry for poor Rita, and maybe had been for some months now. I felt for her. As much as I enjoyed her, we were different women, with different ideas for our lives, and I think maybe that was the very crux of it for her. She'd had plans, big plans, like she'd said so many times before, and she just couldn't see past them. My plans were small, sweet, and simple: marry my Roger and raise a good family. My plans were this very life I had right now, and I wasn't yet ready to fully admit there would be no Roger coming back to it.

"I'm holding up," I answered. "Not sure exactly what I'm gonna do about it all yet, but I'm hanging in there."

She smiled. "What to do about it," she echoed. "Boy, don't I know about that question. I just have yet to find the right answer." She laughed. "And everybody so happy all over the place. Parades and celebrations and 'hurray for us,' and everything. It's about enough to make a person want to run screaming for the hills." She laughed again, harder this time, with a sharpened edge.

"I try to keep myself away from that as much as I can," I said, nodding. "Has a quality of salt in the wound for me."

She looked up, eyebrows raised. "That's it. Salt in the wound. Why yes, Eleanor, you are right, all that show and barely a fare-thee-well for what some of us lost."

I nodded. "That is true," I agreed. "I remember a thing Blanche said to me that day you went to the hospital. She'd called to tell me you were stable, going be all right, and we got to talking about war and all its terribleness. And she said to me, 'The wives get left to pick up the pieces in a thing like this,' or something like that. It came up for me again in the days since Roger's notice. She was right, but I don't half think she knows how right she was."

"Some things only the widow knows," she remarked.

"I'm glad you came by, Rita. Makes me feel just a little less alone than I did before."

She smiled a weary but contented smile. "It is nice to be with someone who understands, isn't it? Even if it doesn't change one damn thing."

The passing of the afternoon lent a darkening shadow to the room. We sat there in yet another quiet, the kind that had fallen so many times between us. There weren't any more words. We had lost, the both of us, and were left only with trying to figure how to get on with it. We each would find a way. Rita had already tried one or two things. For me, I wasn't any surer about my next move than I had been before she came to visit, but I did know I wasn't alone, and that was its own little bit of comfort.

After a while, Rita packed her young ones up, shouldered her coat over her thin shape, and left on promises we both made to see each other again, and to make it a regular thing. But we never did. That afternoon turned out to be the last I saw of her. Rumor was she'd gone back to be with her mother in Minnesota. Not anyone I knew ever heard another word from Rita, but I do hope it all worked out for her somehow.

CHAPTER 31

ELEANOR

Christmastime came around again, heavy with the memory of the year before when Roger had appeared, blowing in on the winter wind like a dose of holiday magic. It had been such a gift. As it turned out, that was the last time I saw him. Of course, if I had only known it was the last time... But I didn't, and what would I have done if I did? So, I let myself reminisce about it for the joyful time it was. I had a good cry, and then I put the memory of it away and got on with the holiday. I even managed to wrangle my brother, Jack, into getting us a tree. He'd been back from overseas since late October.

"Roger'll be glad we got a tree," I told him when we got the thing set up straight in the corner.

Jack shrugged. "Well, I s'pose he can thank me later, then." He laughed, and I did, too. It felt good to joke about it after so many months of sadness.

"He wrote me about you," I told Jack. "Said he wanted to know what kind of action you'd seen."

Jack raised an eyebrow. "That right?" He shook his head. "Woulda been nice to trade war stories with him." He picked at the pine needles thoughtfully. "How about I hang the lights for you, too?"

"That'd be a help." I handed him the strings. "Thank you, Jack." It was a fine moment for us. We had never been close, but the war had changed a lot of things, and it was good to have my brother to rely on.

My funds were holding tight, but only just. The Army was taking its sweet time getting the insurance check cut and mailed, so expenses were never too far from my mind. I was managing to make ends meet with help from a lot of others. Blanche had me baking for her holiday parties, insisting I was better at it than her, which wasn't at all true, but I appreciated her trying to make me feel useful. I refused anything more than the cost of the supplies, but she always managed to slip a few dollars under my sugar jar anyway. I was grateful for it.

Jean and Faye came around pretty regularly. Things were going along fine for them, which was its own kind of distraction. Jean had finally found a man, and it was funny to see her all worked up over it. Somehow this Tony fella had turned her head, and I heard about it every single time she came to my house.

"So, I been thinking about asking Tony to take me dancing," she said. We were doing the dishes after dinner one night. I was washing. She was drying.

"My oh my," I said. "Asking a man on a date."

"Well, that's just it," she sighed. "If I do the asking, I don't want to be so forward as to go all by myself."

"You should ask Faye."

"Remember the fun we used to have in the old days, going to The Riviera on a Saturday night?" she asked.

"I think my dancing days are over. But we did have some fun, didn't we?" I smiled, remembering gliding around the floor wrapped in Roger's arms.

"Your dancing days don't have to be over."

"Oh no, Jean Osborn, don't you start." I pushed my hair off my forehead and went back to scrubbing.

"Start what?" she asked, her voice lifting at the end like a little girl caught.

"Trying to find me a man."

"All I said was dancing." She finished drying a plate and clattered it into the cupboard. "We used to go together all the time."

"Together with Roger."

"I know that, but I do hate seeing you all cooped up here with only bath time to look forward to."

"I think bath time might be the very highlight of my evening, thank you very much." I flicked soap bubbles at her.

"It's just a night out," she said.

"A night of dancing means one of two things: I'm a wallflower or I dance with men. I'm not interested in either of those things." I sank my hands back into the hot dishwater.

She didn't say anything more, and I was glad not to have to defend my widowhood another time. She took a pan lid from the counter, wiped it dry, and tried to put it into the cupboard next to the stove. I knew that cupboard to be small and overfull. I watched her fuss and fight to get the door closed and couldn't help myself—I laughed.

"You organizing things over there?" I chuckled.

"Well, I certainly am," she replied. Then she stepped away from the door and let the lids and their pans tumble out, banging and clanging as if a brass band had just crashed down in the kitchen. The children covered their ears, looked from me to Jean and back again.

"How's that for organized?" she asked, hands on her hips and laughing.

"A fine job, Auntie Jean," I said between giggles. "Just fine."

She picked up two pan lids, banged them together then handed them to Carol.

"Here, honey, let's have a band," she said. Carol didn't hesitate. She grabbed the two lids and clanged them together, softly at first, but harder and harder when she saw I wasn't putting a stop to it. Jean handed Barry a pair and he joined right in. Then she picked Johnny up and showed him how to bang a lid with a wooden spoon. The bunch of them marched around my kitchen, banging and clanging and hollering, making a racket. I watched and applauded.

"You are some kind of marching band, all right." They marched in and out and around the house until the racket wore them out. Then Jean decided to snap on the radio. I gave her a look. She knew as well as anyone that I didn't bother with the blessed radio anymore. All those songs about victory and men coming home from war. I had no need of hearing any of those anymore. Still, she turned the music up loud.

"Let's dance now," she said brightly, swaying Johnny on her hip.

"Dance with me, Mommy," Carol insisted, holding her arms up.

"Me, too," Barry cried.

So I wrapped an arm around each of them, pulled them both up onto my hips, and we swayed to the music. "There," I told Jean, "I'm dancing." And I stuck my tongue out.

"It's a start," she said. The song ended, and I blew the hair out of my eyes.

Then the radio man decided to "slow it down a little," and the first gentle notes of "I'll Be Seeing You" floated out from the box. Jean wrapped Johnny up tight to her.

I hitched Carol and Barry higher up onto my hips and tenderly pressed my face against one, then the other's curly head. They smelled of warm cotton and the rich promise of tomorrow. I could find contentment here—not happiness, maybe, but contentment. Slow and easy, we swayed to the music, thoughts of Roger tripping all over my mind. *At least I have these little ones to remember him by.* I lost myself in the music. At some point, I must have stopped moving. Carol patted my arm.

"C'mon, Mommy," she said softly. "Keep dancing." Barry leaned side-to-side to get me moving again. But I felt foggy and far away. I looked off across the room at the chair where Roger used to sit. I felt like

I could almost see him there, a smile on his face, that easy grin of his turning up the corners of his mouth. He had his work shirt on, the blue one he'd wear to the plant. He winked. My heart jumped. He flashed that smile. I blinked. *Was it?* He nodded. I nearly dropped the children. I took a step toward the table. Carol squirmed down out of my arms. I kept hold of Barry.

"El?" I heard Jean's voice a distance away. "You okay?" She touched my arm. I pulled my eyes away from Roger to glance at Jean, and when I looked back, he was gone, just the same worn wooden chair again.

"Just thinking of Roger," I said, shaking my head. "That song. Brought him back for me."

"Oh, sweetie," she said, snapping off the radio. I looked back to Roger's chair. Carol sat perched on the front edge of it.

"Think I could have a cookie, Mum?" she asked, and my heart jumped.

"What did you say, Carol?" That was just how Roger had always said it. After dinner he'd settle back in his chair while I cleared the dishes and he'd say, "Think I could have a cookie, Mum?" He started calling me "Mum" as soon as Carol was born, and he'd gone on with it even in his letters home: "Miss you, Mum," "See you soon, Mum." The children had never called me anything but "Mommy" or "Mama."

"Could I have a cookie, Mama, please?" Carol said, using her own words again.

"Of course you can, sweetie," Jean jumped in. She took the cookie jar down and handed one to each of the children. That was when I realized I was still holding Barry. He took a nibble of his cookie, then looked at me with a quiet expression.

"Did you see him?" I whispered in his ear. "Did you see Daddy?"

He nodded. "Daddy was smiling."

"He was," I whispered into Barry's ear. "I saw Daddy, too." Barry chewed his cookie like it was a plain old ordinary happening, but me, I was thrilled and hushed all at once. A little slice of magic right there in my kitchen. I set Barry on the floor and looked back over toward the chair. It was empty, but I knew what I'd seen. Jean was watching me closely, inspecting me. She knew something was up. I wasn't about to let on.

"Boy, that song gets me," I said, hoping to blow her worries away.

"Is that what it is?" asked Jean.

"Easy there, mother hen." I dabbed at a drop of sweat at my hairline. "Finish the dishes or start the baths?"

"I'll take the dishes," she said.

"Thanks, honey." I patted her shoulder. She still looked at me sidelong, but I kept on moving.

"Who's ready for a bath?"

"Not me!" cried Barry, cookie crumbs dropping from his lips.

"Me!" Carol hollered.

"Follow me," I said, picking Johnny up off the floor. "You, soldier," I said, pointing at Barry, "help Auntie Jean, then come up in ten minutes."

"Okay!" Barry clapped his thick little hands. Carol, Johnny, and I climbed the stairs, and I ran the tub.

"In you go." I plopped Johnny in, and Carol climbed in behind him. The room filled with the foamy scent of bubble bath.

"Carol," I said, wiping her face with a washcloth, "in the kitchen, was Daddy there? Did you see him at the table?" She was piling bubbles up and down her arm.

She nodded. "He was watching us dance. He laughed when we did it."

"He did?"

"Yeah. Then I sat with him, after." She busied herself putting bubbles on the other arm.

"You sat with him in his chair?"

"Yeah. I sit on his lap sometimes, but Daddy's not real so he doesn't have a real lap. That's how come it still feels like the chair even if I'm sitting with him."

"Is that right?"

"Can you make me a bubble hat?" she asked. I scooped a big heap of bubbles up onto her head and shaped them into a hat.

"Is Daddy here now?" I asked, turning the water off. She looked around the small room.

"No, he's not here. Make it a crown, okay?" She dipped her head, and I dug a circle out of the middle of the bubbles.

"Well, that's too bad. Then he could see your crown."

"Oh, he'll see it. He sees everything."

I looked around the room and had the strangest feeling that I knew just what she meant.

The rest of the evening, a nervous excitement bubbled in the pit of my stomach. I felt like a child—all fidgety and fussy, waiting for a chance to play with her new toy—but I sat with Jean for our usual evening chat. We sat in the living room for the winter months, her on the wing-backed chair in front of the bookcase and me curled up on the corner of the sofa, but I could barely pay attention.

"There's no shame in it," Jean said. "You still have three mouths to feed." She pursed her lips. I nodded, but I barely heard a word she was saying. All I could think about was Roger. Was he in the room right now? I let my eyes flit around, searching. Was he listening? Was he sitting there next to me, or across the way? Maybe he was making faces. He liked to do that sometimes—in the old days. One of my sisters would get going on something, he'd stand behind them, twisting his face into all kinds of contortions, sticking his tongue out or pretending to nod off, and I'd be stuck trying to keep a straight face while he carried on. That was probably what he was doing right now. It made me smile to think of it.

Jean stopped talking and looked at me like she was waiting for an answer. Not having an inkling of what she'd just said, I shrugged.

"Eleanor!" she burst out. "I am trying to help you!"

And now, this was bad, but I laughed. I couldn't help it. I was half-giddy already and Jean was just so serious. But I had to smooth things over, so I said, "You are helping me plenty coming over here night after night. And I thank you."

SOMETIMES A SOLDIER COMES HOME | *Jessica Ciosek*

She took a breath like she was winding up to lecture me. I held up my hand. "But that's all the help I want right now. I'm not going dancing, and I'm not going to meet men. What I want is to stay right here in this house with my children. And that's all I want."

"El..." she started.

"I know you want the best for me," I said. "I do. And I don't want my life going to rack and ruin, either. But for now, I just want to keep things steady and try to find my way on my own."

She shook her head. I could see she wanted to say more, but I wasn't going to hear any more, and she knew it. We were stuck, which wasn't usual for us, but it was my life, and that was just how it was going to have to be. I looked away, nothing more to say.

And then there he was, over Jean's shoulder: Roger, standing just behind her chair dressed in the khaki dress uniform he'd worn the last time I'd seen him alive. He was smiling gently, and he seemed to be nodding. A thrill rushed through me. I squeezed my fists tight and swallowed hard, but I didn't look away. I intended to hold him there with my eyes as long as I could. Jean was still talking, but I didn't hear a word, and I wasn't taking my eyes off Roger for anything.

Finally, she demanded, "What are you looking at?" and looked behind her.

"I'm not looking *at* anything," I said, crossing my arms like I was in a huff. "I'm trying not to look at you so you'll stop going on about how I ought to live my life."

She laughed. "Oh, is that right?" She stuck her head in my line of sight—right between Roger and me—although she didn't know it. "Poof, here I am," she chuckled. "Can't get away from me."

Roger and I both laughed. "Oh, Jean," I said, trying to contain myself when all I really wanted to do was jump out of my seat and wrap my arms around my specter husband come home to me. I took a deep breath. "I'm going to be okay without a man. You wait and see."

"I know you'll be okay. I just don't want you to be alone."

"I know," I said to her, but to myself I thought, *I'm not.* I glanced over at Roger again. He was nodding and flipping his head toward the door, smiling and mouthing "get her going." I faked a yawn, partly to cover my laugh.

"Okay," she said, standing up slowly. She came across and held me at arm's length. "But as soon as you get ready, I'll be happy to do the fixing up." She smiled.

"I will keep that in mind." I walked her to the door, my heart jumping. She stopped in the doorway, and it took all my reserves not to shove her through so I could get back to Roger.

"Call me tomorrow."

"I will." She eyed me like she knew something, but I just smiled. "Nighty-night."

She went out the door, glancing back one time. Still smiling, I waggled my fingers at her.

As soon as she was out of sight, I slammed the door, locked it, and raced back into the living room. He wasn't there.

"Rog?" Nothing. "Bedtime, Rog?" I said, laughing but starting to feel a little foolish. I went around the living room, turning off the lights, trying to spot him out of the corner of my eye. Then I heard the word *upstairs* in my head as distinctive as if someone had said it out loud. I looked over my shoulder, but I felt like I already knew better. I raced up the stairs, and there he was in the children's room, standing between the kids' beds, smiling. In my head, I heard him speak.

"They're sleeping easy, El," he said. I smiled, relieved to see him, but suddenly feeling a little overcome by it all.

"Roger?" I whispered.

"Meet you in the bedroom," he said, and he disappeared.

I pulled the covers up over Carol and Barry like I did every night and hurried into the bedroom. There he was, just as he promised, sitting in the blue chair in the corner of our room. Wearing his blue work shirt and dungarees now, he was filmy and a little bit see-through, but he was there.

"Is that really you?" I whispered, stopping just inside the bedroom door.

"It's me, Mum," he said. The words hummed in my head.

"Oh, Rog," I cried softly, tingles running across my skin. "I don't know whether to laugh or cry."

"No need for tears, darlin'. I'm here. Not quite in the flesh," he said, poking a finger through his middle, "but it is me." A bright grin lit up his face.

"I can't believe it." I dropped onto the end of the bed. "They said you were dead."

His face turned somber. "Well, hon, I am gone now."

"Oh, I know. I mean, I *know*, but then here you are." I waved a hand toward him. "I didn't know this could happen."

"Me neither." He poked the finger through his head this time and smiled his silly smile. "Light as a feather."

I laughed. "You are still a goof."

"Same as always." He winked.

"Oh, Rog, it's so good to see you."

"Wish it was all of me."

"Me too," I conceded, "but this is better than nothing." And I wanted to cry. My husband was home again. He looked like himself, thinner maybe than when he left, and not just because he wasn't whole. I blamed it on the war. "I've missed you so."

"I am sorry, El. It was an accident," he said, his eyes meeting mine. "Just a stupid accident. Fella dropped a gun, it went off."

"That's what the telegram said. 'Accidental gunshot.' I didn't know what to think."

"I wasn't a hero." He dipped his head.

"You're all the hero I've ever needed."

"Woulda been a better excuse for leaving you all alone if I'd saved a platoon or something."

"You must have done at least that to make it through the war."

He shrugged. "I did my part. Still, I wish you could've bragged about me."

"I do anyway." I winked, patted the bed. "Can you come sit here with me?"

"I can." There he was, right next to me as soon as he said it. "But you won't feel a thing."

"I can pretend." I placed my hand on what should have been his thigh, but it rested flat on the bed. All I felt under my fingers was the nub of the bedspread. There was no dent to the bed where he sat, no whiff of cologne or his familiar earthy scent, but I could see him.

"Will you stay?" I asked.

"As long as I can." He reached his hand for mine. I didn't feel that either, but I imagined I did.

"Forever'd be nice," I replied.

"Well, that is what I promised on our wedding day." He winked.

"I'll hold you to it."

"I kept this promise."

"What do you mean?"

"I promised I'd come back."

I laughed. "That you did."

He smiled. "It is good to see you again, El. You're as beautiful as the day I left—more, even."

"You always were a charmer." I ached to lean into him, to press my face to his chest, hear his heartbeat against my ear. He shrugged as if he knew what I was thinking.

"You get your rest now, darlin'," he said. "I'll be here in the morning."

"Will you?"

"Sure as I'm here right now. I came to be with you, El, as best as I can." His face took on a sad kind of twist.

"It'll be fine to have you like this," I said. "We'll make it fine, just like we always did."

He nodded hard. "I do love you, El."

"Oh, Rog, I love you, too," I said, and I wanted so bad to kiss him, to put my hands on his cheeks and pull him in to meet me, taste his lips again. I leaned over and kissed the air. He met me halfway. I didn't feel a thing, but I filled in the gaps with my imagination.

"Better than nothing," he said, grinning.

"Let me wash up, then we can lay next to each other all night." I got up, then turned around. "It was you that day, when it stormed here? You came to say goodbye?"

"I did. That was before I knew I could come back. I had to tell you."

"And in the mirror?"

"Me again." He smiled, and everything in that smile was so familiar. It was Roger here in the bedroom—not fully here, but someone I could see and hear and talk to.

"It did scare the dickens out of me."

"Sorry about that, hon."

My turn to shrug. "S'okay. Maybe it makes it easier for me to believe you're here now."

"Think we can make something of this, El?" he asked, and all his longing for me to say yes was right there in his ghostly eyes.

"Well, we can certainly try," I answered and smiled hard. If there was any chance at all that I could carry on a life with my Roger, I would take it.

I stepped into the bathroom and closed the door behind me. In the mirror, I grinned at myself, giddy like a schoolgirl. I splashed cool water on my face and grabbed the Noxema from the medicine cabinet. But this time, when I caught sight of that Aqua Velva bottle, instead of sadness, a thrill ran through me all over again. Roger was back. And, when I reached for my solitary toothbrush, I decided I'd just go buy another toothbrush to keep mine company. It might never get used, but it wasn't going to be lonely anymore, and neither was I. I slipped the soothing flannel of my nightgown over my head and took a giddy look at myself in the mirror again.

"Rog is back," I whispered, a little thrill catching in my throat. Then, just as quickly, a tangle of doubt curled itself in my middle—what if I'd imagined the whole thing? I looked at myself in the mirror again. "Couldn't be," I whispered, but there was doubt even in my words. So, I yanked that bathroom door open and hurried back into the bedroom before I could think another thought. And there he was still, lying on his side of the bed, waiting.

"You're still here."

"Just like I said." He grinned. "You know, you don't have to close the bathroom door on me, hon, I am still your husband."

I blushed. "Oh, stop it, Roger Mitchell. I'm not used to a man in this house again, let alone in my bedroom."

"Well, I am glad to hear that." He laughed. I tried to give him a gentle slap, but my hand went right through to the mattress. We both chuckled.

I turned the light off, curling myself toward where he lay. "Are you real?" I whispered.

"In a way."

"Have I lost my mind with grieving you, Roger Mitchell? Tell me true."

"I can't explain everything, El, but I can tell you, this is me. Not in the flesh, but if you've lost your mind, then so, my dear, have I."

"Well, I'm not sure that's much of a comfort, you being dead and all."

We laughed, easy together like always. I curled in closer next to him. He put his arms around me. I couldn't feel them, but I could see what there was of them, and that was enough. I drifted off and slept in the arms of an angel.

☆ ☆ ☆

The morning sun peeked in around the edge of the curtains and I woke, half forgetting that I'd fallen asleep next to my dead husband. I tossed the covers back, wondering why I seemed to have a song in my heart. Then I remembered. Roger was back. I looked around and half-expected to find him still sitting there at my side. But the bed held only me.

"Rog?" Nothing. "Well, he'll turn up," I told myself, hoping he might come and reassure me. "Right, Johnny boy," I said overloud. Johnny gurgled a good morning to me, but Roger still didn't show. I got Johnny's diaper changed and dressed him for the morning. The two of us made our way downstairs, and the whole time I was convincing myself I hadn't made the whole thing up. Then, sure enough, there Roger sat, smiling and handsome, in his chair at the kitchen table.

"Morning, darlin'," he said.

"Morning, love," I replied, a sigh of relief slipping out between my lips. "It had me a little worried when you weren't upstairs."

"You know I'm an early riser."

"I s'pose I forgot. Do you sleep?"

"Nah, not really. I kind of just fade away for a while, off somewhere I can't really even understand myself."

"That must be strange."

"It is and it isn't. I'm just happy to be here," he said, and smiled in that earnest way of someone who is trying to convince the other that they mean what they say. I slipped Johnny into his highchair.

"What's for breakfast?" he asked, his voice inside my head like it always was, but overloud this time to change the subject. He patted his belly.

"How 'bout a lumberjack special, eggs, pancakes, bacon, the works?" I planted a kiss on the air that should have been his head. There wasn't the feel of him or the scent I knew deep in my heart, but, somehow, he was there.

"That does sound delicious."

"Da," cooed Johnny.

"We've been working on that," Roger said with a wink.

"'Course you have," I said. "Dada, there he is." I pointed.

"Da-da," Johnny echoed, and just like that, the idea of it seized me: a boy calling out for his dead father. How could it be? Was it all just a widow's wishful thinking? It was impossible. My head went dizzy. My knees buckled. I grabbed the edge of the table.

Roger stood up. "You okay?" He reached for my elbow, but I had to steady myself.

"Sure, I'm okay. Dizzy spell, that's all." I looked into Roger's blue eyes. They were the same blue, but faded and translucent now.

"Honest?"

"Oh, I don't know," I confessed, dropping into the chair.

"Da da da." Johnny banged his highchair tray, looking for Roger's attention. But Roger, patient like a man who has all eternity, looked only at me.

"I just don't know what to think. And when I do think, it all seems to not make a bit of sense. How can it be that my own husband, who the War Department has told me isn't coming home, is sitting here in my kitchen teaching our baby boy how to say "Dada"?"

Johnny chanted on, "dadadadadadada."

"And our boy is saying it!" I half-laughed, half wanted to cry. "You are standing right in front of me, see-through like the window sheers, but you're here. I can see you. I can hear you. I can't touch you, or smell you, but you're sitting right there. The children tell stories of you, so I'm sure there must be something more to it than my own mind playing widow tricks on me, but I can't explain it. I just can't."

Roger took the chair opposite me, reached his hand across the table, and laid it, weightless, on top of mine. He smiled that easy grin I knew so well. The grin that had always meant everything was going to be all right. Only I wasn't sure I was supposed to believe in that grin anymore, or if it even was real. Maybe the whole thing was just the foolish hope of my broken heart.

"It doesn't make any sense," Roger admitted. "Doesn't to me, either. But who cares? The way I figure, if you and me and the three little ones all believe we are together again, then who is there to tell us it isn't true? We aren't bothering anybody, and we don't have to tell a soul. Let's just enjoy what we've got and keep the rest of the world none the wiser." He smiled, his eyes twinkling. And that was him—that was Roger right there saying those things. That was just exactly the kind of thing he would say.

Then he said, "Whaddaya say, Mum?" cocking a grin, and I knew. Even if I was playing tricks on myself, I wouldn't have thought to say that, wouldn't have put those words into my own head. It had to be him, it had to be.

"You're right, I guess," I said, wishing I could lean into his reassuring arms. "Nobody else has to know a thing."

"Just us."

"But from time to time you might have to remind me that I'm not ready for the loony bin."

"Will do," he said, "as long as I still think so." He winked.

"Ha, ha, aren't you a card?" I shot a light push at his shoulder. It went right through. We laughed, and I felt the worry fall off some. Maybe I wasn't crazy with grief, maybe I was just plain lucky.

"Dada," Johnny chimed in.

"Yes, Dada," I said, meeting Johnny's sparkling blue eyes.

"He's a handsome one, isn't he?" I said to Roger.

"Handsome as they come."

"His father's boy."

CHAPTER 32

ELEANOR

t was easy enough to settle into a routine of sorts. Roger joined us around the breakfast table every morning. We'd talk and he'd play with the children over toast and oatmeal. He couldn't play in all the same ways he had before, but he could sing and joke with them and, as time went on, he could make the curtains flutter or wiggle a spoon. Little things like that he could do with ease, and it kept the children caught in a state of wonder for most of mealtime.

"Disappearing Daddy" was a favorite after-breakfast game. Roger would be sitting right there across from them one second and gone the next. They'd look around, and then he'd call, "Betcha can't find me!" They'd run to find him, but finding a ghost is more or less up to whether the ghost wants to be found, and Roger took full advantage of that. He'd pop in and out, sometimes right next to them, and whisper "boo," and they'd scream with the thrill of it. They never did get enough of that one.

Most days, he played with the children while I got around to my chores. He was like a babysitter for me, keeping an eye on them, correcting and guiding as he needed to, and calling me if a real problem arose. It was different than before, but better than nothing, so we got used to it. He'd join us for dinner, and we'd share a meal like a regular family. Not that Roger ate, of course, but he did manage to compliment my efforts even if he couldn't smell it or taste it. Then, we'd get on with the night, baths, and bedtime. Roger could read to the children if they held the book, so that was a nice thing for him. Once they'd fallen asleep, the two of us would head into our bedroom. I'd moved Johnny's crib in with Carol and Barry so we wouldn't keep him awake. Roger would sit in the blue chair in the corner of our bedroom, a smile on his face. I'd climb into the bed and tell him about my day, whatever he didn't already know, and he'd tell me what he did with the children. We'd laugh and worry together, like parents do.

When it came to mix-ups with my sisters and that, he'd hem and haw, but mostly he just listened, same as before. Other times he'd see a little trouble on the horizon, and he'd warn me. "The toilet's about to go haywire, El," he'd say. "You best turn the water off underneath until the plumber can get here." There was a time when I needed a particular screw to fix a wiggly chair, and he told me just where in his garage I might find it. It was nice, the two of us together again. I did feel bad for him, not being able to wrap his arms around the children—or me, for that matter—and love us like he once did. He didn't get to eat a chocolate cake or have some of my sugar cookies, but we were together, so we took what we could get and called it perfect.

Our new life wasn't as strange as it sounded—plenty of people were adjusting to different things after the war. There were other widows, of course, and there were wounded men coming home, too. War did terrible, terrible things to a human body. In those days, it wasn't something you could miss: men on the street missing an arm, a leg, sometimes both; in wheelchairs, on crutches, hooks for hands and the like. You'd try your hardest not to take any notice, to draw the children's attention away so they didn't say something to make the man feel uncomfortable. Oh, but didn't you feel for them, whole and strong once, never to be the same again. Broke a person's heart to think how much was given to war.

There was a fella around the block like that, Paul Gregory. Paul was a good man. He and Roger had carpooled to the plant back in the early days of the war. I knew his wife Winnie to say hello. They had a little boy a year or so older than Carol. And honestly, I might never have known what became of Paul Gregory if it weren't for one morning when I'd taken the children for a walk. It must have been March or so. The weather wasn't warm yet, but you could feel the promise of spring.

"I think I'll get the children out for a walk today," I told Roger over breakfast.

"I'll hold down the fort," he said.

"You can't get out at all?"

"Not out for a walk, no. I'm pretty much here where you leave me."

"Well, I guess it's good to know you won't go getting lost, then." We laughed.

I cleared the breakfast dishes and bundled the bunch of us into our jackets, and off we set.

"We're on an adventure," Carol declared, marching on down the street. Must have been around ten or so in the morning. And, as we turned the corner onto Paterson, an ambulance turned the corner with us. I might not have noticed—it didn't have the sirens blaring—but the red light on top was whirling and it surely caught Barry's eye.

"Mama! It's an ambulance!" he cried and started after it as it drove up the street, a quick walk that broke right fast into a run.

"Stop at the corner," I called after him, but I needn't have, because the ambulance pulled into a driveway midway up the block. Well, that took Barry and I both by surprise. He stopped dead, glanced back once at me, then took off on a tear. I was hot on his heels.

As luck would have it, the ambulance had stopped in the Gregory's driveway that morning. And there stood Winnie on the front walk. Dressed in her brown wool marketing coat, she was a wisp of a thing, her arms wrapped tight around her. I remember she was wearing some short men's rubber boots, and her legs peeked out just above, thin and blue-white, like the legs of a fragile bird. She had her eyes trained on the men climbing out of the ambulance. There were three of them. Two of the men went directly to the back of the vehicle with hardly a glance. The other one had some papers clutched in his hand. He made his way toward Winnie.

Barry, his little legs pumping, ran up to the ambulance.

"Hey there, little fella," one of the men said.

Now, the last time I had anything to do with an ambulance, they were hustling Rita off to have her stomach pumped, and the way those men hurried her in and sped off was a far cry from this chatty Charlie. I made it to the ambulance and took hold of Barry's hand. The ambulance man smiled at me. I nodded politely, but I mostly just wanted to get Barry out of there without making a scene.

Then Winnie saw me. "Morning, Eleanor," she said, easy as you please.

"Morning, Winnie," I said. "Sorry about this." I nodded toward my Barry standing next to the ambulance. Of course, he didn't look anything like he was sorry, a big smile painted across his face and his eyes almost glazed over in a trance for the beauty of this big white ambulance and its red light on the top.

"Oh, that's all right," she said. "My own Michael'd be out here too if he wasn't at school just now."

"Mrs. Gregory?" the third man from the ambulance asked. She nodded. "Sign here and here. We'll get things all taken care of."

She took the clipboard from the man and signed the papers without more than a glance at what they said. The man took the papers and headed back toward the ambulance as breezy as you please.

"Everything okay?" I asked.

"Paul's coming home today," she said, a smile on her lips, half weary, half glad.

"Really? Oh, that's great news."

"He's in there." She tipped her head toward the ambulance.

"Oh, is that right?" I said, none too smartly.

"Bedridden for the rest of his life, they say." She dropped her gaze, tipping her head sideways. "Nothing more to be done."

"Oh, Winnie, I'm so sorry. War is an awful thing."

"It is." She nodded, stuffing her hands in the pockets of her coat.

"At least he's home."

"Yes," she said. "He's home now." Then she turned sharply and met my eye. "I was so sorry to hear about your Roger." She placed a warm hand on my arm. "Not easy for any of us, is it?" she remarked.

"I didn't mean..." I began, because I didn't. I wasn't feeling sorry for myself. Wasn't trying to make her feel like she was luckier than me. I was genuinely feeling glad for her that her husband was home again.

"I know, honey, it's just"—she shrugged—"do they think about the wives, I wonder, the wives and the mothers? Even the other side has wives and mothers."

"Couldn't, or they wouldn't, is what I've taken to telling myself." My turn to shrug.

"I like that, 'couldn't or they wouldn't,'" she said. "Don't know if I believe it, but I like it." She smiled, then reached out her hand. We gave each other a squeeze of understanding, which was just about all any of us had in those days.

The man with the paperwork returned.

"I suppose you need to look around inside?" Winnie asked.

"Yes, ma'am, that would be helpful." And they went off into the house. And I went to inspect to the ambulance with the children. We were admiring the lights on top when they hoisted Paul Gregory out of the back of the car. He looked so frail, no bigger than a skeleton under a pile of blankets and sheets. He smiled weakly, the heartiness I'd recalled about him gone. But his voice was as strong and playful as I remembered.

"Morning, Eleanor," he said. "Nice of you to be here to welcome me home." He laughed.

"Morning, Paul. Forgot my brass band. But it is good to have you back."

"Well, some of me, anyway," he answered, not a thread of bitterness in his voice. This was a man relieved, just relieved to be home again. A man I'd known to be vital and young, brave like my own Roger—to see him here pale and skinny, confined to a hospital bed for the rest of his life and still smiling? Well, that plain showed you the awfulness of war like no words could.

"Don't want to be keeping you," I said. "Probably want to get yourself set up inside."

Paul smiled. "Been a long time since I've seen the inside of the old place." The ambulance man wheeled him gently away up the walk. Paul turned his upper body to call back to me.

"Hey, Roger home yet?"

Winnie came out of the house in time to hear this last bit. She shot a glance my way, her face solemn.

"No," I said, probably more brightly that I should have. "No Roger." What I wanted to say was, "Yes, Roger has come back and life is grand," but that wouldn't do, so I took Barry by the hand. "Come along," I said, leaving Winnie to tell Paul what she would once I was out of sight. And off we went, down the block, Barry and Carol skipping along beside the stroller. There were plenty of questions coming from the two of them, and I just went along with them, all the while thinking what a laugh Roger and I would get out of the story when I told him later that night.

"Why was Mr. Gregory in a bed outside?" Carol asked.

"They were taking him home," I said.

"In a bed?"

"In a bed. Sometimes people do silly things."

"That is very silly." She laughed.

"I wanna ride in the ambulance," Barry said.

"Let's hope you never have to, darlin'," I replied.

CHAPTER 33

ROGER

Eleanor and the children tumbled in the door, refreshed and chattering away. The children talked over each other, excited and full of stories.

"We went to the playground," Carol said while still tugging her coat from her arms. "Nobody was there but us."

"Well, that sounds pretty special. Did you ride the merry-go-round?"

"No." She shook her head and scrunched up her nose. "The merry-go-round makes me too dizzy. We went on the swings. And we saw an ambulance."

"It was a real ambulance!" Barry exclaimed, his nose rosy and damp.

"Is that right? Did it have its siren going?"

"No, just the light," Barry said, shaking his head.

"It was dropping off a man in a bed," Carol answered matter-of-factly.

Roger looked up at Eleanor.

"Paul Gregory's come home from the war. Winnie says he's bedridden for the rest of his days. She was waiting out front to bring him in."

"That's a tough go." Roger shook his head.

"It is. I felt bad for them. Paul asked after you. I just told him you weren't home. Winnie will explain it to him. They had enough on their plate this morning." Eleanor unwrapped a package of crackers. The children milled around her feet, waiting for a snack. She handed Carol and Barry a few each and put Johnny in his highchair to eat his. Then she sat at the table, munching at a bit of cracker herself.

"It was funny, though," she said, looking off out the back window. "I could see in Winnie's eyes that she felt sorry for me, that even as her husband was coming home bound to a bed for the rest of his life, to her I looked worse off for being the widow. That's how it looks to the outside world: I'm the poor widow Mitchell. But I don't feel that way at all. I just feel lucky. Because you *are* here, even if no one else knows it."

Roger came around and wrapped her in his arms from behind. She leaned into him. They had gotten so practiced at the imagining of it that it almost felt real.

"You don't feel the least bit sorry for yourself?"

"No, I don't feel sorry for myself. I'm glad to have what I've got. Could have been so much worse." She decisively nodded her head once. "I'm happy, Rog, I am." She patted her hand where his ought to be.

Roger brushed his lips across her hair and decided to take what she said at face value. If she wanted to believe she was happy with their strange life together, then who was he to argue—even if it felt like maybe she was trying to convince herself.

CHAPTER 34

ELEANOR

The insurance check came in late April, a week or so before Johnny's first birthday. The postman made sure to place the envelope on top of the power bill and a postcard hawking a new washing machine. My heart skipped a beat when I saw its return address: "Department of the Army," it said. Then, I laughed. They had already taken my husband; what else was there to be afraid of? I flipped it over right there on the porch and tore the envelope open. Inside was one thin government check made out to Mrs. Roger C. Mitchell. $10,000. There it was—the end of the Army's responsibility to me. It was as bittersweet a moment as any since the day Roger had shipped out. I needed the money. It would solve so many of my worries. But it wasn't near enough for what I had lost.

"The Army finally paid up," I announced, waving the check as I entered the kitchen.

"Well, it's about time," said Roger.

"I'll say. $10,000 dollars, just like Jack said it would be."

"$10,000? That's what I'm worth?" Roger tried to laugh, tried to make it sound like a joke, but I could tell the very idea of a dollar amount in exchange for his life was a difficult pill to swallow. I went over and sat with him, in the spot that would have been his lap.

"You're worth more than gold to me. Always have been, always will be." I kissed the air where his lips were. He puckered his lips and kissed me back, but the space between us served its purpose as the usual reminder of all we didn't have anymore.

I drove over to the bank later that day. Faye came by to sit the children so I could go by myself. The teller was kind enough, but he made no mention at all about a woman like me depositing a check from the War Department into her savings account. He didn't ask or offer condolences. I'm not sure I wanted them, but it wouldn't have hurt my feelings, either.

I drifted home on thoughts of my full bank account. What a relief! But as soon as I walked in the door, it hit me. There was no more. That was the money I was due, and now it had come and there wasn't another cent promised to me for the rest of my life. My head spun.

"Oh my word," I whispered to myself and grabbed hold of the counter edge.

Faye overheard me. "What? Honey, are you okay?"

I looked at her, gentle Faye, concern written all over her face. "What am I going to do, Faye?" I whispered. "I put the money in the bank, and what now?"

"Oh, El." She wrapped an arm around my shoulder and gave me a squeeze. "You just let yourself breathe for a day or two. It'll sort out."

I nodded, let her rub my shoulder, but not a bit of it steadied my nerves. I should have been smarter. I should have already figured out a plan. I felt like the worst kind of fool.

Faye left after dinner, and after seeing her off, I got the children tucked into bed and went into the bedroom. Roger sat on the edge of the blue chair, waiting for me.

"Everything go okay at the bank, hon?" he asked right away.

"Yes, it did. It was fine."

"But something's bothering you."

I laughed. "You must have heard me talking with Faye."

"I try not to eavesdrop, El. But I can tell how you feel most of the time."

"I guess there's just no hiding from a ghost."

He shook his head. "No, ma'am. Now, are you going to tell me what's bothering you?"

I dropped onto the bed opposite him. "I just don't know what I'm going to do when the Army money runs out," I admitted, my voice breaking halfway through the words. Tears caught in my eyes; I couldn't believe I was crying again. Roger came and sat next to me. I suppose he draped an arm around me, but I didn't have an ounce of my brain to imagine its comfort.

"That money ought to last a good long while," he said.

"It won't last forever. And I have three children to provide for."

"I'm sorry it's come to this. I never meant for you to have to go it alone."

"Oh, I know that. I never wanted to go it alone either, never wanted anything more than to be a wife and mother. But the truth of the matter is that I *am* going it alone, and I've got to figure something out. Maybe I could take in laundry or clean houses with Mother." My mind was running in circles trying to find a solution.

Roger frowned. "Maybe I could think of something to help."

I barked a half-laugh. "Are they hiring ghosts these days?" I wasn't trying to be mean, but it did strike me as funny.

"Maybe I could haunt a mansion or something." He chuckled, that familiar sparkle in his eye.

"Except they'd pay you in ghost dollars, too, I imagine." We laughed, but my current situation wasn't all that funny. I had a real problem to solve.

"The last time I worked was at the five-and-dime back when we were in high school."

"You were cute in that apron." He winked. I smiled, but my thoughts were a million miles away from those childhood days.

"The whole world says there aren't jobs to be had for women," I said, "what with the men returning. But there's got to be something, right?" I looked at him like I expected him to have an answer.

"I think any boss would be happy to have you," he responded. "You're organized and smart, hard-working and reliable. Why, I'd hire you in a second."

"Is that right? A woman who hasn't worked in some years and has three children at home, you'd take me on?"

"I surely would take on a woman who can handle all that and work, too." He nodded, hardy and encouraging, but, in his eyes, I could see a curl of frustration. This wasn't a conversation he wanted to be having. Not because he didn't want to help me solve it, but because he wanted to be the provider, the husband, the father, the man of the house.

"I'm sorry, El. The whole thing is just a damned mess," he said, his tone gone from cheery to tired.

"I'll figure it out," I said. It was my turn now to be encouraging. "Don't worry, Rog." He smiled, but it was laced with sadness. We sat there across the room from one another, not talking, but trying to solve the same problem from two very different places.

☆ ☆ ☆

Later in the week, Jean came by, and she seemed to believe that it was possible I could find a job.

"Men like for their secretaries to be women, El, so there are jobs to be had."

"I haven't typed a letter since typing class in high school."

"Oh, it will come back to you. It's like riding a bike."

"Ha! I haven't ridden a bike since high school, either!"

Jean went and pulled the newspaper from the pile by the door. She flipped it open to the want ads and snapped it flat. "Okay, Mrs. Mitchell, let's see what we've got." We spent the rest of the evening circling "girl wanted" ads and laughing about how I might just become a business lady after all.

In the morning, the very first ad I called was to an employment agency. They sent me out for an interview right away. It was a receptionist's position at an insurance office downtown.

"No experience required," the woman at the agency said.

"That is just about the kind of experience I have for an office job," I said with a laugh.

"Yes, well, that's fine," the agency lady answered, not enjoying my joke. "Tuesday at ten okay for you?"

"Tuesday at ten," I affirmed with only the slightest hiccup of nerves.

With the interview all set and ready, everybody lined up to give me advice. Roger had answers on what to say during the interview and Jean told me what to wear. I took it all in, even wrote some of it down, but in the end, I mostly just crossed my fingers and hoped for the best.

The morning of the interview, Faye came by to look after the children while I got ready. Roger offered more encouraging words while I got dressed, then sent me off with an air kiss and a "good luck."

Downstairs was more reassurance from Faye. "Don't you look smart," she remarked as I came into the kitchen. Jean had me kitted out in a blue shirtwaist with a tidy beige cardigan.

"I think it fits all right," I said, pulling at the front. Jean was a good bit tinier up top than me.

"I'd hire you in a second," said Faye with a wink.

"Me too, Mommy," chimed Carol around bites of toast.

"Let's hope this Mr. Dabbs fellow agrees with you." I kissed each precious head, feeling not at all sure that what I wanted was to be away from my little ones all day every day. But we do what we have to. So, I slipped my coat over squared shoulders, grabbed ahold of my handbag, and decided to do my best.

"Wish me luck," I called, walking out the side door. It was springtime and the air was light with the promise of new beginnings. *Yes, this might work out just fine*, I thought, climbing into the car.

I found the office and parked down the block in an open lot. It was a storefront place where a person could walk in off the street. I pulled open the door, and a bell jingled overhead to announce my entrance. Not a soul showed at the sound. Inside, the air felt stale and dry. Dark brown paneling covered the walls, and the worn floor tile made a thin path from the front door to the closed office door at the back. I imagined that must be the office of Mr. Dabbs, the man I was here to meet. I waited a moment. When no one showed, I went and knocked at the closed office door.

"Just a minute," called a man's voice. He sounded a little impatient, but I was here at his behest. So

I settled into one of the two metal chairs lined up in front of the windows, folded my ankles up under me, and took a look around. The place was a mess: papers and files piled here and there and everywhere, dust bunnies under the desk in front of me, empty coffee cups on the table behind the desk. The place needed seeing to and cleaning up was something I was an expert at, if nothing else. I folded my hands over my handbag and waited.

After a while, the door at the back of the room swung open and out stepped a little man, short with a protruding lower belly that called to mind a stout teapot. His hair was slicked heavy with pomade and he squinted at me through smeared glasses riding so low on his nose that he had to tip back to see. He wasn't a very welcoming sight, but I pressed on. Taking a strong step across the room, I offered my hand like Jean said I ought.

"Good morning, Mr. Dabbs," I said, the quiver in my voice only barely noticeable. "I'm Mrs. Mitchell." But I guess he didn't operate like the men Jean worked with, because he looked down at my hand like I was holding a dead kitten and made no effort whatsoever to shake it. Without a word, he motioned for me to follow him into the next room. I went after him, but already my hope was dimming.

This office was just as cluttered as the outer one and smelled of old salami. The windows were situated high on the wall and covered over by dirty, yellowed sheers, giving the room a muddy glow. There was a row of lights along the ceiling, but only one of them had a working bulb in it. And the dust,

I cannot tell you. I waited while Mr. Dabbs picked his way around his desk. It was heaped with the same sloppy piles of papers as the one out front. He dug around among them until he came up with one.

"So, Miss ahh," he said, holding the paper up and squinting. "*Mrs.* Mitchell." He emphasized the Missus part in an odd way, then smiled at me like he was doing me some kind of a favor in having learned my name.

"That is me, Mr. Dabbs," I said, as pert and cheery as could be. I took a seat on the edge of the frayed burlap of the chair opposite him.

"You're here about the receptionist position?" he asked, peering over his glasses at me.

"That's right," I answered.

"Have you ever *worked* in an office before, Mrs. Mitchell?" He raised his eyebrows.

"Not in an office, no, but I did work in a five-and-dime when I was a girl." I smiled and felt a bead of sweat race down the small of my back.

"But never in an office," he said dryly. He pushed his dirty glasses up on his nose and grimaced like he'd suddenly been overcome by indigestion.

I probably should have thrown in the towel right then, but I pressed on. "Why, no sir, not in an office. But I'm a quick study." I smiled hard.

"Yes, I'm sure you are smart as a whip, Mrs. Mitchell. Smart as a whip." He nodded, then looked up at me again, his eyes beady. "I am wondering, is there a *Mr.* Mitchell?"

Well, the nerve. But I answered, I surely did. "There was a Mr. Mitchell," I told him in a stronger voice than I was feeling. "But I am a widow of the war now."

"Oh. Well, sorry for your loss," he said, without sounding like he was sorry at all. "Are there children for you and the late Mr. Mitchell?" This he said while sliding his glasses down his nose and fixing those beady little eyes on me, as if he thought I planned to lie.

"Yes, sir, we have three. A girl and two boys."

"Isn't that nice?" He smiled a mean little smile and wrote something down. "And how old might they be?"

"They are children, Mr. Dabbs," I answered. The beads of nervous sweat running down my back were turning hot with annoyance now. "My daughter will be starting school next fall, and the boys will be home for a few more years." I faked another smile. "And the position—it's nine to five, then?"

"Nine to five, yes." He leaned back in his chair, looking bored like I was the mouse and he was the cat who had me in a corner. "And what would you do with the children if you were to get a job that was nine to five?"

"*...If you were to get a job...*" That's what he said, the snotty little chicken liver. Bet he hadn't left the safety of this dirty old office in the war years for anything more than a bologna sandwich.

"Well, I suppose that's my business, but I have worked out an arrangement for my children to be taken care of while I earn a living to support us." *So there you go, Mr. Fancy Pants,* I wanted to say. But that self-satisfaction lasted only about a second for me, because the old buzzard starting laughing.

"Ho, ho," he chortled like some department store Santa. "That's all very nice." He pulled his tie straight over his round belly. "But I doubt you'll be supporting a family of four on what we pay here." He laughed even harder, as if it was the funniest thing he'd ever heard. Oh, wasn't he having a lovely time at my expense. But there was something about his rudeness that made me press on.

"That may be, but I have been looking after my family with some success for a while now. And while this job would help me along, either way I'm sure I will continue to manage." This seemed to strike some interest in him.

"How long have you been on your own, then?" he asked, shooting a morbid leer my direction, as if he had some grim curiosity about mourning. Well, that was the last straw for me.

"I'm not sure as to what that might have to do with my being qualified for answering phones in this office, but I can tell you I took my first job the day I turned thirteen. I've been working in one capacity or another since that very day. I know how to read and write, and I know how to manage a bucketful of details, seeing as I've run a household day in and day out for nearly six years now." I paused here to catch my breath. A huff of anger was building in my throat.

"Now, if you could tell me a little more about the job," I tried. "The hours are nine to five, and I imagine there's a lunch break. Would that be thirty minutes? And what other duties might there be beyond answering the phones and greeting people at the door? I've just finished up a typing course down at the secretarial school. Would you care to have me take a typing test?" I rattled this all off my tongue like I knew what I was talking about, and I hadn't taken any such typing course, but that hardly mattered.

He looked at me through his smeary lenses like I was the most pathetic little child needing his careful guidance. He tented his fingers up in front of his chest and took a deep breath.

"No, I don't think we'll be needing a typing test. And as for the lunch break, I imagine that's only important if you're offered the position." He paused long enough to re-straighten that ugly tie over his enormous belly, and then he sat up in his chair and looked dead at me. "But it seems to me, Mrs. Mitchell, that this job is more appropriate for a girl who isn't, shall we say, so encumbered."

He said "encumbered," but what he really meant was burdened.

"I do appreciate your need to support your children," he went on, those dirty glasses like a mask he was squinting through, "but given that they are as young as they are, I'm sure you are more needed at home with them than you would be out earning a living." He smiled at me in a know-it-all way, like he was giving me the advice of a lifetime.

"If I were in your predicament, Mrs. Mitchell," he continued, "I would be looking for a husband rather than a job."

Well, didn't that take the cake. This man who didn't know a doggone thing about me figured he had the right to tell me I ought to marry. The *nerve!* I stood up from that awful ratty chair and smoothed my skirt.

"I thank you for your time, Mr. Dabbs," I said, seething with outrage, "but I'll decide the best way out of my predicament for myself. Thank you." I turned on my heel and walked out of the office without one more look at his squinty face.

Still fuming, I marched toward the parking lot. What a pile of nonsense! Who on earth did he think he was? Lord in heaven, that dirty old office, but he thought he'd got advice to be giving *me?* Ha! I wouldn't work a minute there anyway.

Climbing in behind the wheel of our Buick, I thought of Roger. I had him, didn't I? I had Roger and the children waiting for me at home, no matter what this Mr. Dabbs thought of me. But I will admit, a part of me just wanted to cry.

Of course, Faye and Roger were both ready to hear all about it when I walked in the door. Faye was none the wiser that Roger was in the room, and I put the best spin on it that I could for her sake, but after Faye left, I poured my heart out to Roger.

"Oh, Rog, it was awful, just awful." I wanted to cry, but I wouldn't.

I told him all the gory details, and when I was done, he smiled and said, "Well, El, I think you can safely say you got the worst interview out of the way first. It'll be all downhill from here now." And we laughed, me especially, long and hard, but the whole situation was starting to lose all of its humor for me.

CHAPTER 35

ROGER

Eleanor got an idea to have Jean and her new beau, Tony, over for dinner.

"And you come, too," she said to Roger. "Sit there at the table with me. They won't be any the wiser and it'll be fun."

"You sure it won't be hard for you?" Roger asked. "What if they notice you looking my way?"

"It'll be fine," she said. "Jean's different with Tony around. She won't notice a thing."

So Roger did what she asked. It felt like old times, watching her move around the kitchen, sure of herself and her meal. Still, when the new couple rolled in on a warm May breeze, Roger would have liked to have offered the man a firm handshake, would have liked to let Jean know he was looking out for her like a brother-in-law ought to. He'd always felt a little protective of Eleanor's sisters. But he could only watch.

Tony presented Eleanor with a bouquet of yellow tulips. Eleanor accepted them with a high blush in her cheeks, then subtly turned and winked at Roger, already impressed by her sister's new friend. Roger returned her nod, but his first thought was that charmers knew how to charm, especially when it was only women in the room. Roger intended to reserve his full opinion until after dinner.

When dinner was set on the table, Roger took his usual seat. Eleanor had pushed the table up into the corner so no one would take his chair by mistake. The food looked delicious: a baked chicken, mashed potatoes, salad, and green beans. The guests were full of compliments to the cook, which let Roger know that Eleanor still had her touch.

Throughout the meal, Eleanor shot looks at him, nodding ever so slightly, smiling, even winking a time or two. Roger never failed to return her smile, to nod, to agree with her. Pretty in the soft lamplight, Eleanor looked content. He watched the ease with which she handled the conversation and the dinner. She was more confident than the woman he'd left behind. She had grown into her own in their time apart. She still loved him and wanted him around, but her need for him had changed. She knew herself now, could handle herself. It was clear everywhere he looked: the way she had chosen the menu with no need to ask his opinion, the certainty she had about how to situate the table, the way she chatted with Tony and carried on with Jean. He knew it ought to make him proud, and it did, but it broke his heart just a little, too. A person, alive or dead, doesn't really want to think the world goes on without them. And yet, Eleanor had carried on perfectly well during the war, and was doing just fine without him now.

Roger stayed nearby through dessert, watching as the dishes were washed and put away, nightcaps sipped and swallowed, and goodbyes said. He would have liked to help, would have enjoyed his own sip of brandy. Instead, he kept a keen eye on things and told himself he was happy to be able to do that much.

Upstairs afterwards, Eleanor was giddy with the evening. "He's a nice fella, don't you think, Rog?" She had tucked into bed but was too excited to sleep. "A little short for my taste, but just right for Jean."

"Seemed like a fine man. I'm sure they will be happy together."

"Do you think he'll marry her?"

"Well, I s'pose he will, if she'll have him."

"Seemed like that, didn't it? Seemed like he was downright smitten with her."

"It did."

"You okay?" she asked. "You're a little quiet."

"Oh, I'm fine, darlin'. You did a beautiful job. The chicken looked delicious."

She smiled. "It was tasty. Tony took seconds."

"The way I remember, you never did make a bad meal."

"Aren't you the charmer?" She laughed.

Roger shrugged. "Not saying a word that isn't true."

Her face dropped a little. "Is it hard for you, Rog?"

"Hard?" he echoed.

"Being here but not really being here."

"Oh, I don't know." He came over and sat on the bed next to her. "It's great to be with you and the children. I am lucky for that. It's just that I feel a little useless sometimes, and all the good food, laughing and kidding with good people... I'm there and I see it, but I'm not really a part of it."

"Oh, Rog, I'm sorry."

"Don't be silly." He reached to grasp her hand. "I'm lucky to be here at all. So I'll take what I can get."

"I do think I know a little of what you mean," she said. "Right now, I'd like you to hold me, kiss me, love me, but we can't. It's a piece missing, for sure." She sighed. "But I'd rather have you like this than nothing at all."

"Me too. At least we have this." He lay down beside her. They curled into each other like spoons, and they fell asleep, filling in the spaces with memory and imagination.

~~CHAPTER 36~~

ELEANOR

"I think I'll leave the car in the garage today," I told Roger that morning. I had marketing to do, but I was keeping an eye on expenses.

"Not too much to carry?" he asked.

"I'm only picking up a few things, and I'll have the buggy."

"It wouldn't be so much to take the car," he said.

"I'm thinking I might sell it. Jean can drive me where I need to go, and that would save me a good bit every month."

"It's come to that?" He shook his head. I could tell that watching me count every penny was just about breaking his heart.

"Just until I get some work," I said, trying to reassure him. "Jack knows a guy who might want to buy it. I could sell it to him, get the money, and then if I find real work, I could buy it back."

Roger shrugged. "I s'pose that's a fair option. For now."

We left it at that, and I went off to the market with Johnny in his stroller and Carol and Barry by my side. It was a sunny and blue-skied day, a day a person could breathe a sigh of relief no matter their circumstance, which might explain why I made the foolish choice I did.

I took care of the shopping; it took longer than usual with the children in tow, but I got most everything I needed. But I hadn't calculated right, and we simply had more than I could manage to carry, even with the stroller. I could have asked for delivery from the store—people did it all the time—but I was fixated on saving my dimes, so I loaded up the stroller's undercarriage, gave Carol and Barry each a small something to carry, and even put a few things on Johnny's lap. The rest I packed to overflowing in one bag and carried that on my hip. It was going to be a long journey home, with stops and starts for sure, but we set off.

Then, while we were waiting at the corner for the light to change, a burly man in cut-off sleeves and saggy dungarees appeared out of nowhere.

"Can I help you with those bags, ma'am?" I didn't say anything, keeping my eyes on the traffic signal. "Sure is hard, a woman all alone with three little ones," he went on. I eyed him. He wasn't the cleanest soul I'd ever seen. Looked like a day laborer, the sort who goes from house to house asking after odd jobs. A good number of them used to come around during the Depression.

"Don't know how you women do it with your men away. Woulda done my part, you know, ma'am, if they woulda had me."

"My husband's returned by now, sir," I said.

"Well, aren't you one of the lucky ones?" He grinned, baring a set of grungy yellow teeth. "Doggone if I didn't have the fever when I was a boy. My hearing ain't never been the same. I don't see why that ought to have mattered. Seems likely one of them old Nazi guns going off might be loud enough for anyone to hear." He laughed, the old snake.

"Yes, I s'pose that's true," I said curtly.

"I have been aiming to do my part here at home, though, with the stronger men away. I'd be happy to help you carry those bags home, if you'd like." He reached for the one I had balanced on my hip. I wrapped an arm tighter around it.

"I mean no harm, ma'am. None at all," he said and held his hands up, palms facing me. "Just thought I might be able to help you."

And now I was embarrassed. The heat of it ran up my face. Maybe I was just being suspicious. It was a heavy load, after all, so I gave in. "I s'pose it might make the trip easier," I said.

He smiled in a nice way, no menace in his dark eyes, and it felt like maybe I had read the man wrong. Carol looked at me sideways when I handed him the bags, but I didn't pay her any mind. That was my next mistake.

The man talked the whole way back to the house, on and on about his mother and the war and the good the men had done and I don't know what-all. I do recall he took the time to find out if my husband had found work since he'd been back. I lied and said Roger'd gone back to his job at the AC plant, which turned out to be yet another foolish thing.

Finally, we reached our block and made the turn. I was nearly home free, or so I thought. Next time, I told myself, I'll be getting the grocery boy to bring my bags home, tip or no tip. I stopped outside the side door.

"It's fine if you leave them here," I said. "The children and I will put them away." He nodded, set the bags on the driveway, then wiped his brow with a rag he pulled from his back pocket.

"Those bags sure were heavy, ma'am. Might you have a drink of cold water for me?" He lifted his chin toward the screen door. And that worrisome feeling I'd had back at the traffic light came over me again. Here I was with a child in a stroller, two others at my feet, a mess of groceries to get in the house, and this "helpful stranger" was now asking for a glass of water. I should have told him to take a drink from the garden hose and get on his way. But I was still trying to be polite.

"Yes, water," I said. "I'll bring it out." I handed a bag each to the children and took Johnny into my arms. "Be right back," I said clear as a bell and went in the side door, leaving the stroller and the groceries underneath out there with the man. I'd see to all of that once I got him on his way.

"Just drop the bags here, kiddos," I said, trying to sound cheery. I put Johnny on the floor and grabbed a glass from the cupboard; I flipped the tap on, filled it and turned around. And there the man stood, smack dab in the center of my kitchen floor, his arms heavy with the rest of my groceries.

"Thought I'd save you a trip." He set the bags on the kitchen table.

"I'm sure you've done enough already but thank you." I handed him the glass of water. He took it but didn't drink. Instead, he offered me his hand.

"Name's Herman, Augustus Herman," he continued, as if it wasn't the oddest thing to come into a woman's kitchen without an invitation and decide it was a social call.

"Pleasure, Mr. Herman," I said, trying to be cheery. I even reached out and shook his rough hand. "Eleanor Mitchell."

"Eleanor," he repeated with a drawl. "Please call me Augustus." He raised the glass in a kind of leering toast, tipped it, and drank the entire thing down in one pour, his Adam's apple jumping.

"Mama, I'm going out back," Carol called, halfway out the door.

"Me, too," Barry echoed.

"Take Johnny with you," I called, and he toddled after them. Now I was alone with this man, but at least the children were safe. I scanned the room for a sight of Roger, but I came up empty. It was me and this man in my kitchen, and I wasn't at all sure where it was headed.

"Ahhh." The man wiped his mouth with the back of his hand. "I do thank you, Eleanor," he said, winking. The back of my neck was prickling with dread now.

"You are quite welcome," I said, "but I'll be needing to get these groceries put away now."

"That was just right," he said and handed the glass back to me, a murky sort of grin on his lips. Now, every single alarm in my body was going off like the fire department on an all-hands call. I set the glass down carefully in the sink. My small kitchen felt like it was shrinking by the second. And his odor was overwhelming, the dirty grime and salty sweat of a man who needed to bathe; I wanted to gag, it was so thick in my throat. From out in the yard, I heard one of the children giggle.

"Well, Mr. Herman, Augustus, I do appreciate your help. Honest I do, but if you'll excuse me."

"Elllle-a-nor," he said with such a drawn-out bit of emphasis it sent a shiver up my spine. "Isn't Eleanor the name of a poem by Edgar Allan Poe?"

"That's Lenore," I answered, trying to sound firm. "My husband reads a good bit."

"Is that right?" He tipped his head sideways, but he didn't seem to have any idea to be getting on his way. Then it hit me, he must be looking for a tip. Stupid me, I thought I'd save on the tip with the grocery boy, not thinking a stranger might expect at least that in return. I fumbled in my dress pocket. There, tucked in among a small circle of thread, my fingers grabbed ahold of a nickel, the bit of change from my groceries.

"Well, thank you, then, Augustus, for your help with that heavy load." I took a step toward him, my hand outstretched with the coin pinched between my fingers. He grabbed my hand along with the coin. His hand was hot and damp, and so big it wrapped around my whole fist. I pulled away, but I wasn't going anywhere.

"No need for money to change hands between us, Eleanor," he said, pulling my arm in toward him, nearly against his chest. I held on to the edge of the sink. "We all know a good war wife must count her pennies. What kind of man would I be if I took the little you have for myself?" He was thick and nearly six feet tall. He took a step toward me, wrapped his other arm around behind and pushed me back against the counter edge, his body pressed hard against mine. He pulled my hand, the one that offered him that stupid nickel, to his mouth and started running his lips along the length of my fingers.

"Get off me," I hissed, pushing with my shoulder against his chest and trying not to have the children hear. "Let go."

"You poor girls," he drawled, his sour breath wet and foul in my face. "All alone while your man serves his country. Doesn't seem right."

"No," I said, twisting and lurching trying to get loose of him. "Get off," I spat like an angry cat. I pushed and I shoved, I even stepped on his foot, but the beast moved only where he wanted. Over his shoulder, my tiny yellow kitchen seemed not to care a bit what was happening, and still no sign of Roger. I hoped he might push the icebox over on the brute, but I caught no sight of him.

"Now there's no need for all that fuss, woman. No need to protest. I know you young ones get lonely. And Ol' Augustus is ready to help. I been thinking that's why Uncle Sam left me behind, to see to the lonely ladies waiting for their men to return. Ha!" He pulled his mouth wide to laugh, and I could see all the years of brown neglect. I gagged, pulled back from the stench. He took that opportunity to push his knee between my legs. Now, he had me off the ground and up against the cabinet like a child on a pony ride, the countertop's edge cutting hard into my backside. He grabbed hold of my one free arm with his hand from behind so he had the both of them pinned against my sides. He pressed his wet mouth against my neck and I nearly vomited on him. Wish I had. I squirmed and squealed, kicked and tried to bite him. Anything I could think of, but still I couldn't get loose of the bastard. He laughed.

"You're a hot little number, ain't you?" He reached up and squeezed my breast, pinched it as hard as he could.

I began to scream but cut it short. The children. I bit my lip and moaned. I would rather take whatever this bastard was here to dish out than let him near the children.

"We can do this the nice way, or we can be rough. I'll get it either way," he growled.

I fought and twisted. The dirt scent of him nearly overwhelmed me, and I retched. He took this as a sign to press his thick wet lips over mine and shove his tongue into my mouth. I pulled back and away. He dipped to mouth my breast and his grip slackened. I pulled my right arm free and boxed his ear with all my might. He reared back, his face red and screwed up into an angry mess of bulging flesh and snarling teeth.

"Bitch." He bared his rotten teeth, yanked on my hair. He was making a beeline to sink his teeth into my breast. As he dipped his head, I reached behind me into the sink, and I felt it, the smooth side of the water glass. I wrapped my hand around it. He bit me and the pain seared up through my whole body into my head. Fighting back a scream, I gripped that glass with a force from somewhere deep inside me and slammed it against the side of his face. It shattered like I'd thrown it against a brick wall. He yowled, and a stabbing pain shot up my arm. I hardly noticed. I pressed the broken glass against his leathery skin, twisting and turning the jagged edges again and again. Then I shoved that fat beast as hard as I could off of me. He stumbled back. I grabbed the dulled butcher knife from the rack.

"Now you get out," I growled, jabbing the knife in his direction. "Get out. NOW!"

The beast glared at me, his right eye wild, his left blinking hard. He pressed his fingers to the side of his head, pulled them back. At the sight of his blood, he smiled.

"Well, well, looking for a fight, are we?" He swiped his sleeve against the dripping blood and stepped toward me. I lowered the knife to a level even with his groin. If you ask me now, I couldn't imagine sticking it in a man's flesh, but that day, right there in my own kitchen, I didn't have a qualm about it. If it was gonna be him or me, then I'd be damned if it was gonna be me. I leaned forward from my waist, lowering in toward him.

Just then, a heavy ceramic vase fell from the shelf over the refrigerator, landing with a hard *thunk* directly behind the beast and shattering into a million pieces. It would have taken an earthquake to move that vase from where it sat. The beast turned. Had he not been moving in to have another go at me, the thing would have landed squarely on his head, and he knew it. He looked back at me, his eyes rounded in confusion. Then, from that same shelf, a glass salad bowl dropped. This one smacked the beast's shoulder before shattering just beside him. He yelped, looked behind him, saw nothing that would make those dishes move, and turned back at me, his face twisted in fear.

"You are a crazy bitch," he spat and made a beeline for the side door. I ran after him, the knife still tight in my fist. All I saw was his sweaty, ugly back running off down the street.

I ran into the backyard. The children were fine, playing peacefully, none the wiser. I breathed a fearsome sigh of relief and Carol looked up.

"Mommy, why do you have a knife?"

I looked down and saw my hand wrapped tight around the handle of the butcher knife. My first instinct was to hide it behind my back, but she'd already asked.

"Oh, I just forgot to put it down before I came out." I laughed halfway and laid it on the picnic table, my hand shaking.

"That's silly. Look at my mud pie." She held up a metal toy plate with a pile of mud on it.

"Well, that looks yummy," I said and wrapped an arm around her, kissing her head. "You smell like the great outdoors." And she did, fresh with the scent of the spring air. It soothed my nerves to drink her in.

"Wanna bite?" She grinned.

I laughed, really laughed, this time. "Don't mind if I do." I swiped my finger across the top of the mud and pretended to eat.

"Mama, your hand is bleeding," Carol noticed with concern. I looked at it. Sure enough, my palm was covered with tiny little cuts like a constellation of heaven's own stars right there in my hand.

CHAPTER 37

ROGER

R oger knew there was trouble as soon as the side door opened. There was an anxious edge in Eleanor's voice and a heavy, dark feeling around what should have been a normal grocery delivery. Roger went to the side door, tried to catch Eleanor's eye. She seemed to be searching for him, too, but she couldn't see him in her fear.

"I'm here, honey, send him away," he said, but she couldn't hear him, either. She hurried into the kitchen, Johnny in her arms. Roger watched the man push in behind her, a look of menace on his face. He tried to stop him, tried to push against him. He even grabbed the door, aiming to force him away, but his own distress prevented the kind of concentration he needed to make it happen.

He followed the man into the kitchen and kept at it, kept shoving and pushing, trying to throw things in his way. The man noticed him only like a gnat or a fly; he swiped at the small bother that Roger was, but kept on his course of terror. Eleanor's fear clutched at her as she tried to distract and quell the man. She gave him a glass of water, made conversation, offered him money. The beast would have none of it. Roger was frantic to intervene. He hurled himself at him, but the man only tipped onto his other foot. He snarled in the man's ear. But the man was so horrible, so hell-bent on taking what was not his, that he hardly noticed.

Eleanor fought like hell, and finally Roger found his strength. He shoved the vase and it crashed to the ground. It startled the beast but didn't chase him away. Roger shoved the glass bowl, and it glanced off the man's shoulder. Roger was preparing to drop a skillet on his head next when the beast ran off.

But Roger was devastated. *I'm no use,* was all he could think. *I'm no use to her at all.*

🌟 🌟 🌟

That night, Eleanor did not look for Roger when she came into the bedroom. She didn't look up at all. Instead, her arms full of folded towels, she marched toward the linen closet inside the bathroom. She buried herself inside the muffled space and took her time, folding and refolding, tucking the towels carefully into their places. She would not rush because she had no wish to confront the day's happenings with Roger. He could feel her frustration, her anger, could hear the bitter questions spinning around her mind. All she had ever wanted was a normal life, and this far from normal.

Roger's joy, his contentment at being with them, was weighed more heavily every day with the guilt of holding Eleanor back from being happy. He could see this now in a way he'd never let himself recognize before. It had been foolish to hope that their life together could last. It was not enough. If he was honest, he had known it wouldn't be, and likely Eleanor had, too. But they had agreed, without words, to ignore the limitations; to pretend that this life could suffice, a new version of the love they had known before the war. The vagrant's attack had pointed up their folly. Love might be able to cross the great divide, but safety and security could not.

Coming out of the bathroom, her arms empty, Eleanor stopped just inside the room.

"So," was all she said. Hands on her hips, she eyed him, a challenge of sorts.

"I'm so sorry, sweetheart," Roger said. "I wish I could have done more."

She waved a dismissive hand. "Nothing to do," she replied. "He's gone and I'm okay." But her shoulders dropped as she spoke, betraying her exhaustion.

"Come. Sit." He patted the bed. She eyed his transparent hand, the barely there-ness of his smile, and opted instead to drop into the blue chair.

"I feel like a fool, trusting that man," she said. "I should have been more careful."

"You can't blame yourself." Between them the air hung tired, empty, ready for rest. Eleanor rubbed her eyes, yawned, then looked him in the eye.

"You pushed that vase off the shelf, didn't you?"

"It was the best I could do. I tried pushing, shoving him, closing the door on him. Nothing worked. It was all I could get to move. I hoped it might knock him out."

"And the glass bowl? That scared the old bum."

"I'm sorry for all of it, El."

"It isn't your fault. If you were alive, you'd have been at work."

"But you wouldn't have taken that many groceries by yourself. You'd have waited for Saturday, like we used to do. I'd watch the children, you'd take the car," he protested.

"Like we used to do." She sighed.

"It's not what I promised."

"That was a silly war promise. Nobody expected you'd keep it."

Roger was stunned. "Nobody?"

"Well, I did, but I knew it was a fool's gamble... or maybe I didn't." She came over and dropped onto the bed with a heavy sigh. "Okay, yes, I believed, but I knew I shouldn't. I knew it was childish, but I did believe."

"I meant it."

"I know you did. But it was war. Who could promise anything? I just never, ever thought it would turn out like this for us. I loved you, Roger. I love you still. We were supposed to be together, a happy family. Forever." Her eyes welled with tears. He nodded, admitting to what felt like every failing. She looked off out the darkened window.

"I s'pose I just figured if I did it all right, if I followed the rules, it would all work out. We'd be back together again. We'd have a thousand stories to tell to find our way back to knowing each other, and you'd be in my arms again." A slow tear dripped from her eye.

"The war changed me," Roger said quietly. "The man you'd have gotten back, he wasn't the man you married. Not by a long shot." He rubbed a hand across his jaw, a gesture Eleanor recalled from Roger's father: a show of resignation.

"What do you mean?" She pulled herself upright in the chair.

"I couldn't come back," he murmured, refusing to look up.

"Why not?" she asked, leaning down to catch his eye.

He met her gaze. "I wasn't the same."

A flash of irritation ran across her face. "I have no patience for guessing, so what was it? *Was* it an accident? Or was it something else that took you? Tell me now and tell me straight. After today, there isn't much that can throw me too far off-track." She leaned forward, hands on her knees.

"Too much had changed, El. I was shaking all the time, couldn't sleep—cried out when I did. I barely ate. Look at me now; you can see I'd gone thin." He pulled at his ghostly shirt. "And I was jumpy, startling at every breeze that blew through the trees. I didn't know myself," he said. Her mouth hung half-open, a drawn look of surprise on her face.

"Wouldn't have mattered to me," she said, shaking her head.

"I tried to fix it," he went on. "Quit smoking, tried to nap, tried to exercise. I even talked with the chaplain a few times. There weren't any answers, and nothing was getting better. It felt like I was already a ghost." His eyes begged her understanding.

"I would have taken you any way you came."

"How could I be a husband, a father, when I couldn't even steady my hand?"

"But it was an accident?"

"It was. I didn't take my own life, Eleanor; you can believe that," he said. "But I had this feeling, even after the fighting ended, that one way or another, I wasn't coming home. I s'pose every soldier thinks that, but I couldn't picture it—kept thinking of you and the children, us being together again, and I couldn't get a bead on it. Every time I tried, my stomach would start to churn, my head would go a little dizzy, and my heart felt like it might seize up and give out. I put it off to fear, fear that I wouldn't make it home.

"Then the accident happened." He looked at his hands. "And it all made sense. I wasn't fit for this life anymore. I'd known it, but I couldn't admit it. At least that's what it seems like now; all the nervousness was trying to tell me something, to warn me."

"Oh, Roger, it wouldn't have mattered."

"It's better," he said, his voice thick. "You're better off without me."

"Better off?" She cocked an eyebrow. "No, I am not better off without you. All I ever wanted was you."

"I'll find you someone new, El. A better man."

"There isn't anyone better than you, not a single man in the world better than you." She wiped at her eyes.

"Lay with me, honey," said Roger, sliding under the bedcovers. "Let's be as together as this fool mess will let us."

She stood up slowly, made her way to his side of the bed and curled in toward him, pressing the pillow against her back to pretend it was him. He wrapped his arm tight around her, recalling her warmth from so many nights spent in each other's arms. He ached to make love to her, to feel her body supple against his own.

"Let's figure it out in the morning," she said, more to herself than to him.

"Mmmm," he answered noncommittally.

In the morning, he would convince her it was best that he go. Not right away, but slowly, steadily, over time, he would leave. This half-life would never do for her. She'd never admit it, never give it up—she wasn't a quitter—but he loved her too much to ask it of her. She was alive and real, a woman with needs and responsibilities. His lingering like this was only making it harder for her to get on with her life, such as it was. For tonight, he held her in his heart, if not his arms; he held her and lived in the memories that would have to last them both a lifetime.

He spent the night next to Eleanor, an arm wrapped about her shoulders. Then, before dawn, he moved into the children's room to lay with each of them in turn. He would miss this intimacy, an intimacy that a dead man had no right to. The time had come for him to let them go on without him. What that meant for him, he wasn't entirely sure. He'd lived in this limbo state for enough months now to feel the pull from both sides. The goodness of the life he had known with Eleanor was both evident and consoling, but the beyond invited him with a gentle kind of peace. He could never go back, this he knew, but he could release Eleanor and himself from the bondage of what could never be.

The morning dawned bright and cool. Roger took his usual place at the kitchen table, and the muffled sound of his family's waking wrapped itself around him like a quilt of warm contentment.

"Hi, Daddy," Carol called, coming into the kitchen.

"Morning, honey," Roger said. "Where's Mommy?"

"She's changing Johnny." Carol slid into the chair opposite him.

"How'd you sleep, sunshine?" Roger asked.

"Okay," Carol said, making shadows of her hand in the sunlight on the table. "Only one bad dream."

"You had a bad dream?"

She nodded, playing with the sun. "A bad man came. But I hid under my covers."

"Did he go away?"

"I guess so. I fell back asleep."

Roger chuckled. "Do you have bad dreams a lot?"

"Not really. If I do, I just tell them to go away."

"That's very brave."

Carol shrugged. "I'm hungry."

"Mommy'll be down in a minute."

"Could you make me pancakes, Daddy?" The innocence of the question threw him. His heart caught in his throat. A father ought to be able to make his daughter a tall stack. She waited, her blue eyes wide.

"Oh, sweetheart, I can't cook anymore now."

"How come?"

"I'm not real, remember?"

"But daddies are real. My friend Madelyn has a real daddy. I saw him. He makes pancakes with syrup and butter."

"Madelyn is very lucky."

"I want pancakes."

"Me, too. Let's ask Mommy when she comes down."

She looked at him sideways but made no more demands. For Roger, it was yet another dagger of truth driven straight into his heart. She'd accepted his avoidance without protest, but that wouldn't always be the case. He watched her trace circles in a small bit of sugar spilled on the table. His resolve strengthened as his heart broke just a little bit more.

Eleanor came around the corner of the stairs and into the kitchen with both boys, one on either hip. She gave Roger her bright morning smile. Yesterday was a nightmare she had decided to forget. Roger knew she was faking it for the sake of the children.

"These boys were both too lazy to carry themselves down the stairs, so I had to do it for 'em," she declared with a laugh. "Now, I've got to get the breakfast on." She popped them into their chairs one at a time. Roger watched her deft moves appreciatively and even with a touch of envy. He wished he could hold his children again, nuzzle and cuddle, carry and caress.

"Carol asked for pancakes," he said to Eleanor.

Carol hollered, "Pancakes!" The boys cheered. Roger grinned, every bit the proud papa, but underneath he felt the sharp pinch of a necessary farewell, harder this time for its finality.

☆   ☆   ☆

After breakfast, the children darted off to play in the other room. Eleanor busied herself at the sink. Small and lovely, her movements were practiced and nimble. Roger admired her efficiency.

"How are you this morning, Mum?" Roger asked.

"I'm just fine," she answered, without looking at him. She clattered the dishes into the cupboard. She was strong, he thought, watching her. Strong and tough like women all around the world had had to be during the war. But many of those women could let their guard down now, share the burden with someone again. Not all of them, not by a long shot; but enough that Eleanor knew what she was missing. No end to the heartbreak. She cried sometimes, in the tub, or late in the middle of the night, when she thought he wasn't watching. Sometimes out hanging the laundry, a heavy sadness would overcome her. If one of the kids came running, she'd smile through her tears. But Roger knew how lonely she was—how weary, in spite of his presence. She was, in the end, all by herself.

Still avoiding him, she wiped the sink for the umpteenth time.

"Buffed to a fine polish now," Roger said. She laughed, couldn't help herself. Then her face turned serious.

"You can't leave me again," she said, frowning. "You can't."

He patted the chair next to him. "Come sit." She poured a cup of coffee and joined him at the table.

"You can't get on with things while I'm still here, El. We both know that."

"I don't want to get on with things. I'm fine this way. I'm sorry for what I said last night." She sipped her coffee, her eyes holding his, a frown sagging her lips.

"Life can be better than this for you."

"I'm perfectly happy." Her frown turned to a straight line of determination.

"But think of it: someone to take care of you, someone to watch over you."

"I can look after myself," she said quietly.

"Of course you can, but you don't have to. I'll find someone for you. I don't know how just yet, but I will, a good man. A man that'll make the years ahead easier on you."

She stared at him. "Roger, don't..."

"It'll be okay. I'll figure it out."

"It's not that. It's... I just..." she started, her mouth sagged with grief, her shoulders slumped. "I've got nothing left, Roger. No love left."

"That's not true. Look at the love you give the children, and even you and me, how we carry on in our way. You're full of love."

"Oh, I'm full of something, that's for sure." She barked a bitter laugh. "Piss and vinegar, as Mother used to say, or maybe it's just a whole lot of nerve. Mostly I think it's anger. I'm just so damn mad most of the time. But what I'm not full of is love. Once I was, and I do love the children, and I love you. But full of love? No."

"I'll send you love, Eleanor. The kind of love to last a lifetime."

She leaned her elbows on the table and shook her head. "The day you weren't coming home anymore was the day that changed it all for me. I got as scared as I ever was gonna be in my whole life that day. More scared even than yesterday, with that beast here in my very own kitchen. No, the day the telegram came, a fright came over me. A fright so full and so bone-deep I wasn't sure I could breathe one more breath. My hands were shaking, my mind raced, and my throat seized up. I hadn't known a person could feel so afraid, so broken, so lost all at once. I wondered if I was losing my mind." She stopped. Roger waited. She took a deep breath.

"That night, after crying so many tears I didn't know if my eyes would dry up, I went up to bed. I lay in the middle of our bed, staring at the ceiling in the dark. And I wondered if I could go on—if I was even meant to go on without you. Maybe all this I was feeling was some kind of death boiling up in me and it might take me in the night. I almost hoped it would. But then I rolled over and my eyes fell on Johnny sleeping the sleep of angels in the crib, his little chest rising and falling with tiny breaths, his lips open just so.

"And it came to me—watching Johnny, I was watching life, all fresh and sparkling new, hopeful and trusting. It made me think about those fairy-tale dreams you and me used to have. The plans we made. Start fresh after the war, we said. Pretend the war never happened. We were gonna live happily ever after. It didn't work out that way, but looking at Johnny in the crib, he didn't know it hadn't worked out. He had no idea things were supposed to be any different than this—no father, just a mother. He was born into this mess none the wiser. And that's when I realized I couldn't quit. I had to carry on, for the sake of that baby boy lying just a few feet from me. I had to fight; the fear was mine to beat for the sake of that baby, and his big brother and big sister sleeping in the next room. I had to keep going for these three little people who had no idea about war or accidents or any other sort of nonsense that make life the battle it is. They were depending on me. I couldn't let them down.

"So, I took a deep breath and I buried the fear down deep. It's still there somewhere, but every time it tries to push itself back up and cause me some trouble, I swallow hard and shove it back into hiding. And that's what I've been doing since the day you weren't coming home anymore. Life isn't fair, it isn't ever gonna be fair, but I'll be damned if the son of a bitch is gonna beat me while I've got three children to raise."

She turned and smiled in bitter relief at having unburdened herself. "Bet you never thought you'd hear me curse, did ya?" It was a challenge as much as a joke.

"I can see why you would."

"So, what I got here is strength, conviction, and resolve, and that's what's gonna carry me through, come hell or high water. But what I don't have, what I can't do, is try to love again. I just can't open my heart up again. I've thought about it long and hard. I can't find a way back into a place where I might love and lose again. I won't do it."

Her fingers circled the edge of her mug. Roger didn't speak, just let her sit with the words between them. He wouldn't force her to accept love, but he would send her love wrapped in a package of warmth and sincerity. And he would hope that she could find a way to let it in. He moved next to her on the chair; neither one of them could feel the other, there were no hugs to be had. Still, he sat there with her and she with him.

"I won't leave just yet," Roger said quietly. "But I do have to go, sooner rather than later." She pinched the bridge of her nose as if she were pinching back tears.

"Well, take your time about it, huh? Just a little more time?" she pleaded.

Roger nodded, kissed her head, and wished it all had come to a different end.

CHAPTER 38

ELEANOR

And so he was gone. Not right away, though; he left slowly, fading over a long set of weeks. Almost like he was erasing himself. At first, I couldn't see him as well. His voice dulled to a whisper. The children spoke less and less of him. After a while, all I could see was his blue eyes. Like a change of season, he went bit by bit, until one night I went into the bedroom and he wasn't there at all. I had known the day was coming; he'd indicated as much the night before. Sitting right there in that blue chair, he had blown me a kiss, just like the kiss he'd blown me at the train station. I had known it was coming, but that first night without him took my breath away.

I went into the bathroom, trying not to think too hard about it. The bathroom was a place he hadn't come into since the day he died, so I could pretend nothing really had changed while I was in there. Then I went back into the bedroom. I tried not to look around too hard. It was quiet and empty, like the air had leaked out of it, just the plain old room again, boring and ordinary in a way it hadn't been for months. It reminded me of a forgotten Christmas stocking, all forlorn and empty. I lay down in bed, and stared at the ceiling again, my old, bleak friend. It hung there, blank and unconcerned.

"Roger," I whispered, knowing it was useless. "Don't go." The empty room swallowed my words. Nothing remained but quiet. I understood the wisdom of his going. I supposed I needed him to go so I could get on with things. We lived in two different worlds now. It was never really going to work. But I would have lived that way with him forever if I could have, or at least until I could join him on the other side.

The old fear inched its way back into my brain, the same fear I'd felt when the Western Union man showed up on my doorstep. Only this time it felt like a grizzled friend, and I knew exactly how to handle it. When my heart raced, I held tight to the bed until it slowed. When my throat tightened, I drew tiny breaths until it opened again. I'd been here before. *You will breathe again,* I told myself, *you will live.* And I did. I lay there and I lived, my eyes fixed on that blank ceiling. Eventually, sleep took me. In its fitful arms, I dreamt of empty rooms, old people lost and alone in the middle of fallow fields. I woke with a chill. Nothing had changed; I was alone now. I rolled over, buried my face in Roger's pillow, and fell into a fitful sleep.

In the morning, sunlight and Carol woke me.

"Mommy," she said, her hand shaking my shoulder. "Wanna wake up?" I turned. Her face was inches from mine.

"Morning, sweetie," I said.

"C'mon," she said, clapping her hands, "let's get this day going." I smiled at her, but I felt glued to the bed.

"In a minute," I said, but I didn't mean it. I rolled onto my back. There was the ceiling. "Welcome back," it seemed to be saying; welcome back to nothing.

Carol leaned on the bed, her chin propped in her hands. "Mom-my," she whined. I pushed myself up onto my elbows, but it felt like a weight was pressing on my chest. I wasn't sure I could lift myself any further.

Then from downstairs we heard a familiar, "Yoo-hoo!"

"Auntie Jean!" Carol cried, her eyes round and bright. She dashed out of the room.

"Morning, sunshine," I heard Jean say. "Where's your mama?" Seconds later, she and Carol appeared, hand in hand, at the bedroom door.

"Still in bed?" she squawked when she saw me. "Good Lord, El." She checked her wristwatch. "It's after eight."

And I might have been embarrassed, but I wasn't; I didn't have the slightest inclination for embarrassment or anything else. I dropped onto my back again. She came to the side of the bed and placed a cool hand on my forehead.

"I'm not sick," I replied, a little too gruffly. "I'm just tired."

"Okay, grumpy pants. Maybe you ought to sleep a little longer."

"Maybe." I turned toward her. "Would you mind seeing to things for a bit?" She looked worried, but I couldn't fix that. I just needed some more sleep.

"Sure, okay. I'll put the coffee on, get the kiddos fed. You catch a few more winks."

"Thanks, Jeannie," I said, rolling away. She pulled the covers up over my shoulders, gave me a pat on the back.

"C'mon, Carol, let's see about your brothers," she said.

Jean greeted the boys with the same cheer she'd rolled in on. I listened and I was grateful. My sisters were my saviors; always had been, always would be. But I'd be lying if I didn't say I knew I ought to be getting up and getting around. I knew I ought to get moving; I knew I ought to be strong and brave and resilient. But I had done it so many times before: bucked up like a good war wife when Roger was called to duty, pulled myself together after that awful storm, and carried on again after the telegram. I saw to the children, saw to the house, cooked and cleaned, rationed and scrimped, all of it, and all it had left me was alone—alone in my bed, alone in my life, alone and trying, time and again, to pretend it was fine. I just couldn't do it one more time.

I had wanted more for my life, and maybe that was where I'd gone wrong. Maybe I hadn't the right to expect anything more than the scraps from the table that I'd had as a child. Swaying in Roger's arms at the high school dances, I had dreamt a whole world of contentment. Pressed tight against his side out on the back porch surrounded by crickets' music, I had imagined sharing a home with him. In the tizzy of his kisses on the sprung seats of his father's truck, I had conjured a little family, a dream life of picket fences and perfect bliss. A life different than the one I'd grown up with. I'd dreamt of it and for a minute I'd had it. Then the world laughed. Right in my face, it laughed like an old bully.

So I stayed in bed. It worried Mother and them—I could tell by the lines across their foreheads when they came in to see me. But they didn't say much about it, just stepped in and started taking turns. They wouldn't let the children get lost in my grief. They'd drop in my room, bring me juice or tea and toast. They never said much, not in the first few days, just brought me a tray and took it out again.

I heard them whispering from time to time outside my door: "This long after?" they asked each other.

"Well, I was surprised when she just kept pressing on."

"It took a while, but it's definitely laid her low now."

All their observations trickled in on hushed air. I heard them, but I didn't care. I knew the real reason it had taken me so long to feel my pain, to believe my grief. And yet, it hardly mattered. I was mourning, early or late, and god bless if I didn't feel entitled to it.

I lay there for seven days, a full week, getting up only to use the toilet and wash myself from time to time, usually in the hours just before dawn when the house was asleep and I was feeling every bit of my broken heart. It was Mother who lost her patience first, although she tried to be understanding.

"Eleanor," she said, marching into my room 'long about the fourth or fifth morning. "I'm here, dear, to change your bed. But I'd also like to remind you that you weren't raised to take to your bed like a princess." She pulled the covers off me, rolled me over, and pulled one side of the sheet out from under. "Your children need you." She rolled me the other way, grunting and straining, and pulled the bottom sheet clean off. I could have gotten up, but Mother seemed to prefer to work around me, so I lay like a corpse and listened.

"Women the world over have kept going for their children," she continued, fluttering a fresh sheet up to the edge of me. "It's what women do: we keep going. There aren't any easy roads for anybody here. And if you think you find someone whose road looks simple, why I'll tell you, you just haven't looked deep enough." She rolled me onto the fresh side of the sheet, tugged it underneath me, and tucked it into the edge of the bed before flipping me flat once again.

"The world works the way it does, and we are to do our best with what we get. That right there is the long and the short of it, my girl." She shook a clean sheet over the top of me and followed that with a quilt. She tucked the both of them in. Finally, she straightened and looked at me from the foot of the bed.

"Now, you take another day or so. Then you're done, and you get up and you get on with it, you hear me?"

I nodded, pushing myself a little up more toward sitting. She went and stood in the doorway, studying me with a mix of pity and frustration in her eyes.

"Of all my girls, I figured you had the grit of survival," she sighed, and then she turned and walked out.

I listened to her footsteps fading away as she descended the stairs. The scent of line-fresh sheets wafted around me like a hug and a scold all at the same time. I wasn't a princess, and I wasn't weak, but maybe I wasn't as strong as I'd thought, either. And I didn't care a bit who knew it.

It was a few days later, the seventh day, that I felt a shift in the air, and I knew someone was at the door.

"El?" It was Faye, her voice soft and easy. My heart jumped a little at the sound.

"I'd like to come in, El. If that is okay," Faye said.

Staring at the ceiling, I answered, "If you want." My voice came out raspy and thin for not having been used. I liked the sound of it; it reminded me of some old woman, a witch who lived out among the trees and spoke only to her cats.

"May I sit?"

I flipped a hand toward the edge of the bed, still not looking. When Faye sat, the edge of the bed dipped in a way that rolled me sideways. Twisting to find a flat place, I found myself looking at her back. Faye had chosen to sit turned away from me, not looking at me in the same way that I chose not to look at her. I shifted my eyes back up to the ceiling again, but the idea of Faye choosing not to look at me still stuck with me.

"Just wanted to check in on you," said Faye quietly. "See for myself."

"See for yourself? Like I'm a roadside attraction?" I cleared my throat for an argument.

"We are all worried about you, Eleanor," Faye rejoined with a slightly scolding tone.

"I'm all right," I answered, my voice croaking again.

"You s'pose?" asked Faye.

I didn't answer. Faye sighed. *Here it comes,* I figured—a lecture, a different version of Mother's reprimand. I braced myself. But sitting on the tiniest edge of the bed, her back still turned toward me, Faye didn't echo Mother, not at all.

Instead, she whispered, "I'd do the same if I was you."

My breath caught in my throat. Tears immediately welled in my eyes, tears I thought I'd cried out ages ago.

"I'd get in my bed," she went on, "and come out only when they carried me off to join him. Babies or no babies, I just wouldn't be able to go on." She was hitting the one nerve I had left, and I felt it. The way she spoke felt like recognition, like the truth I couldn't put a finger on all these days.

"I'm just so damned mad," I whispered.

SOMETIMES A SOLDIER COMES HOME | *Jessica Ciosek*

"Oh, honey, of course you are." She put a small hand on my shoulder, and it loosened the words in me, the words I'd been choking on for months now.

"Just downright angry as a hornet is how I feel. And I got no one to be mad at. I got no one I can yell at. At least Mother could be mad at Daddy for leaving her. How can I be mad? At Roger? *My* Roger? My poor Roger..." I was crying openly now. The tears dripped off Faye's cheeks, too. She said nothing, just letting me rant.

"It just wasn't supposed to be this way—he wasn't supposed to die! He was supposed to come home and get old with me. We were supposed to be that couple in love for all our lives. Doddering old fools, together, like Roger's folks, a matched set. Not like our family, no daddy, no man in the house. Roger was a good man, for me, for the kids." I sat up, pulled my knees to my chest, and wrapped my arms around them, holding on tight. I glanced sideways at Faye.

She blinked at me slowly, seeming to have a similar longing for how life had once been. "I know, El. I loved you with Roger. I loved you and Roger together. Looking at you two made me feel like I could have those dreams, too. You and Roger made it seem possible."

"I just loved him so much, Faye," I moaned. "So much I thought love could bring him home."

"It should have been enough."

"It sure should have."

She wiped at her own tears. "I'm sorry, El. I know it's not fair for me to cry."

"It is fair," I said. "We all lost him. Besides, I'm sick and tired of crying alone." We smiled through the tears. I hugged her hard.

"I do miss him, El, but mostly I miss you with him," said Faye. "You were so happy, so carefree when Roger was around."

"Was I?" I asked. "Sometimes I think I made the whole thing up."

"No, you were. You really were happy." She grabbed my hand, squeezed it.

"It all just makes me so mad," I repeated, but the edge of my anger had gone, the bitter twist of my loss now finally clear to someone other than me. And it was okay—not good, never great, but it was gonna be okay.

She sat with me a while. We didn't say anything more. I tipped my head back against the headboard, closed my eyes, and listened. The sounds of my life floated up from the main floor. Johnny was fussing; sounded like he was due for a nap. Carol was helping Grandma find something in the kitchen.

"Momma keeps them next to the fridge," I heard her say. Must be Mother was looking for a grocery sack. I listened to see if I could pick out what Barry was doing. Then I heard footsteps, small but heavy. And there he was, at my bedside. Faye moved sideways to let him in.

"Momma," he said, leaning on the edge of the bed. "Are you gonna come downstairs today?"

"Oh, I don't know, honey."

"Can I stay with you?"

"Why sure, pumpkin." I pulled my arm back to let him climb in.

He clambered up and snuggled into the curl of my body. Faye smiled and tiptoed out of the room.

"Grandma gave Carol the rest of the juice," he said, his pudgy fingers twisting the ribbon on my nightgown.

"Did you have some juice?"

"Yesterday I had it, so Carol said she got the rest."

"Mmmmm," I hummed. "When Auntie Jean comes over tonight, I'll ask her to get some more. How's that?"

He smiled but stayed tucked up next to me. I held him and we laid there in silence together. After a while, we both dozed off.

When I woke, he was gone, and the house was quiet. It felt empty. I listened hard for any signs of movement. Nothing. Where were the children? My brain told me they'd gone to the playground, or over to Mother's, but that they'd gone without me knowing. Then that terrible dream I'd had some months before came rushing back to me: the dream where the children had been taken away and I was running and calling, unable to find them. It gave me a fright. I'd already lost Roger; did I want to lose the rest of them? Every bit of all I held dear could disappear, I realized, if I never got up and back to my life again.

And, in the end, it was that fear that pulled me from my bedcovers—the fear of nothing more, of nothing special, the fear that it all would go on without me and I'd just fade off into nothingness.

I threw those covers back so fast. I got up and ran down the stairs. And, just like I thought, no one was around. And no note, either. I expected they thought I wouldn't come down to see it anyway. I ran back upstairs and turned on a hot bath. I washed the grime of grief from every bit of myself and I got going. I went on downstairs, dressed for walking and determined to find my family again, when there they came marching in the side door, cheeks rosy and bodies sweaty from playing hard. Faye was with them.

"Mama!" Carol screamed. "You're up!"

I pulled her into my arms. "Yes, I'm up! And I'm wondering where you've been." I kissed her damp forehead and held her at arm's length.

"We've been to the park. I hope you don't mind," Faye chimed in.

"Of course I don't mind! The park sounds like fun!" I exclaimed, too excited by half. But I was as about as relieved as I could be to see them; I couldn't help myself. The chatter began from there, the children telling me of all their adventures, and I finally felt it. I felt the reason for my carrying on: it was here in the faces of these small cherubs, just like it had been all along.

CHAPTER 39

ELEANOR

Summer went along, hot and dull, after Roger left. My heart was broken, but it was mending as best it could. In the fall, Carol started kindergarten. I dressed her up in a school-day pinafore and black Mary Janes. She was pleased to be going, and it gave us a new routine, which was probably the best way for getting on with things. But it was bittersweet, knowing how tickled Roger would have been to see his bright little girl get her start in the world.

To help with finances, I started a small sewing business. Really, it was Blanche who got it off the ground for me. She'd taken notice of a pretty red velvet dress I'd whipped together for Carol for the holidays. It was a fine bit of work, if I do say so myself: a full skirt trimmed in black grosgrain ribbon. Blanche remarked on it at church one Sunday morning, and the next day she came by asking if I could make a dress like that for her new granddaughter.

Her boy, Frankie, had come home from the war with an Italian wife, and she was already expecting by the time they arrived. Sophia, they called the baby. She was a beautiful little girl with brown eyes and dark curly hair. Lucky she was so pretty, too, because Blanche was none too thrilled about her boy bringing home a war bride. But the birth of little Sophia was enough to mend any rift between the two women, and they doted on that baby like she was a perfect angel. So I made the same red velvet dress for Sophia. She was such a tiny little thing, it didn't take but a minute. I used a cream-colored grosgrain ribbon for the trim on hers. It was a dear dress, and the red set off her dark baby curls nicely.

Blanche insisted on paying me for it, even when I told her I wouldn't take it. Then, she went and showed it off to all her friends, and next thing I knew, the phone was ringing with ladies I knew and ladies I didn't, asking if I could make something for their own little girls, daughters, and granddaughters. From there, the whole thing took off, and I was making little girl dresses and ladies' dresses for all the seasons. So that kept me as busy as I needed to be and took a little money worry off my shoulders.

Faye moved in with me, too, which kept me from having to sell the house. It wouldn't be forever. She had a new beau, Bob, and they were pretty serious, but it was a help for the time being, and the time being was all any of us had anyway.

I thought about Roger a lot and carried on as best I could, but I did sometimes feel a touch of envy seeing the other men returning from the war. Life was back to normal in those homes; wives were held again, the children had daddies again, the chair at the head of the table was warm again.

Saturdays were the hardest, it being the day for families to spend time together. One particular Saturday, I'd gone over to the fabric store to pick up some thread. Faye was sitting the children. Walking along, not thinking about too much, I came across a cute little family. The husband still sported his uniform, must have only just come home. With him were his wife and daughter, both of them blonde and pretty. The little girl was all kitted out in a cute pink cotton jacket with a matching polka-dot dress underneath. Adorable. And the wife was a pretty lady, too, slim and blonde and dressed in the same pink cotton as the little girl, only Mama's dress fit quite a bit closer to her body. And, to go along with it, she had her hair combed over the side of her face like she was Veronica Lake or something. But that peekaboo hairdo really only works when you are not wrapped up in a snit at your husband.

I didn't have any idea what the trouble was all about. There were no words exchanged that I could hear, but she was tapping her foot to beat the band, arms folded like armor across her chest, waiting for her soldier husband to hurry around and open the car door. While at Daddy's side, the daughter was jumping up and down calling, "Daddy, look at this."

From where I was, I couldn't see what the little one wanted Daddy to look at. Whatever it was, it was as tiny as a ladybug and probably of less consequence, but she wanted Daddy to see it. And poor Daddy, he wanted just as much to have a look, but Mommy was having none of it. She was as ready to go as a race car driver at the starting line, so Daddy found himself caught betwixt and between the two girls in his life. Well, I could have told him that by the firm straight line of his wife's lips and the tense hold of her shoulders, there'd be no pleasing the Mrs., so he might as well take the half a minute his little girl needed from him.

It gnawed at me some that she could be so mad at this man, a man who was standing right there wanting nothing whatsoever but to please both her and her precious little girl. I wanted to take her by the shoulders and make her understand what it was to not have that man anymore, to not be able to get yourself in some fool twist over how he held the door or which mayonnaise he took from the shelf. I wanted her to know what it was to be left to do these things all on your own now. She had no idea, not one. Oh, that drippy long hair, and that dress too snug. Her husband was probably worried sick the whole time he was away.

Finally, the husband got around and opened the door for her, and she huffed her way into the front seat, nearly pushing him aside as she did. Well, I stopped and I stared. Wasn't fair of me, but I couldn't help myself. I wanted her to know she was lucky to have that man at all, when so many of us didn't. I caught her eye, and she got a little uneasy. She squirmed, her hard expression softened, she nodded ever so slightly, and I nodded firmly back.

Now, I can't be sure she understood what I was trying to tell her, but I do know when her soldier husband climbed into his seat, she reached across and laid a hand gently on his shoulder. He looked over at her, surprised. She smiled; on her lips I read, "Sorry." His face broke into an easy grin. He pulled her hand to his mouth and kissed it quick. Then they drove off. I watched them go. The blonde woman, I'll give her some credit, looked at back me and gave me a small wave. In her eyes I think I saw the tiniest bit of realization.

I took no satisfaction in it. Took no satisfaction in them being happy again. Sure, good for them, but as I watched that green Buick drive off, all I kept thinking was that I loved mine more. I loved my Roger more than anyone loved another, more than life itself. We hardly argued, and we surely didn't bother being foolish over silly things. No, our love was real. Our love was perfect, whole and unending from the very day we met. And now I stood here alone while that pretty lady drove off in a new Buick with her soldier husband home safe again by her side. I might say that a thickness gathered in my throat, a tear stung in the corner of my eye, but I was so used to living with that thickness and that wet eye that I hardly noticed.

PART THREE

CHAPTER 40

ELEANOR

B y June of the next year, 1947, Jean and Tony were engaged. Tony worked at the same plant that Jean did, but he was an electrician, not in the office where she was. One Saturday afternoon, they talked me into going along to a company picnic for all of the General Motors factories. It was going to be a big to-do downtown in Kearsley Park. I can't say why I agreed, except it was a beautiful early summer day, and the thought of getting out seemed like a nice idea. I made a batch of cookies and dressed up the children, and off we went in Jean's big Cadillac with Tony at the wheel (the day Jean let Tony take the wheel of her Cadillac, I knew she was smitten). The drive out was soothing, the wind blowing through my hair, Jean and Tony a pair of lovebirds in the front seat. For a minute, I felt like I didn't have a care in the world, and it sure felt nice.

We got to the park soon enough, and Tony rolled the Caddy up to the edge of the grass.

"Why don't we drop you and the children first?" Jean suggested.

"All right," I said, "but be quick about it. I don't know a danged soul here."

"Oh, you'll be fine. Take your cookies and go make yourself useful," she said, waving a hand at me.

They pulled away. Carol went to find someone to play with, and Barry followed after. There I stood with Johnny by one hand, the cookie platter in the other. The place buzzed and chattered with happy families. The men were dressed in summer slacks and short sleeves and greeted each other like old friends, clapping backs and tipping cold beer over dry throats. The women scurried around with blankets and baskets, pulling out bowls of potato salad and foil-wrapped platters of fried chicken. Cake pans and pie plates were put on another table for later. I couldn't help but think how much more a part of things I might feel if I'd come along on Roger's arm instead of with my sister and her fiancé, but there wasn't a thing to be done about that.

"Cookies," I said to no one in particular. I slipped the platter onto the dessert table.

"Perfect, yes, put those there," one of the ladies said, smiling. "So much food! I hope there's people enough to eat it."

"That bunch looks like they can put a dent in it," I said, tipping my head toward the gathered men.

She laughed. "Yes, I guess they do. I'm Sadie." She offered her hand.

"Eleanor." I grasped her cool fingers in mine. "I'm here with my sister, Jean." Immediately after saying that, I felt that I shouldn't have. It made Sadie smile at me the way people do when they feel sorry for you.

"Isn't that nice," she replied.

"Can I give a hand?"

"Not much left to do," she said. "But those cookies do look good."

Johnny tugged my arm. "Swing, Mommy," he pleaded.

"You go have fun," said Sadie. "We'll take care of things here."

I followed Johnny as he toddled to the playground. I was used to being one of the few who didn't have a second set of eyes for watching the children. Carol stood near the pavilion, talking with two little girls who were holding hands. I could tell by the turn of her head that she'd soon be off romping with them for the afternoon. She took after her father in that she made friends so easily. I looked around for Barry, but he was nowhere to be seen. I scanned the swings and the slide, even the sandbox. Not a sign of him.

"Let's go find Barry," I said to Johnny, "then we'll do our swinging." I pulled him onto my hip and carried him over to where Carol stood with the other girls.

"Carol, honey? Have you seen Barry?"

"He ran away, Mommy," she said, then laughed with her new friends.

My heart jumped. "Ran away? Where?" I put a hand on Carol's shoulder.

"Over there," she pointed toward a small hill, an easy slope that led down to a creek. I looked up and down the length of the hill. No sign of Barry.

To the girls she said, "C'mon, let's go find fairies," and they ran off.

"Stay away from the creek," I hollered after them. With Johnny on my hip, I made a beeline for that creek. My eyes raced along the bank, scanning for those brown curls. Then, just as I reached the crest of the hill, a man's voice called out.

"S'cuse me," he said. "Ma'am?" His voice was so collected, so gentle, I couldn't imagine he meant me. I was panicked, worried my four-year-old was drowning in the creek. But something made me glance in his direction. A tall man with dark hair and an easy smile on his lips, he had a hand raised to wave at me. I looked away. Only after taking three more strides toward the creek did it register that the man was holding Barry by the other hand. I wheeled around.

"This one claims he's yours," he said, tipping his head toward Barry. My body flooded with relief.

"Barry!" I cried. "Thank God! Yes, he's mine. I was worried sick." Barry ran up and buried his face in my dress. I pressed a hand against his back while he hugged my legs. Johnny squirmed in my arms, but I dared not let him down.

"I found him headed off toward the creek," the man explained. "I didn't think it was a good idea for him to go alone."

"Carol was mean to me," Barry said, looking up.

"We went and threw some stones in that old creek then, didn't we?" The man looked down at Barry with an encouraging smile.

Barry pulled back from my legs. "I threw the biggest rock. It splashed so big, Mommy."

The man laughed. "Figured if I tried to just pull him away from the water's edge he might not be too pleased, so we tossed a few stones, then decided we ought to look for Mommy."

"That was a good idea," I said, smiling. The man returned the smile, and a warm rush of ease came over me.

He offered his hand. "I'm Hank," he said. "Hank Hall."

"Eleanor Mitchell." I slipped my fingers into his hand briefly. Callouses peppered his palm, but his grip was gentle, his eyes kind.

"Wanna see me throw some rocks, Mommy?"

"Just a couple," I said, looking over my shoulder to search out Carol. She was wrapped up with her new friends.

"Let's go!" Barry cried. Hank and I fell into step next to each other, and Barry ran ahead. I put Johnny down and he hurried after Barry.

"I looked all over for him. One minute he's with his sister, the next he's nowhere to be found," I explained. "These kids can be so quick."

"That they can. And this one has a mind of his own."

"Does he ever." I laughed. An easy silence fell between us. I could see how Barry might be happy to throw rocks with this kind man.

Near the water's edge, Hank made a pile of rocks for the boys. Barry was choosing the largest and throwing them, while Johnny tossed the smaller stones. Hank kept the supply of rocks steady, cheering every time there was a splash. I tried not to stare at him, but he was a handsome man: thick black hair, tanned skin, and eyes the color of warm earth. He moved like he was comfortable in his skin.

"I imagine you work for General Motors," I said to fill the silence.

"I do," Hank said. "Skilled trades. I'm a welder."

"My sister, Jean, works in the hiring department over on Dort Highway."

"I'm out there at that plant, too. Maybe she hired me in." He smiled that easy way of his, and I got a little thrill in my middle. I may even have blushed. I glanced down at his left hand. Not a ring on it. Not that I had any right to even be looking.

"Your husband work at the plant, too, then?" he asked.

"I'm a widow," I blurted, "of the war." It was like my mouth had a mind of its own, only I couldn't be sure if it was flirting or justifying.

"Oh, I am sorry," Hank said, setting a handful of rocks on the pile for the boys.

"Well, thank you," I replied. "It's been some time now."

"Don't suppose it gets any easier."

"No, not really. But we get on with it." Then I blushed. "Don't know why I'm saying all this."

He looked at me gently. "I imagine you don't get much chance to talk about it anymore."

And I felt another wave of ease wash over me, a loosening of my shoulders. I think I might have sighed. "No, I don't talk about it much. The world's moved on, as it should."

"But none of us should ever lose sight of the sacrifice."

"You are very kind. My husband worked at the AC plant before he left." Hank nodded solemnly.

We watched the boys toss rock after rock and when the thrill wore off, we made our way back to the picnic. We filled our plates and I asked Hank if he might like to join us. He agreed, and I introduced him to Jean and Tony as the man who had saved Barry's life. Of course, Hank laughed it off as not as bad as all that, but for me, it might as well have been.

We ate potato salad and hot dogs and got to know each other. Naturally, Jean had to ask after Hank's history, how long he'd been at the plant, where he was from, all of that. They were things I wanted to know, but I might have waited a minute or two before I started quizzing him. Turned out he had been hired in during the late days of the war. Jean didn't remember him. He had grown up in Arkansas and had tried to enlist, but they had sent him packing for his flat feet. From there he bounced around, doing farm work and the like, he said, until he made his way up to Flint for the factory work.

We had some good laughs. It was all as comfortable as it could be. Jean kept shooting me looks, nodding her head and winking, but I tried not to pay her too much attention. Truth be told, I was looking for a sign from Roger, some hint that this was the man he had sent for me. It might have been a little early to be thinking that, but the way he'd dropped right into things so easy and kind, well, it seemed too good to be an accident.

With the sun taking a dip toward the horizon, we all decided it was time to pack up. It had been a fine day. Tony went around to pull up the car. Hank took a seat next to me on the picnic bench. His warmth beside me set my knees shaking. I took a breath, scolded myself for being a fool, then smiled my best smile.

"I'd like to call on you, Eleanor," he said, turning to meet my eye, "if that'd be all right."

I blushed. I could see it coming, his question. And I had wanted him to ask, but when he did, I hesitated—feeling afraid, I guess, or unworthy. I wasn't sure. He waited, calm and patient, for me to figure out what to say.

Finally, my voice barely above a whisper, I said, "Are you sure you want to do something like that?" I can't say why I said it, can't say even what I meant exactly, except to check that this kind man wasn't just being polite.

And he laughed, his eyebrows raised. "About as sure as I can be."

I blushed, and he smiled as warm and generous as the moment we met, his eyes gleaming the golden brown of a rich topaz stone. And I felt something, a tug, a pull at my heart—something about his smile, his tender eyes.

"Well... yes, I'd like that."

And Hank laughed. "All right, that's a start," he said. "That's a start."

CHAPTER 41

ELEANOR

ank called that very next afternoon and asked for a proper date. I agreed without any fuss. I'd thought about him most of the night, looked for Roger to show me something there in the house, tried to reason it out that he might have sent me a sign I had missed. But, at the end of the day, I was a lonely woman with three children and along had come this kind, gentle man. I'd have been a fool to look the other way, sign or no sign.

Jean was pleased, of course. "Now, aren't you glad I made you come along to that picnic?" she said. And I had to admit that I was.

It wasn't long before Hank and I were spending every day together. He'd come by after work, staying for dinner most days. Or he'd take me out on a Saturday night for a bite to eat or dancing with Jean and Tony. Hank stood about as tall as Roger, but his coloring was as different as it could be; Hank's hair was straight, thick and jet black, a far cry from Roger's light brown curls. And Hank had an olive tone to his skin that browned nicely in the sun, while the sun had turned Roger's skin to red after an hour or so. I tried not to compare the two of them, but in those early days, I couldn't much help it.

The children took a fine shine to Hank and his country-boy ways, too. He could make a blade of grass sing or twist an old piece of twine into something that would have them screaming for more. Roger had been like that, too—handy with things, clever.

I learned Hank had two brothers: Robert and Kenneth. They'd come up north for work in the factories with him but had both gone to war. They were back now and working again alongside one another at the plant. He had a sister, Pauline, who was married and lived with her husband and son out near Bristol Road. Hank was renting a room from them for the time being, but he did aim to get his own place soon. His mother had stayed down south in Arkansas, and his father had passed about ten years before. He told me all of this over the first few of our dates together. "I want you to know I'm a man of good character, Eleanor, with a nice family."

After a while, things between us were going along well enough for long enough that I figured it might be time to let the rest of the family meet him. So I invited Mother, Helen, Jean, Tony, Faye, and my brothers Bill, Perry, and Jack over for a family cookout. Sister Mary had married the man she moved to California for and had settled somewhere out there, sending postcards from time to time and train tickets for Mother when she would go visit.

And when it came to brother Earl—well, there wasn't any of us who could find Earl very often, so I just let Mother know he was welcome, if she saw him.

While I was no longer a young girl hosting her first get-together, I did want the day to be nice. I put together some summer salads and made a fresh blueberry pie that morning. Jean was bringing the corn. Faye had asked Bob's butcher friend for some nice steaks and burgers for grilling. I was planning to have Hank handle the grill so Mother and them couldn't get too much of a hold on him.

'Long about ten or so, I pushed out into the yard to get things set up. Lord, it was a hot one that day; the heat lay like a wool blanket over the whole yard. I stepped onto the grass and it nearly crunched under my feet, everything was so dry. Made me wonder if maybe a quick sprinkle with the hose might be a good idea. I was just saying this to myself when Hank peeked around the edge of the house.

"Hi, beautiful," he called. He was smiling that easy smile, and he looked just as handsome as he could in his crisp white short-sleeve shirt and dark pants.

Carol skipped over to him. "Hank, we're having a picnic. Wanna come?"

"Don't mind if I do," he said. He turned to me. "You look worried, darlin'."

"Little worried the grass is too dry for a grill."

"No trouble, I'll put it on the driveway. It'll be fine."

"So you'll be the cook, then?"

"If you'll have me."

I couldn't help myself—I went over and kissed him right on the lips with Carol and God and maybe even Roger watching. Hank looked surprised when I did it. I suppose I surprised myself, too.

"You do make my life a breeze," I said, blushing and explaining at the same time. We laughed and, gentleman that he was, he didn't say a darned thing about it one way or the other, just accepted my kiss and let my blush pass off unnoticed.

"C'mon, Carol," he said. "Let's get our fire going."

"Okay!" Carol jumped right in, leading Hank into the garage. I went back into the house. From the kitchen window I could hear the two of them chatting away, and it felt like old times again. Barry came down from upstairs, his ears perked, curious.

"It's Hank and Carol. You go ahead out."

I went to find Johnny, who'd been playing with his toys in the living room. There he sat still, happy as a lark with his toy telephone. I picked him and his phone up. And walking back into the kitchen, I heard someone whistling the first notes of "You Are My Sunshine," that old tune that Roger favored. Seemed like it was coming from just behind my shoulder. I turned around, but nothing was there. Still, the whistling went on. I followed the sound, and it led me to the back window. Peeking out, I saw Hank kneeling several safe steps back from the grill, one arm around Carol, the other around Barry, while they watched the first flames lick its top edge. And it was Hank whistling that tune.

I felt a little prick of tears in my eyes. Here was my sign. After all this time, here was Roger telling me this was the love he had promised to send. I took a seat there at the window, put Johnny on my lap, and we watched Hank keeping Carol and Barry safe while the fire took. And I realized that's what Roger had been doing—waiting to make sure it took, my interest in Hank and his in me, before he let me know it was okay to move on.

CHAPTER 42

ELEANOR

I married Hank that September, on a crisp bright blue morning. It was a beautiful day, tinged just a little bittersweet with all that I was leaving behind. The truth of it was that this new marriage would always sit somewhere between heartbreak and happiness for me. No matter the joy in my new life with Hank, I would always be a war widow trying her level best to move along. I knew this, but it didn't mean I wasn't ready for the next chapter of my life, and I was grateful to be getting a fresh start.

The very morning of the wedding was a flurry of mix-ups and fussiness, like it tends to be when a person has big plans. First off, I could barely push Carol out the door to school. Her dress itched, then her socks were wrong, then she didn't want oatmeal, then her tummy ached; one fuss after another, like she knew something was up. Then, Mother was set to come watch the boys, but she was late, so I got them playing and left the kitchen a mess.

I hurried up the stairs and into the bedroom. I looked around. This was the room I'd shared with Roger and no other. Come this evening, it would be the room I'd share with Hank. I went and sat in Roger's blue chair. I closed my eyes. I felt something—not a touch, but something at my left shoulder. I opened my eyes and there he stood, next to me, in his navy blue suit, handsome and filmy.

"Eleanor," he whispered in that gentle way of his. "Be happy with him."

"No chance you're coming home, then?"

"I'm always with you."

"Not really."

He smiled. "I am with you, Eleanor, now and always." His hand squeezed mine, a touch of pressure against my palm, and he was gone. I leaned back, closed my eyes tight. I held a picture of him as I had always known him: young, handsome, and carefree as he would now always be. I had loved him so, would always love him. But I was a young girl full of hopes and fairy-tale dreams when I fell in love with him. Now, I was a practical woman with a life to hold together—a life to scrape some joy out of, if I was lucky. So, I let him go, off to wherever he would go. And I hoped against hope he'd wait there for me until I finished my own earthly business. Maybe we could meet again that day.

"Eleanor!" Mother hollered up the stairs, bringing me around. "You'd best get a move on."

I took a deep breath, steadied myself, and put my makeup on. The curlers fell from my hair in a tumble. I teased it into a pretty, off-the-face 'do. For my wedding clothes, I'd made an off-white linen suit. The finishing touches had gone on just last night. It was a beautiful suit, if I do say so myself, with faux pearl buttons and a flared skirt. I slipped into it, and didn't I look grown-up. I tucked my toes into a pair of matching heels, brushed a pale pink across my lips, and looked in the mirror.

"*I'd* marry me," I whispered.

"Mama," Barry said, a little breathless and unbelieving as I came down the stairs. "You're so pretty." I guess the poor kid had never seen his mother dressed in anything fancier than a day dress.

Mother came over and gave me a look up and down. "That's a nice suit," she said.

"Made it myself."

"Well, I imagine you did." She pinched my waist to test the fit. "Flatters you."

"I must look like a million bucks for you to be saying that." I smiled. She peered at the hem and the buttonholes.

"You did some nice work."

"No Jean yet?" I asked.

"Not yet."

"Carol's home around noon. She likes to eat right away. She can get cranky when she's hungry."

"I'm sure we'll manage, dear."

"Okay, then." I took a deep breath and let it roll out slow over my lips.

"He's a good man, Eleanor," Mother said sincerely, giving my shoulder a reassuring squeeze. "You and the children, you'll be all right now."

"Thank you, Mama," I whispered. Then Jean beeped the horn. I kissed the boys—and Mother, too—a quick peck on the cheek. I never once did it again in my life, but then it was the right thing to do.

"Get on, now," she said, and smoothed a wisp of hair off my forehead. I felt a certain calm come over me, like maybe everything *was* all gonna be okay.

I slipped into the car next to Jean and she started chattering. "Once we get the hitching done," she began, without so much as a hello, "there's a lunch for the group of us. Then later on, the guys from the plant have organized a party at The Riveria for the two of you. Some of your lady friends from the neighborhood said they'd come by, too. Did Hank tell you? No? Good. He wasn't supposed to. Eight o'clock tonight. Mother'll stay with the children. We knew if we told you too early, you'd make some excuse, and we had to throw a party to celebrate the end of your wild widowhood." She laughed like a schoolgirl.

"Well, ain't the whole world full of surprises today," I said.

"Why? What happened?" she asked.

"Mother just gave me her blessing," I said.

"She did not."

"She did, said we'd be all right now."

"I don't believe it."

"Makes me wonder if I don't give her enough credit sometimes."

Jean laughed. "I don't know about that," she said. "But it is nice she can rise to the occasion."

"You're right," I agreed, laughing. "She is still Mother."

☆　☆　☆

Jean dropped me in front of the courthouse and went off to park the car. I tucked my purse under my arm and went clicking along in my smart heels, making a beeline for the door. To my right stood a man, handsome and all dressed up for his own special day. I buzzed on past, must have gotten ten feet beyond him, when I heard, "Eleanor?"

I stopped and turned around. The man smiled and stepped out. Still I couldn't place him. It was the strangest thing. Then he reached for my hand.

"Sugar?" he asked tenderly. And I found him, there in among the dress-up clothes and the busy morning.

"Hank," I said.

"In the flesh." He smiled. "Good morning, beautiful." He leaned in to kiss my cheek.

"That'll be enough of that, now," Jean called from across the plaza.

Hank laughed and snuck a peck on my other cheek. Then he took my hand and slipped it into the crook of his arm. "Would you marry us, judge?"

"As good looking as the two of you are, I s'pose I would," replied Jean, laughing.

Hank's brother, Kenneth, wheeled around the corner. "Morning, folks," he grinned. "Ready for the hitching?"

"Ready as we'll ever be," said Hank.

"Yes, we are," I added, and I was ready—ready to marry this good man, ready to try again. Wiser, stronger—smarter, even—I hadn't given up on love. Or maybe I had, but I'd found it again.

The four of us made our way into the courthouse. I meant to say something—meant to tell Hank how handsome he looked, how glad I was to be marrying him, to give him a kiss that meant something. But, next thing I knew, the clerk called "Mitchell/Hall," and we were up. The jitters started in me; my head got a little light. I grabbed hold of Jean.

She wrapped an arm around my back. "It's fine now, just fine," she whispered.

In front of the judge, Hank took my hands, and I got a touch steadier looking into his eyes. He smiled. This was my husband-to-be, and he was a fine man.

"You clean up awful nice," I said finally.

"Why thank you, ma'am," he winked.

"I hardly recognized you outside."

"Hmm, not sure if that might be good or bad."

"It's not bad. I thought you were too handsome for me."

He smiled that gentle smile. "Never for you, darlin'."

I think I might have blushed.

The judge cleared his throat, we said our "I do's," and Jean and Kenneth took the party from there. The luncheon was nice, just the four of us and some fine laughs and good times. Later that evening, we went on to the party nobody had thought I'd come to. I let myself loose and had some fun, comforted by the thought that when I left to go home for the evening, I wouldn't be going alone anymore.

Back at the house, the children were tucked in for the night. We thanked Mother and said our goodnights. And there we were, Hank and I, husband and wife in the house alone. Not that we hadn't been alone before, but we hadn't been married, and I can guarantee you the man had not been into my bedroom. We stood there in the half-light of the kitchen, the house quiet, our ears still ringing a little from the band at the party.

"Do you want a little coffee? A slice of pie?"

"I think I'd just as soon get to bed. The morning's gonna come before we know it."

"All right, then."

He checked the doors, and that had a nice feel to it. Then we climbed the stairs together. Me first, him coming up after.

"That was a nice party," I said.

"Those boys from the factory know how to throw a shindig," he laughed.

Walking into the bedroom, there sat Hank's bags. He hadn't come with much—a suitcase and his toiletries.

"Space in here for you," I said, pulling the dresser drawer open.

"I don't mind living out of a bag for a while," Hank said, seeming unsure if he ought to look at me or not.

"Cleaned 'em out special for you," I said, winking.

He smiled. "In the morning, then."

"Suit yourself," I said. Then I shut myself into the bathroom, my hands shaking and a thrill in my middle. I hadn't ever once been alone with a man but Roger, and now Hank was standing on the other side of my bathroom door, expecting me.

I washed and pulled on the lace nightgown I'd bought special. I wasn't gonna think one bit more about all of this. I pulled the door open and there he stood, my new husband, handsome in the dim bedroom light, his shirt unbuttoned, a smile on his lips.

"Well, look at you there, beautiful," he said, whistling low. I blushed.

"Oh, this ol' thing?" I flirted. I went to him, let him wrap me in his arms. Against me he was solid and sure. His lips against mine felt more urgent than the kisses we'd had until now. I must have tensed.

"We can take it slow," he whispered. I kissed him harder, pulled him to the bed. His hands were large but slow in their touch, patient, tender. I swooned, and that is the last of what I am willing to put into words.

☆ ☆ ☆

The next morning, I put his clothes away for him and stowed his luggage up in the attic next to mine. His toothbrush and shaving kit fit with room to spare in the medicine cabinet but filled it in a way it hadn't been full for nearly three years. That old Aqua Velva bottle—well, I took a small sniff near the cap just for old times, and then I placed it ever so gentle in the bottom of the trash basket. Hank wore Old Spice.

☆　　☆　　☆

Pork chops and scalloped potatoes were what I served on Hank's first night as head of the household, with tomatoes fresh from the backyard and a loaf of homemade bread. The pork chops were browned and crispy, fried in bacon grease—my specialty. Hank ate three, plus two helpings of potatoes. He slathered two slices of bread thick with butter and finished the plate of tomatoes. I always thought it was nice to watch a man eat. They went at it with such a sense of purpose.

"Dee-licious," he said and smiled.

"Yes, Mommy, dee-licious," Carol echoed, and we all laughed—like a regular family.

THE END

ACKNOWLEDGMENTS

So many wonderful people helped bring this book into being — starting, of course with my remarkable husband, Bob. Without him the true story of Roger's death might never have been revealed to me. Also, an enormous thank you to SSgt. Edward J. Skalitzy, a brave soldier who read our message on a message board way back in 2003 and, as witness to Roger's passing, was kind enough to share the story of what really happened and the impact it had on the other men.

I'd also like to thank my grandparents – Eleanor who was a like a second mother to me, Burrell (Hank) who was like a second father and Roger whom I didn't know but who surely must have been a wonderful man.

I'd also like to thank the many, many workshop teachers and participants over the years who gave me meaningful and sometimes pointed input on various sections of this manuscript. There are many, but by name I'd like to acknowledge: Martha Hughes, Tom Jenks, Carly Yuenger, Lisbeth Redfield and the Women's Writers Circle at Pen + Brush. From the NYC Pitch Conference, Ann Garvin, whose contagious enthusiasm made me believe my book had a place in the world. That group of women as a whole has been a wonderful addition to my life, specifically: Meg Nocero, Suzanne Strong and Lisa David.

A million thanks to my insightful, tough beta reader — the incomparable Lisa Rose.

Thank you to the team at GenZ who showed interest when I felt like the world had moved on from stories of WWII and this one still hadn't been told. Specifically, L. Austen Johnson, Stephanie Marrie, Destinee Thompson and all those behind the scenes bringing new stories into the world.

And thank you to my children, Ava and Quincy, who always believed in my dream.

I am also grateful to authors who came before me especially Emily Yellin author of *Our Mothers' War. Don't You Know There's a War On?* by Richard Lingeman and *Soldier From The War Returning* by Thomas Childers also provided essential context for the book.

Finally, I'd like to thank the soldiers of WWII who fought and died so the world could know peace — and the families who loved them.

THANK YOU FOR READING

SOMETIMES A SOLDIER COMES HOME

Please consider leaving a review so that other readers can find this title.

Discover more titles from other GenZ authors at Genzpublishing.org